# Take the Shot

James Korom

**Take the Shot**

First Edition: 2023

ISBN: 9781524318574
ISBN eBook: 9781524328559

© of the text:
  James Korom

© Layout, design and production of this edition: 2023 EBL

*This novel is dedicated to my loving and supportive wife, Lucia. Thank you!*

# Table of Contents

This is a work of fiction. All names, places and events depicted in this book are the product of the author's imagination.

# Chapter 1

## 1998

"Take the shot."

Acting Assistant Special Agent-in-Charge Jonathan "Jake" Mott spit out the order as if the bullet were coming from his own lips rather than the muzzle of the rifle of an FBI sharpshooter. He had a confidence in himself and in his training that helped him bring order and clarity to the chaotic-looking scene spread out below him. From his second-floor Command Post across the street from the First National Bank branch in downtown Milwaukee, he'd made a decision that would change his life, and that of so many others, in ways he would never see coming.

He had gotten the call at home around 9:15 am. It was a Saturday, and he was supposed to be going to a child-birthing class with his now very pregnant wife, Kathy. He had put the class off too many times, blaming the demands of his new job in the FBI's Milwaukee Field Office. So, when he told Kathy he was needed at a hostage situation, he could see from that look on her face that he would need to do some serious fence-mending when this was over.

As he drove downtown from their home in suburban Brookfield, Steve Marks, one of the agents assigned to his team, briefed him by radio on the situation, "the branch office opens on Saturdays at 9:00. A few minutes after opening, some amateur walked up to the teller, flashed a handgun, and demanded money. The guard quietly radioed the local police, but rather than waiting for backup, he confronted the perp, and took a bullet. We know the guard is alive, but we don't know how badly he's hurt. The locals responded "red lights and siren" in force, set a perimeter, and then called us. They're pissed off. Apparently, the guard is retired MPD. You better get here quick."

"What else do we know from inside the Bank?" Jake asked.

Steve went on, "our perp was smart enough to lock the front doors and corral the tellers and the customers behind the counter, so we don't know much more about the situation."

Jake asked how many hostages there were, but Steve could only be sure of one assistant bank manager, two tellers, and a few early morning customers. Jake had many more questions, but knew Steve was in over his head and Jake didn't want to be critical. Jake would need Steve's help as this unfolded.

"I'll be there in 15 minutes. Are the sharpshooters on site yet?"

"Do you really think it might come to that? This guy seems like a goof, not a professional," Steve asked with a noticeably shaky voice.

Jake knew the FBI's SOPs required the dispatch of at least two sharpshooters to every hostage situation, so he knew they'd be on station soon. But the question showed just how unprepared Steve was for the type of leadership now expected of Jake. Even though Steve had more years of seniority in the Bureau, and had applied for the job of ASAC, the FBI had promoted Jake instead. Jake merely replied, "How do you think the hostages would feel about the use of force right about now, Steve?"

Steve gave no answer.

Jake was ready for this opportunity, as tragic as it could turn out to be. Born in Ann Arbor, Michigan to loving parents, he'd attended a Catholic high school run by Jesuits. They instilled in him the importance of leadership and commitment, and the need to do the right thing, even when it was difficult. Four years at Georgetown reinforced that message for Jake graduating cum laude with his degree in criminal justice. Hired by the FBI, he breezed through the Academy at Quantico. He worked for two years as an agent in Oklahoma City, earning accolades for his commitment and leadership. So here he was, only a few months into his first leadership position in the Milwaukee office. He was green, but he felt ready.

Normally, the SAC, Arnie Dunn, would handle a high-profile event like a bank robbery with hostages, but Arnie had suffered a heart attack three days ago and was still at Saint Luke's Hospital. Jake realized with a twinge of guilt he had not visited or even called him yet. In Arnie's absence, the Assistant SAC, Mike Glover would normally step in, but Mike had been placed on administrative leave the day before after being accused of harassment by some of the female staff in the office. So Jake got the call. "Only time will tell if I'm as ready as I feel," thought Jake as he pulled his sedan as close to the barricades as he could, before getting out and looking for Steve Marks at the scene.

To the reporters corralled behind a barricade, things must have looked chaotic. All traffic on Water Street and Wells was closed for two blocks in every direction. The Milwaukee PD had set up barricades and crime scene tape, and curious onlookers stood outside the perimeter, hoping to see something more exciting than another routine shopping trip downtown. The press had the best view, Jake thought, hoping no doubt for the worst possible ending to this story. "If it bleeds, it leads" was a cynical newspaper adage that was all too true. The press would take a perverse pleasure in filming a dead perp, and even wouldn't mind a dead hostage or two. They could sell papers for days with the sob stories from the victims' families, not to mention putting those who had to make the tough decisions under a microscope. "Ah well," Jake thought, he'd learned in the Academy that dealing with the press is part of the job, and that making decisions primarily to keep reporters off your back is a waste of time.

Inside the barricades, Jake saw Marks talking to the senior MPD Captain on the scene. Jake flashed his credentials and was ushered inside the perimeter by a young but attentive officer. Demeanor was important to leadership, Jake had learned. He knew he was not gifted with a powerful personal appearance. Jake stood a very average five foot eleven, 180 pounds, ten of them he would like to shed if he just had more time. He had brown hair, brown eyes, and a forgettable face. Because of that, Jake knew he had to use a strong voice, effective body language, and an air of confidence to command others. The stress of the situation, and the emotions of the local cops would test that leadership style today.

"Where are we set up?" Jake asked.

"No Command Post yet, sir. Waiting for you." Steve replied. He handed Jake a hand-held radio. "We're all on Channel 2."

Jake took it all in. The bank was on the first floor of an office building on the southwest corner of Water and Wells. Windows faced east and north but were tinted. Visibility from the street was limited. The northwest corner housed a deli, evacuated by MPD. An old four-story office building, half unoccupied, held the southeast corner. The last corner, opposite the bank, was Johnson Bank, with windows on the second floor overlooking the entire scene. Perfect.

Jake pointed. "I want the Command Post set up there. All communication to run through that office. I want a direct line into our hostage taker, now. And deploy our two sharpshooters, one into that deli, and the other on the second floor of that old office building. Have them report to me when they are in position with fire options." Steve and the MPD Captain, a Robert Stawski, turned to make it all happen. Before they got too far, Jake called Stawski back. "I know the guard is one of yours, and I'm sure your men are itching to do something about it. Please trust me that I am too. Have your guys work with me, and I promise I'll do everything I can to get that guard out safely."

Stawski looked appraisingly at Jake, paused, and nodded. "I'll trust you for now. Thanks for asking me. It shows you understand."

Jake began to walk the scene to get his bearings. While there were lots of moving parts, between the press, the local cops, medical emergency vehicles, the crowds of onlookers, and his own agents, he was pleased everyone seemed to be playing nicely so far. As the tension built, however, Jake knew that wouldn't last long.

Within ten minutes, Steve called Jake on his radio to tell him the Command Post was ready. The manager of Johnson Bank apparently had some sympathy for his competitor and was falling all over himself to help. Jake walked into the lobby, bounded up the stairs, and walked into the CP, a converted conference room. Wires, radios, and law enforcement people bustled throughout the room. A video camera had been set up by the Bureau, taking in the view across the intersection and south down Water Street, another SOP in this situation. He asked Marks if the dedicated phone line to the lobby of the bank was set up yet. It was. He asked about his sharpshooters. One of the radios on Jake's desk crackled to life.

"Jake, this is Mark Olsen. I'm set up in the deli. I can't see shit with those tinted windows. I can see some movement when somebody is under the lights inside, but I've got no idea who I'm supposed to be shooting at. And I have no idea what the bullet will do when it hits that glass."

"Who is in the office building?" Jake asked into the radio.

"That would be me, Jake, Todd Chen. Same situation up here, but my angle might be better than Mark's if this asshole stays behind the counter instead of coming out into the lobby."

Jake had met Todd at the Academy. He knew he was a great shot, and reliable in his reports. If Todd said he had a shot, the perp was done.

"OK. Todd and Mark, I'm going to call this guy. Listen in on the call and see if you can figure out which one is our HT when he answers the phone."

"Steve, put me through," Jake ordered. The phone in the bank rang four times before someone picked up. "This is Jake Mott of the FBI. Who is this?"

"Th-th-this is Mr. Peters. I-I-I'm the assistant manager. I'm scared. Please get us out of here!"

"Calm down, sir. We'll do everything we can. How many people are in there with you?" Jake knew gathering information was his top priority right now. But before he got an answer, he heard Peters cry out in pain. Then, a rather high-pitched, nervous voice said,

"Oh no you don't. The less you cops know, the better chance I get out of here alive and with my money."

"Who is this?" Jake asked.

There was a long pause.

"For now, how about you call me Willie? You remember Willie Sutton, don't you? Now listen to me. I've collected the money this bank took from me and my friends, no more, no less. I expect to walk out of here with it and disappear into the crowd. You don't know what I look like, or anything about me, so this can work if you want it to. But if you don't, I've got a bunch of hostages, and a wounded guard who looks like he's bleeding pretty good. Their lives are in your hands."

Jake knew the reference to Sutton, the criminal who, when asked why he robbed banks, replied "because that's where the money is." But the hostage taker's comment about taking only what the bank took from him and his friends was intriguing and could be the basis for a dialogue.

Jake replied, "I want to make this work, but I need to know how the bank took your money. If that is true, there are ways to get it back without taking hostages. Help me to understand what is going on here."

"What is going on here is that you are not listening!" Willie screamed. "You're just another part of a system that sucks money and power from people trying to get by in the world, care for themselves, their loved ones, and their... children. Don't you think I already tried to get my money back? Do you think I'm stupid? I told you lives depended on you getting on board, and instead you just say you 'want to understand'. Bullshit! I'll show you I'm serious!" Jake then heard a shot go off in the bank, and one of the plate glass windows on Water Street exploded out onto the sidewalk. The line went dead.

Before Jake could decide on his next move, Todd Chen came on the radio, "Jake, I think our perp just fucked up. Let me check something out. I'll call you in two minutes."

Jake's mind went over the exchange with Willie. Clearly, he was an amateur. There would be records of his attempts to 'get his money back' but that would take time, time Jake didn't have right now. Willie was pretty wound up, probably from the stress of the situation, his perceived injustice over whatever he thought the bank had done to him, and a feeling of powerlessness. Hence the gunshot, to try to reassert control. Little did Willie know that his gunshot hurt his own chances of survival. Jake now had one more factor weighing in favor of the use of force rather than prolonged negotiations. Willie had just foreclosed options. But that hesitation before Willie mentioned taking care of 'children'. What was that about? Jake hoped he'd have the chance to find out.

Chen interrupted his thoughts. "Jake, I was right. He screwed himself. I moved one office to the south, and I now have a direct line of sight through the broken window to the phone the perp was using. I can't see him right now, but if you can get him on that phone again, just give me the word and I can end this."

"Roger that. Good work. Be ready. I'm going to give him a few minutes to cool off, and then call again."

Now the moment had come. Should he pursue protracted negotiations? The perp was obviously unstable and unpredictable. He clearly felt aggrieved, and claimed he was trying to right an injustice against him and 'his friends'. Jake had learned that this victim/hero complex made hostage takers very dangerous, especially when backed into a corner. That fact endangered the currently unknown number of hostages. The extent of the guard's gunshot wound was also an unknown, so any delay jeopardized at least one innocent life. "Damn, I wish I knew more!" Jake thought.

Jake knew any order to take human life was grave and serious. But he also knew that this decision came with the job. He had spent many hours drinking beer with some of his Jesuit professors at Georgetown. They had assured him that the Catholic Church condones the taking of human life in order to protect innocent life. No problem there. And he certainly wasn't afraid of the press. The Academy had taught him the "FBI two-step" in his Public Relations class: When the press starts asking questions, if credit was to be taken, the FBI steps in front of the cameras; if things turn to shit, the FBI blames local law enforcement.

Jake would not be human if somewhere in the recesses of his mind, he didn't think about the career opportunity this gave him. He was in a new assignment, his first with real leadership responsibilities. He had a child on the way, hopefully with more to come (if he could mend those fences with Kathy when this was over). His superiors in Milwaukee and at Headquarters in D.C. would go over this whole event with a fine-tooth comb. If he impressed them, who knows where he might end up? Jake knew he wouldn't be so callous as to give the order to shoot just to advance his career, but it did help focus the mind when making this type of call.

In the end, Jake knew only two things mattered. First, Jake's world was simple: There are good guys and bad guys. This perp decided to be one of the bad guys. The reasons didn't really matter. And second, Jake had to save innocent lives. If the chance came to save those lives, to take them out of danger and return them to their families safe and sound, Jake knew what he would do.

"Chen, are you ready?" Jake asked.

"Roger," came Todd's reply.

"Ok. Call him back, Steve." Steve Marks looked uncomfortable. "What are you planning to do?" he asked. "This guy doesn't need to die today. I think we have lots of options."

Jake choked down the reply he wanted to give. It would have included the words 'chicken shit', 'ass-covering', and 'above your pay grade'. But Jake also knew that if this went bad, having Marks as an enemy inside the Bureau during the inevitable inquiry wouldn't help. So instead, he said as gently as he could, "I'm going to try to talk him down, but if he does anything to further threaten the hostages, I'll have no choice." Marks only nodded. A nod was the best Jake was going to get. Steve put the call through to the bank.

Peters, the assistant Manager, answered on the second ring. Jake asked him how everyone was doing. "He told me not to say anything, and he's got a gun. Sorry. Hold on, he's been talking to someone on a walkie-talkie off and on during this mess. I'll get him."

"Todd, be ready," Jake reminded his sharpshooter.

Willie spoke next, "are you ready to get me out of here now, or do I need to show you I'm even more serious than the last time?"

"Listen to me carefully," Jake said in the sternest voice he could muster. "I have one priority here, and that is keeping these hostages safe. You just threatened them again. I want you to live through this, too, but you will not be leaving with that money. So far, if that guard lives, you are looking at charges a lot less serious than murder, and maybe even an opportunity to have your grievances against the bank be heard by the press and the public. If you've been screwed by the bank, surrendering now might even help you at sentencing."

Then Jake played what he hoped would be his trump card. "But it sounds like you might have children that need you. Think about that. Now how about you hang up that phone, walk to the front doors, toss out that gun, and end this?"

Jake's gamble about children struck a nerve. The wrong nerve. Willie first started to sob into the phone. Then he started shouting at Jake, "How dare you talk to me about kids! That is what this is all about. I just wanted my son to be born and raised into a world where folks like him and me are treated right. Where he could see justice done! I wanted to have some money so I could give him a home, and some things I never had! Now I know that will never happen. But still, someone needs to pay so that someday, my son will know his dad wasn't useless! And they will pay with their lives!"

Jake was surprised by Willie's reaction, but his instincts took over. He knew the situation was unravelling fast. It was time.

"Take the shot."

Todd Chen was ready. The .45 caliber bullet flew unobstructed the 150 yards or so from the sharpshooter's rifle to the HT's forehead. It barely slowed as it passed through blood, brains, and the back of Willie's head before lodging itself in the polished wood panels behind him. The good news was that Willie never felt a thing. One moment he was there, angry, tearful, and alive. The next he was simply... gone.

Standing at one of the barricades south on Water Street, a tall, dark-haired woman heard the shot echo off the buildings. She knew it was over. She turned and started to walk away, pausing only to drop a walkie-talkie into a nearby trash bin. As she walked down Water Street, she wiped away a single tear with one hand, and rested the other on her slightly bulging belly, saying, "One tear is all I'll shed. But they will pay, young one. Someday, they will pay".

# Chapter 2

## 2020

"So you really are going to retire? I never thought that you of all people could pull the plug after only twenty-five years."

Todd Chen flopped down in the standard, government-issue pea green chair in Jake's office at FBI headquarters in Washington D. C. with an incredulous look on his face. His old friend only shrugged, gave him a grin, and nodded. "I sent the paperwork upstairs this morning. How did you find out so fast?"

"I've got eyes and ears everywhere in this place. You don't survive the politics here without making lots of friends who will tip you off to these juicy tidbits when they happen. You've got to stay ahead of the curve." Chen smiled. "I'm going to miss you, buddy. When does it happen?"

"June 1, if my vacation payout is approved, later if not. We'll see. And I'll miss you too."

Jake meant it. He and Todd had crossed paths many times on their respective postings in the Bureau, none more important than their encounter in Milwaukee. After the shooting, Todd could have told the Review Board he was just following orders, and let Jake take the heat alone. But he'd told them he agreed with Jake's assessment of the situation and fully supported the decision to take out the HT. Jake chuckled when he later found out Todd had even told them that if Jake hadn't given the order, Chen would have shot Willie anyway. Jake had always respected him for that and knew he could be trusted. That was especially important in the political swamp that was the FBI.

Over the years, the two men stayed close, even if their assignments did not. After being exonerated in the Milwaukee case, Jake got a plum assignment to the New York office, arriving only a few months before the Towers fell on 9/11. After working brutal hours for nearly four years in the aftermath and helping in the arrest and prosecution of several of the terrorists involved, Jake was offered his choice of assignments. Knowing he wasn't yet ready for FBI Headquarters in D.C.; he'd contacted Chen for advice. Chen had just finished an assignment in the Bureau's Denver office, and both thought Tampa would be nice. They were both sent there, and enjoyed a four year assignment together, where their friendship grew.

They also spent time getting to know each other's families. Chen had a beautiful wife, Carla whom he had met on the job in Denver. After a whirlwind romance and a Vegas wedding, their first child, a daughter, was born. Chen insisted on pointing out to everyone that Angela's birth was more than nine months after the wedding. Twin boys followed, Ed and Ted. Chen only shared with Jake and a select few that he named them after Edmond Heckler and Theodor Koch, the famed German gun manufacturers. After his family, weaponry was Chen's true love.

Jake's family loved spending time with the Chens. Jake's oldest, Charlie, had been born two months after the Milwaukee shooting. Three years older than Angela, he loved teaching her, playing with her, and generally showing the protective instincts that would eventually lead him to consider following in dad's footsteps in law enforcement. Nobody messed with Angela when Charlie was within earshot.

Jake was able to mend fences with Kathy, but not without some conflict. His attention to his career, and the stress he went through after the shooting and the Review Board made her wonder if their marriage would be able to last. He convinced her to stay with him, with promises that he would do a better job at home. Shortly after Kiley, their beautiful little girl was born, they moved to New York. Jake's workload there after 9/11 convinced Kathy that his promises would never be kept. He loved what he did too much. But she loved him and respected the work he did. He was a good man, and that is what she thought the kids needed in their life. So, they stayed together, but no more children would come.

"Why retire so early, buddy?" Todd pressed. He knew he could pry a little because of their long friendship.

"So many reasons, but it comes down to family. I owe it to Kathy, mostly. She put up with a lot and was the bedrock of the family while I pursued my career. Now that the kids are both in college, I want to give her the companionship she deserves. Maybe more of me is the last thing she would want, but I have to do right by her after all these years of her carrying me and the kids. She and I have been kicking it around for a while, and when I told her I was going to submit the paperwork today, she was as happy as I've seen her in way too long."

"I am also worried about Charlie. He graduates this spring from Georgetown, and he's talking about applying for a job at the Bureau. Did he pick Georgetown because I went there? Is he choosing the Bureau because he wants to live up to some ideal he has in his head about pleasing Dad? I just don't know. My hope is that if I retire now, it might take away some of that pressure and let him make his own decisions. Looking back, I know I didn't spend enough time with him growing up, so now I'm a bit at a loss to know what he really thinks."

Chen hesitated. He knew his dedication to his own career had forced compromises in his family life. "Don't beat yourself up too bad about it, Jake," Todd said. "I always believed that being 'the good guys' and 'fighting crime' made the sacrifice worth it, and you did too. Are you sure that's the real reason?"

"That's the real reason, Todd. I love my wife and want to take the time to try to make her happy. Simple."

Todd shrugged, saying, "Just don't let Carla know."

Jake laughed.

Jake's administrative assistant, Paula, came in just then, saying, "The boss wants to see you upstairs, pronto." Jake and Todd both rolled their eyes, and Paula just shrugged. She knew the history. Paula had been Jake's assistant ever since he hired her when he came to the D.C. office. Of her many skills, the one trait Jake insisted on was loyalty, and Paula had always been that. He could trust her to watch his back.

"The boss" was Steve Marks, the little weasel that had tried to hang Jake out to dry those many years ago in Milwaukee. During the Review process, he had worked behind the scenes to plant seeds of doubt in the minds of the investigation team about Jake's decision-making the day of the bank robbery and shooting. He offered up other options he thought should have been considered, and solutions that, in hindsight only, might have been better. But when it came time to give a formal statement, he ducked all the tough questions, and never went on record openly criticizing Jake's handling of the case.

Sadly, Marks was particularly adept at the politics that often dominated decisions within the Bureau. While the FBI had recognized Jake's superior leadership and law enforcement skills when they promoted him over Marks early in his career, Marks worked his magic behind the scenes to move up in the bureaucracy without having to stick his neck out. Jake had to give him some credit. For a man with Marks' limited abilities, he had risen to a position of authority in the D.C. office, no small feat.

"Did he say what it was about?" Jake asked.

"No clue," Paula replied, "but he had your retirement papers on his desk when he asked for you."

Jake plodded up the one flight of stairs with mixed emotions. He really did dislike Marks, so spending any time in his presence, especially at Marks' insistence, was distasteful. On the other hand, at some point, Jake looked forward to telling Marks what he and the rest of the 'real' cops in the Bureau thought of him. Maybe today was the day.

When Jake entered, he had to admit that Marks knew how to play the game. His desk was at the farthest point from the door, so his guests had to walk the entire length of the room to greet him. Marks, as always with an underling, waited behind his desk for Jake to approach. As Jake walked in, he also noticed the "ego wall" along the left. Pictures of Marks shaking hands with past Directors if the FBI, various politicians, framed Awards and Commendations he had somehow collected through the years, and a framed copy of the Mission Statement of the Bureau. Exactly what a career weenie would display, thought Jake.

After a few banal pleasantries, "How's the wife and kids? Still swimming every day? Blah, blah, blah," Marks got to the point. "Jake, I got your retirement request today. I need to ask you for a ... Wait, let me rephrase that. The Bureau needs to ask you for a favor. We need you to delay your retirement for six months."

Jake shook his head no. "I've made up my mind. It's June first. I'm firm on that."

Marks took a long pause, rearranged a few things on his desk, and wiped away an imaginary speck of dust. Finally, he looked up. "Look Jake, I know you and I have never gotten along. I know you think I'm a bureaucrat, but this organization needs bureaucrats, too. Let's not let that get in the way of the good of the Bureau. This request isn't coming from me but from the Director himself."

Jake just nodded and said, "I'm listening."

"As you know, this COVID-19 pandemic has screwed a lot of things up. Our case backlog has swelled, we can't get agents out to meet with witnesses, and many key businesses are shut down. Our supply chains are messed up, the courts are backed up on processing prosecutions and on issuing search warrants for pending investigations." Jake began to protest, but Marks held up his hand and continued. "I don't need your help on those things. We will figure them out. But this is what we need you to do. As you know, we had to cancel our Spring class at the Academy in Quantico, sending everyone home after only three days of classes. What I am asking...what the Bureau is asking, is that you take over the leadership of the Academy for the Summer semester."

Jake, a lifetime Agent focused on practical work in the field, not teaching, was surprised.

Marks continued. "It won't be easy. We will be trying to run as many students as we can fit into the dorms there. We will need more new Agents as soon as possible to help with the backlog of cases we have now, and to replace the retirements we have on the schedule already. The Director thinks you have the organizational skills to handle it. On a broader scale, we always worry the Bureau is losing its passion for the nuts and bolts of law enforcement. You have always had that passion, and we are asking you to pass that along to the next generation of agents."

Marks could see Jake was intrigued but needed a push. "I've heard Kathy has been bugging you to go on a Mediterranean cruise with her. The Bureau would be willing to pay out your accrued sick leave in a lump sum. That would be more than enough to allow you to cruise in style. Plus, you'd have full control over staffing, curriculum, the works. I'll be your liaison here at Headquarters, but you'd be the boss on site."

Marks paused. He could see the indecision in Jake's face. Then, "Jake, the Bureau needs you. You have never let us down before. Can I... I mean, can we, count on you?"

Jake stroked his chin. Marks couldn't know that the most persuasive thing he had said was that Marks wouldn't be at Quantico with him. But he kept that to himself. "I need to talk to Kathy about it. I'll let you know tomorrow."

Marks nodded. "OK, but if you decide to do it, you need to formally withdraw your retirement application, or your retirement is automatically approved effective June 1. I've drawn up the forms for you to sign. Take them with you and get them back to my assistant as soon as you can. Good luck with Kathy tonight."

On the drive home, Jake tried to make sense of all he was feeling. Even before Marks' request, Jake was scared to death of the prospect of retirement. Financially, they would be okay. Even the smaller twenty-five-year pension from the Bureau, plus some smart investing over the years and a small inheritance from when Kathy's parents died would be enough to live on comfortably. But Jake thought, a few more years of income would be better.

Jake shook his head. He had to stop himself from using money as an excuse. He knew the money wasn't his only worry, or even the most important one. It was more his sense of who he was. His place in the world. His mission. In retirement, he would need to figure out how and where he would add value to society, and law enforcement was all he knew. Facing the unknown was intimidating, especially for someone who wanted—no, needed—to be in control. That was his real fear.

Jake mulled over his career. It had been a good one, he knew. The way he had handled his first big leadership test in

Milwaukee was a good start. The work he did in NYC after 9/11 made a difference in people's lives. He had worked many other important cases in his later postings, boasting one of the higher case clearance rates in the Bureau. However, he wondered about his legacy with the Bureau. The FBI had hundreds of dedicated Agents who worked as hard and as passionately as he did. This new assignment at the Academy would be a way to cement his reputation, and to pass along to a new generation of agents some of what he had learned on the street. That was tempting.

As he pulled up into his driveway, he still hadn't figured it all out. But what he had decided was that his old way of making life decisions unilaterally was going to end. This decision affected Kathy too, and he would talk to her about it first. Knowing how excited she was when he told her he was handing in his retirement papers, he suspected he knew how she would react.

When he opened the front door, he noticed the music first. With both kids away at school, he was used to hearing the sewing machine, vacuum cleaner, or the evening news on the TV when he came in. Romantic music was different. Then he smelled the aroma of cooking from the kitchen. Was that his favorite, baked salmon and fresh bread that he smelled? As he walked towards the kitchen, he heard his wife ask if he wanted a cold beer. He said he did, and she met him in the doorway. Her short blonde hair was styled differently than usual. She had applied a little extra makeup, even though she knew Jake always told her that her eyes were her best feature. She was wearing her favorite apron. She handed him the beer, raised up on her toes to kiss him, and then turned back to the kitchen.

"How was your day, dear?" was all she said, as if nothing was out of the ordinary. When Jake didn't answer right away, she looked over her shoulder, gave him a sly smile, and said "Is something wrong, honey?"

Jake finally managed a smile back, saying, "No, everything is just great now that I'm home." He meant it. Kathy had been a runner when they first met, a passion she continued until both kids needed her. With some guilt, Jake realized that if he had been home more to help out, Kathy might have continued to be a runner. Nonetheless, she shifted to using a stationary bike, a rowing machine, and yoga whenever time permitted, and it paid off. She was still strong, fit, confident, and attractive. How could he have failed to pay closer attention all these years? But her message was clear tonight: She was in a romantic mood.

Jake's very male initial instinct was to take full advantage of this very new and exciting opportunity. Let's just let this play out, he thought. After dinner and some much-too-rare time in the bedroom, we could talk about delaying retirement. But Jake had a conscience and knew he couldn't go that route. If he was going to reform the way he and Kathy made decisions, he couldn't start out with a lie, even one of omission.

"How long until we eat dinner?"

"About 30 minutes. Why, is there something you would like to do before then?" Kathy asked, suggestively raising her eyebrows.

Jake's mouth went dry, but he swallowed hard and said, "Can we sit down for a few minutes and talk first?" Kathy could tell it was serious. They sat on the couch, and Jake poured out everything that was on his mind: the job offer, how he was afraid of retirement, his legacy at the Bureau, the opportunity to spend a little more time with Charlie, assuming he got into the Academy, the sick leave payout offer. Everything he could think of. No reaction from Kathy. Just as he finished talking, the timer on the oven went off.

Kathy got up and told him to sit down at the dining room table. She went into the kitchen, plated the dinner, and joined him. He saw the bottle of wine she had opened and filled their glasses. She lit the candles she had set into the candleholders that Jake remembered they had gotten as wedding gifts from his parents. They said grace, as they always did, and began to eat. It was a fabulous setting, and great food, but the silence from Kathy was eating him alive. They were nearly done eating when Jake finally asked, "So, what do you think?"

Kathy looked surprised. She finished chewing, swallowed, and said "What did you decide to do?" She said it without malice or sarcasm, but Jake knew it reflected the selfish way he had treated her for so many years.

Jake replied, "I know that I have spent most of our marriage deciding things on my own. Things that have affected you, our kids, and our lives. Important things. I realize that I was wrong. Whether or not my decisions later turned out to be the right ones, you deserved to be part of them. I'm so sorry for that. And I am so thankful for your love and support for all these years. So, I really do want to know: What do you think?"

Kathy stared out the window at first, saying nothing. Jake then noticed a tear form at the corner of her eye. She put down her fork, and wiped away that first tear, and many more that came after. Jake was frozen, uncomfortable with any display of emotion from the usually strong and stoic woman he loved. Finally, she composed herself, reached for his hand, looked into his eyes, and said, "Jake, you have been a fine man, but as a husband, not so much. There were so many times, I'm sure you knew, that I questioned whether we should stay together. We had both drifted into our own routines, career for you, kids, the house, and volunteering for me. Like the Earth and the moon, circling each other, but never coming together. When the kids went off to college, I was as worried about our marriage as you are about your career. I'm still worried. But tonight, you have made me as happy as you have in a long time just by asking my opinion.

It gives me new hope that you... we... can change a lifetime of bad habits. Thank you for that."

Jake was truly moved but didn't know what to say. Always on task, he rather lamely asked, "so, what about the job?"

Kathy rose. She untied the apron, took it off, and dropped it on the chair. "If you really want to know my answer, you're going to have to work for it. I have a few special tasks for you in our bedroom that need your attention. Oh, and hurry up, please. I'm still hungry." She smiled and wiggled her hips a little more than usual on her way down the hall. Jake did as he was told.

Hours later, Jake and Kathy were wrapped up in their sheets in bed. They were tired but comfortable in ways only long-married couples can be. Jake asked if he had properly earned her answer. She smiled. "If you want to pull the plug now, I'd support your decision. But I think you should take the job at the Academy. Use the time to pass along to your son and the rest of the new recruits the values of honesty and integrity you have always shown in your life. Let that be your legacy. And when you are done, you are all mine! Now, I have another request for you if you're not too tired." Jake wasn't.

# Chapter 3

## 2001

Nadia Trulenko could not feel the joy that most new mothers felt as she nursed her own child. Of course, she could look down at her precious son with pride, hope, and excitement about his future and hers. But the concept of love had been drained from her since the very beginning. The life that had been forced upon her, from her childhood right up to the time she saw the father of her child gunned down, killed by an evil and heartless representative of a power structure that continued to oppress the weak and the needy, removed any semblance of emotion that might be compared to love.

She had named him Sean when he was born a little over two years ago. He looked up into her eyes now, his tiny mouth smiling around her breast. He had known only her since birth. No babysitters. No father. Nobody else had so much as held him. Nadia was his whole universe, and the source of all his food, warmth, and security. It was she who comforted him when he cried, fed him when he was hungry, and slept with him in their only bed. So different from her own sad life, Nadia thought. Nadia remembered how her own mother told Nadia the family history and knew she would someday tell Sean her own story.

Nadia's parents had come to the States from the former Yugoslavia in 1973. Much of the strife that would tear apart that area of the world was still to come, but it was clear even then to Nadia's paternal grandparents that the future there was going to be ugly. The constantly shifting political factions, and the religious conflicts and divisions, foreshadowed nothing but heartache for its inhabitants in the decades to come. So, when Nadia's father Nico, and his new bride, Talia, were married, Grandpa insisted they leave his farm for America right after the wedding. By the time passage on a ship was arranged, the immigration paperwork was finished, and the goodbyes were said, Talia was pregnant. Unsure how the pregnancy might affect their immigration status, she and Nico told nobody. They arrived in New York unable to speak the language, unemployed, and pregnant.

The only thing Nico knew how to do was farm. He stayed in a seedy tenement with his wife for a few days until he learned of the need for farmworkers in Texas. The large corporate farms there needed workers, and Nico saw what he thought was an opportunity. An unscrupulous recruiter promised Nico and Talia free travel to south Texas in return for a commitment to work for three months on the harvest of the spring citrus crop. They took the deal.

They soon learned they were trapped. The long hours in the heat and humidity of the Gulf Coast were brutal. They earned just enough money to pay for their food (bought from the store owned by the company they worked for) and for shelter in the form of run-down barracks shared with dozens of other primarily Hispanic migrant workers. They knew they were better off than the illegal immigrants who were always living in fear of deportation if they had the temerity to complain. However, Nico and Talia were not able to speak either English or Spanish, leading to greater and greater isolation. Even worse was that by the end of three months, when the citrus crop was in, Talia's pregnancy began to show.

When he went in for his final paycheck, his field boss, George Henry, praised him for being such a hard worker, and asked him what he planned to do next. In the very broken English and Spanish he had picked up from his fellow workers, Nico told George about Talia's pregnancy. George explained how this ‹farming thing› worked. As the summer went on, many of the workers migrated north with the harvest season. They would continue to work, as they had in Texas, in places that Nico had never heard of: Oklahoma, Nebraska, Iowa, and Wisconsin. They would harvest corn, soybeans, cabbage, and other staples. George told Nico that with his work ethic, he could earn enough to let Talia work fewer hours until the child was born, and then take off a few weeks until she felt able to return to the fields. Once the winter came, the company would bus everyone back to Texas and it would all start again the following spring.

Nico felt he had no choice. It was 1974. Unemployment was high. Inflation was double-digit. The political and financial world after Nixon's resignation was in turmoil. This was no time for Nico to take big risks with his wife and unborn child. So, he agreed. Just for one season, he told himself.

Three months later, he found himself on a large farm in Iowa. He had proven himself to be a hard worker, even taking on some lead worker responsibilities at George's insistence, with some extra pay. He held the other workers to his high standards and berated them when they fell short. They resented him, but his loyalty was to supporting his wife and family, not to currying the workers' favor. He also picked up a few extra hours in the evenings feeding the hogs on the farm, so Talia could rest in the heat of the afternoons.

August 14 was the day Nadia was born. Not that Nadia would ever celebrate her birthday in any meaningful way, but her mother at least told her it was her birthday every year. Nico was working in the fields that day. It was hot, and Talia was resting in the barracks, alone, in the hottest part of the afternoon. Her water broke, and she felt the labor pains start. She managed to call out, and fortunately for her, a veterinarian was visiting the farm that day to inoculate the hogs. He heard her calls for help and knew enough to help her through the birth. Talia had heard what to expect, but the reality still was a shock. Her mother had told her before she and Nico left Yugoslavia that labor had always been quick in their family, and Nadia was born in less than an hour. So, when Nico returned, tired and sore from his day, he was shocked, as well as a little sad and even embarrassed that he was not there for the birth of his own daughter.

Talia was able to take time off to be with the baby, but that only put more pressure on Nico. He worked more hours, drove his subordinates harder, and was saddened by every moment he was away from his family. With no friends, no rest, and no support, he was inevitably drawn to the home-made alcohol the other itinerant farmers made in the barracks. It was foul-tasting, made from potatoes, beets, or any other vegetables they could steal during the day, but it quickly and effectively numbed Nico. As his guilt and powerlessness grew, so did his dependence on the warm feeling the clear liquid made as it slid down his throat. As the summer and fall wore on, and Nico continued to stumble down the path that fate seemed inevitably to have placed him on, the hopeful and hard-working émigré to the land of opportunity slowly died. In his place grew an abusive and demanding tyrant, with no memory of the good values he was taught as a child.

As Nadia learned from the earliest time she could remember, Nico's intolerant behavior applied to everyone, including his wife and child. Symbolic of his own failures as a provider, and emphasizing his absentee status, he grew increasingly resentful towards them. He saw any failure on their part as making his hard life even harder. The drinking prevented him from showing any kindness towards them. He couldn't let his guard down for even a moment lest the men and women under his supervision take advantage of him, so he wouldn't even accept kindness from others, especially those closest to him. Nadia never felt any sense of love from him.

Yet, it was still a shock to her four-year-old eyes the first time Nico hit her mother. By then, the three of them had survived three more cycles of harvests, following the sun and the heat through the midsection of the country. As hard as they tried to save enough money to end the cycle, something always came up. The company would raise prices on the food and clothing they were forced to buy from them. A poor harvest would reduce income for a time, depleting their savings. Nico was injured one September, and while he could still oversee the work of others, he could not help with the harvest, and so lost money.

The December after Nadia's fourth birthday, she came down with a bad cough. Talia tried the usual remedies she knew, and even some the other women had suggested, but nothing seemed to help. Nadia's fever grew worse, and Talia finally took Nadia to a clinic in the small town in Texas where they were staying for the winter to see a doctor. He was very concerned, and prescribed a strong antibiotic, warning Talia that if Nadia did not improve quickly, she might need to be hospitalized. When Talia returned home, Nico had been drinking. He flew into a rage about how she should have asked him before taking Nadia to town. When Talia asked Nico for the money to buy the medicine, he checked their savings, which he kept hidden away in their battered suitcase. He kept close watch on their money and was shocked to find twenty dollars was missing. He demanded to know if Talia knew anything about it.

Talia explained that Christmas was coming, and Nadia had never had either a birthday present or a Christmas present so she had taken the money to buy Nadia a doll. Nico erupted. He began blaming all their problems on Talia and Nadia. Why couldn't they be more supportive? Why were they always wasting his money? Why didn't Talia work as hard as he did? Why couldn't Nadia start helping with the harvest? As his rant went on, his voice got louder. He got closer and closer to Talia, who was standing between Nico and Nadia. Then his fist lashed out, catching Talia flush on the right side of her face. She crumpled to the ground and tried to cover herself and her daughter. Nico continued to rage. Talia told herself it was just the alcohol and the stress, but Nadia only saw the blood coming from her mother's nose and mouth. The gentle soul who had cared for her and nurtured her since her birth was bleeding. Nadia would never forget that moment.

Nadia now looked down at her own child, sweetly nursing as he fell asleep. She remembered how her childhood had shaped her. Now, she would begin to shape the life of her own son. She would use all her skills to shape him into the tool that would avenge his own father's death. She would show the world the difference between a mother who is a loving but powerless and weak victim, and one who will do what is necessary to control her own life, and that of her son.

# Chapter 4

## 1998

As soon as Tony Chen announced the perp in the Milwaukee bank was down, the EMTs on stand-by got the go-ahead from Jake to get into the bank and check on the wounded guard and on Willie. Within a few minutes, Jake learned the guard was going to be okay, but that they needed to get him to the emergency room. He'd lost a lot of blood but was awake and alert and no major arteries had been hit. As for Willie, they told Jake he could send in the Medical Examiner whenever he wanted. Willie was dead, and there wasn't a lot of doubt about the cause of death.

Jake knew the situation now moved from an emergency response to a full-out investigation. A man was dead, at Jake's direction, no less. The Agency now had two main objectives. First, it needed to run down every lead to be sure those responsible for this situation were brought to justice. Was Willie a lone wolf, or was he part of a greater movement? Who had helped him, and might they try this sort of thing again? Jake had to find out who Willie was talking about when he referred to taking back money for his friends. And who was he talking to on that walkie-talkie?

But Jake also knew the Bureau had a second objective, this one far more personal to him. The press and the brass in DC would ultimately judge every decision Jake made that day. As the new guy, pressed into a leadership role only because of the unavailability of both the SAC (because of his heart attack), and his deputy (because of alleged sexual misconduct), the scrutiny would be even more intense. Jake would have to be perfect so nobody could later claim he'd missed something.

Jake first got Captain Stawski, the MPD commander on the radio. He told him to get his men into the bank and see to the hostages. "Nobody is allowed to leave the bank lobby, no matter how much they scream. Get all of their names, and give the list to the Public Affairs officer, so he can communicate with their families. Make sure the hostages are calm and let them use the bathroom. Let's get them some sandwiches from the deli across the street. The deli owner probably will be glad for the business after having us shut him down all morning. Then I need your men to separate the hostages from one another and take detailed witness statements from each one."

The captain was as professional as Jake could have asked for. "I'm on it. The statements will take a few hours. I've only got two detectives on scene, and all my other guys are tied up with crowd control. You just want the usual open-ended 'tell me what you can remember' statements, or do you need something specific?"

"Nothing special. The more detail, the better," Jake told him. "Also, get your crime scene guys to take pictures of the crowd as soon as you can. This creep was talking to someone on the radio, and I want to see if I can figure out who. And on the witness statements, drill down into anything they can remember about the reason he was pulling this stunt, and anything about the walkie-talkies. Thanks."

Everything seemed to be going by the book. The local MPD cops were working well with Jake's guys, something that didn't always happen. The medical examiner was on his way. Jake's team would follow all the FBI protocols. They were well-trained and, at least today, motivated. While he would normally stay in the Command Post in case something came up that needed his attention, Jake was an impatient man. He grabbed a radio and told Steve Marks he was going to take a look around. He told Marks to be sure to make several copies of the video from the camera set up at the CP for the investigators and left the room.

By the time he walked across the street and got into the bank, the MPD officers were in place. A few of the hostages were complaining about being kept isolated, so Jake walked over and told them the FBI needed their help if they could just be patient, they'd be released as quickly as possible. They all calmed down.

"You have to love Midwesterners," Jake thought. "Salt of the earth, and always willing to help."

Then Jake walked over to the sheet that had been draped over Willie's body by the EMTs. He had seen dead bodies before, some quite gruesome. Most had been victims of violence; some were perps killed by his fellow agents. But Jake had never been personally responsible for a death before, so he knew he might look at this body differently. When he pulled back the sheet, his first impression was that Willie was sleeping. His eyes were closed, and his facial muscles showed none of the ugly grimace associated with violent death that Jake had seen on other victims. Just a small hole with a bit of blood above the right eye. When Jake looked closer, of course, he saw that the back of Willie's head was gone. There was blood-matted hair around the fringes of an exit wound the size of an orange. When Jake looked up at the wall behind the body, he saw what a supersonic bullet from Chen's rifle did to a man's head.

Jake was curiously calm about what he was seeing. He'd read enough about PTSD to know that he may be able to process the scene logically and dispassionately now, but that later he may need to talk it through with the Bureau's shrink to avoid having it build up and start to cause a problem. He reminded himself to make an appointment to do just that next week. The Bureau hadn't yet made such a visit mandatory, but Jake knew it could only help.

An MPD Crime Scene tech was hovering near the body. Jake asked if the body had been processed, and was told it was ready to be moved, but that Jake should minimize any contact. Jake asked about ID, and the tech handed Jake a sealed evidence bag with a wallet and driver's license. The license showed that 'Willie' was actually William Landry. His address was listed as 7247 Springfield Road, Lodi Wisconsin. Jake knew that was in a farming area a little north of the state capitol in Madison. Weird. Why would Landry have come all the way to Milwaukee to do this?

Jake pulled one of his agents off to the side and gave him the address. Dave Earle was new to the Milwaukee office. "Grab a car and get up to this guy's place as soon as you can. If someone is home, get as much information as you can, and try to get permission to search. If not, sit on it until I can get someone up there to help. We probably won't be able to get a search warrant until Monday, so I don't want anyone in or out until then. If this guy had an accomplice, the house will probably give us our best leads. Got it?"

Dave nodded and left. Jake's mind continued to race, trying to think a step ahead of anyone else who might have been involved. He spotted the walkie-talkie in the box holding all the bagged evidence that had been gathered so far. He asked the evidence tech if he had tested it before bagging it. He had. Nothing from the other end. The tech told Jake that once the lab got hold of it, they would be able to identify the frequency, and match it to any other radios found. Jake radioed to his team to search for any discarded walkie-talkies within four blocks of the bank in any direction. Probably a waste of time, but it didn't hurt to try.

The last thing Jake could think of was to try to chase down the motive. He asked to see the Bank Manager and was shown into his office. The nameplate on his desk read George Varney. Jake introduced himself, and complimented George's assistant, Mr. Peters, for remaining calm when they spoke on the phone during the crisis. The manager perked up at that, as Jake hoped he would.

"Any idea who this guy was, or why he was here?" Jake asked.

"No idea," George said. "He was very upset, and kept on about how the bank had ripped him off, as well as some of his neighbors. He had a list of specific amounts with people's names on it. The total was about $204,000. He showed me the list, and demanded I put that much money, to the penny, in a bank bag for him. I didn't recognize him. Sorry."

"His name was William Landry. Ring a bell?"

George hesitated a beat too long. Jake gave him a hard look, and said he better not hold back. A man was dead, and Jake wanted to know why.

George hesitated another beat, but then told Jake "In some of our management meetings we talked about some deadbeat loans in our Madison branch. Apparently, this Landry guy was raising quite a stink about it when he couldn't make the payments. Blames the bank, somehow, but then most of our delinquents say that. At our last meeting, they told the Madison branch to refer Landry to the main branch here. When he called last week to set up an appointment with me, I told him to contact our lawyers. That's all I know. He never said anything about it today, so I never made the connection."

Jake told him to start getting all the paperwork together on Landry's loan, as well as the collection efforts by the bank. Jake also wanted the contact information for the Madison branch manager as well as their corporate legal staff. Jake told the evidence tech to get George a copy of Landry's list of names and amounts, and told George he would need the loan documents, if any, for those names as well. George, true to his banking pedigree, said he would need a subpoena before he could release those records.

"Just get them together," Jake growled, "You'll get your subpoena on Monday morning."

Jake had done all he could think of at the scene to get all the right wheels in motion. Now he would need to begin the painful process of waiting for his people to do their jobs, sift through the evidence, and then try to understand why, on a beautiful Saturday morning in otherwise peaceful Milwaukee, Wisconsin, Jake had given the order to kill a man.

As Jake's mind began to slow down, Nadia's began to race. She had some vague idea of how the FBI and the police would act in response to the events of this morning from television and movies. She knew she would have to move fast if she wanted to cut the ties that would lead them to her door. Immediately after wiping her prints from the walkie-talkie and dumping it in the nearest garbage can, she moved as quickly as she could to their car. Fortunately, they had borrowed Bill's neighbor's car, so even if the cops put out a BOLO on Bill's car, they wouldn't find her that way. The car was parked in the Grand Avenue shopping mall parking garage, only a block away. She was out of the garage and on the expressway in a matter of minutes. She kept the speedometer at five miles over the posted limit as she drove west towards Madison. The last thing she needed was for a State Trooper to pull her over.

What a mess! She had been hopeful Bill would be able to pull this off. Their plan was for him to get the money and be miles away before the cops even were called. When the bank alarm went off, their back-up plan was to have him run into the crowd with the money, knowing he'd be caught. But if, in the confusion, he could slip the money to her before he was nabbed, she'd hide it in some shopping bags she was carrying and get away. He'd lawyer up, refuse to cooperate, and take the punishment, but at least his farm, and those of his neighbors, would be saved from foreclosure. His naivety, willingness to help others, his fundamental goodness, was what had attracted Nadia to him in the first place. Now he was dead, and she was on her own facing criminal charges for being an accomplice to a bank robbery, pregnant, and on the run. She had to become a ghost, severing all ties to the first man who had ever loved her.

She remembered the first time they had met, two years earlier. She had been working the same migrant worker circuit as her parents had for years. While all the companies that ran the migrants took full advantage of the workers, the one she was working for since she broke away from her abusive father was happy to have a younger, brighter, and more experienced worker than the ones who usually applied. She knew the ropes and interacted well with the farmers who hired the company to help harvest their crops.

One of the smaller farms she had done some work for, Black Earth Growers, asked her to help them sell their organic vegetables at the Madison Farmer's Market on Saturdays. She normally had Saturdays off, but could use the extra money, so she agreed. The experience was a revelation. The entire square around the beautiful white marble domed State Capitol building was packed. Vendors set up booths one next to another, selling all manner of things. During a break, she walked the square, delighting in the pastries, specialty coffees and teas, flowers, fruits, cured and fresh meats and cheeses; in short, everything a Wisconsin farm might have to offer.

Of equal interest were the people. Most of the customers were students at the University of Wisconsin-Madison, but because of its international draw, Nadia saw and heard people who came from all over the world. Many former students settled in the Madison area, working for the State Government or the University, so the eclectic and well-educated nature of the student body extended to the older customers as well. She also took in all the political groups trying to sell their particular messages to that same customer base. Student advocacy groups, anti-war groups, pro-choice and pro-life groups, pro-labor groups, and political parties from the Green Party to the Young Republicans and every stripe in-between, were represented. For someone whose childhood was limited to moving from one farm to the next, interacting with poor and generally uneducated migrant workers, and reading whatever books she could get from the local library, the Farmers Market was a veritable feast of sights, sounds, smells, and experiences.

When she got back to her own booth from her break, still overwhelmed by all she had seen, she first noticed the man in the booth next to theirs. His eyes were what struck her first. They were blue, but not that soft sky-blue you see in children. They were a darker blue, almost turquoise, and they smiled even before the rest of his face did. He was about thirty she guessed; a bit older than her twenty-four years. He was wearing a blue plaid flannel shirt and jeans, both showing the dirt that is part of the life of a true working farmer. His hands were callused, and his nails were dirty, but his face was both serious and kind. When he noticed her looking at him, his smile was both instantaneous and warm. He extended his hand, and introduced himself as William Landry, "but my friends call me Bill." His voice was gentle, like his demeanor. She instantly liked him.

"I'm Nadia Trulenko. I'm helping out at Black Earth Growers. Glad to meet you." Nadia had no idea how to act. She knew that physically she had nothing to worry about. She was a bit taller than average, but thin. Her breasts and hips were curved enough that the men she worked with had no doubt she was attractive. Normally, the clothes she wore in the fields covered up her charms, but today she was wearing a sleeveless knit top and shorts, which showed off her long legs, and well-muscled arms. She was a hard worker, and her body proved it. That hardness may not be what every man was looking for, but to Bill, it was the feminine ideal.

Her upbringing, or more precisely her lack of it, made her reluctant to talk. She knew being a migrant worker was not something to be proud of. The abuse she and her mother suffered for years didn't open any lines for discussion about her childhood, either. What, if anything, would she and this gentleman find to talk about? She needn't have worried. Bill started asking her questions about the one thing she knew a lot about: Farming. She instantly felt at ease, and they fell into a comfortable dialogue about all things agricultural.

Their conversation, in between waiting on customers, gradually revealed Bill's story. He owned a small farm north of Madison, inherited from his parents. His mother had died four years ago, her loyal and devoted husband followed her within the year. The farm was large enough to financially break even every year if the weather was good, and for the past four years, it had been. But he always worried how he would cope if his luck ran out. He and his neighbors helped one another to plant and harvest the crops every year and could be counted on if a piece of equipment broke down or there was an illness or injury. But bad weather would hurt them all, so there was no true safety net for them.

"We do have some hope, though. Two winters back, one of the vice presidents from a Madison bank approached my neighbors and me. He said they had done a lot of research and financial analysis on organic farming. According to the bank, backed up by a detailed report, the Madison area was ripe for significant expansion into the organic food market. There was little supply, and demand was going to rise, and so would prices. There was some risk, he said. We would need to let a portion of our farms lie fallow for up to two years to leech them of any chemicals or pesticides in order to meet Federal and State regulations. To make ends meet in the interim, the bank would extend a loan to each of us, at favorable rates. Then once we are certified 'organic', we could raise prices on our produce, repay the loan, and increase our profit margin on a yearly basis thereafter."

Bill explained he and his neighbors struggled with the decision. None of them, including Bill's dad, had ever wanted to have a mortgage; the farm was all they had. However, they also knew the economics of the small family farm didn't work long-term and selling out to a large corporate farm was the only alternative. Ultimately, they all decided to take a chance on something new. So, for the past two seasons, they had all left one-fourth of their land lie fallow, trying to increase their yield on the remaining acreage to make up the difference as best they could. Meanwhile, the interest was accruing on the mortgage, and the first payments were due a year from now. The next year would determine their fate.

The afternoon had raced by without Nadia even noticing, so captivated was she by this man's story. The life she had lived, trapped in a cycle of harvesting crops for a wage that was never quite enough to end the cycle, was the same as Bill's. That he was willing to risk all he owned to try to escape that cycle inspired her. She wanted a chance too. So, as they packed up their booths and prepared to head home, she promised to return the next Saturday. He promised to be there as well.

The following Saturday, and over the three weeks after that, Nadia and Bill became closer. Nadia felt more comfortable sharing many of the details of her difficult life, and Bill was understanding and supportive without being condescending. She noticed his clothes and hands were cleaner than their first meeting, and she convinced one of the female workers to let her use a bit of makeup. She found herself thinking about him during the drudgery of her week and couldn't wait for Saturday to come. Hope for the future was not something Nadia had ever experienced. It was both odd and exhilarating.

The Farmer's Market had its last Saturday of the season in late November. Nadia was at a crossroads. She would be returning to Texas by Thanksgiving, as she had her entire life, to begin the harvest cycle again. She needed a way out, and this hopeful and gentle farmer might just be it. He seemed enamored of her, and she had been thinking of how she might take advantage of that to start a new phase of her life. It's not that she didn't enjoy his company, or even admire him. But she knew in her heart that love was never going to be an option for her. She had seen what "love" had done to her mother and had never had anyone in her life model self-sacrifice. People were only a means to an end in Nadia's eyes, and Bill, as nice as he was, would only ever be a way out for her.

So, after they had packed up for the final time, she asked him to join her for a farewell dinner. She told him the Black Earth Growers truck was her ride back home and asked him if he could drive her there himself. He agreed. They ended up at a small diner just off the square. After they were seated and ordered their food, she excused herself to freshen up.

When she returned, she was a different woman. She had combed out her hair and put on more makeup than her usual light touch. The silk blouse, black skirt, and sandals she had borrowed from the daughter of the farmer she was working for showed off her beautiful, tanned skin and animal grace to full advantage. Many men's heads turned to watch her, but she was only interested in Bill. His eyes never left her.

As she sat down, he told her how nice she looked. She knew it was time to make her pitch. "Bill, these last few weeks have been wonderful. I have been looking forward to Saturday every day, and I think you have been as well. I am amazed to have so much in common with someone so handsome and hard-working." Nadia had learned how to read people, and she knew Bill was buying it. She continued. "You need someone to help you on the farm. I know farming, love to work hard, and I'm willing to work for room and board. In all the years I've worked as a migrant, I've never been able to save anything for the future anyway, so helping you is no different. Will you let me help you?"

Bill began to look uncomfortable. Remembering that he had been raised by two loving, married, and likely conservative parents, Nadia quickly added, "I'm not suggesting anything improper. I'm sure you have a spare room in the house I could sleep in. I'd be glad to cook and clean to help earn my keep in addition to sharing the farm chores. We would make it crystal clear to the neighbors that nothing improper was going on. At the end of the day, you get full-time help, and it costs you nothing except a little bit more food." Finally, she took his hand in hers, leaned close, and said, "And if by being together more, the feelings we clearly have for each other lead to something more, that isn't a bad thing either. Now, what do you think?"

Their food came just then, giving Bill a reprieve. As they ate in silence, Nadia knew she had to give Bill time to digest her proposal. After a decent interval, she slipped off a sandal, and rubbed her foot against Bill's calf. He looked startled. He finally spoke. "I'd be lying if I said I hadn't thought about spending more time with you. I was dreading the day you went back south. So, this is all very unexpected. I've been so lonely on the farm since my parents passed, so company would be welcome. That the company would be such an attractive and interesting woman was more than I could hope for. But I have two problems. First, my reputation in the community. Having a young woman living with me would be hard to understand for the folks around me."

Nadia gave him a disarming smile. "I know that. But if we are both open about the purely platonic nature of our relationship with them, I think we can bring them around. What is the other problem?"

Bill hesitated, but finally got it out. "I like you. A lot. If you come to stay with me, I don't think I could look at you as just another farmhand. It would be difficult for me to pretend I didn't want more than that. But I wouldn't want to take advantage of you, or have you feel any sense of obligation to pursue a relationship with me."

Nadia thought to herself, "I've got him!" While her foot travelled further up his calf, she leaned in close. "What makes you think I wouldn't be the one who wants to take advantage of you? I've been imagining exactly what we might do together since the first day we met. Why don't we head out to your car and discuss this some more?" Bill couldn't pay the check fast enough.

Suffice to say Bill agreed to Nadia's proposal. She picked up her things at the Black Earth Farm and spent the night on Bill's farm. And not in the spare room. That was two years ago. Now Bill was dead, and she was speeding along on I-94 West trying to figure out how to escape her ugly past.

# Chapter 5

## 2020

Jake was starting to get excited about the opportunity to work with a bunch of new agents before they developed all the bad habits they would later learn in their first assignments. Traffic had been light on the forty-five minute drive from his home to the front gate at Quantico. The FBI Academy is a unique facility. It is a large collection of buildings and land wholly enclosed within the confines of a U.S. Marine base in Quantico, Virginia, a short drive from downtown Washington.

The Marines took their security seriously and required Jake to show a picture ID while the gate guards checked in and under his vehicle, including his trunk. After a computer check of his license, Jake was waved through the fortified entrance. He continued driving through the grounds until he arrived at the front entrance parking area to the FBI's prime training facility, The Academy.

Jake had been here many times, first as a new agent-in-training, and then later for several refresher courses during his long career with the Bureau. He had also been an instructor on occasion when the Bureau invited representatives of local law enforcement to attend training at the Academy, a plum opportunity for many local police chiefs and future leaders in law enforcement. Jake had always enjoyed the cloistered nature of the environment, and the lack of outside distractions the physical isolation of the Academy created for the students here.

During the COVID pandemic that swept the world, the Academy had suspended classes, creating the urgency that led to Jake's current assignment. But the confined nature of the Academy would actually be a benefit during the upcoming semester. Following the lead established by many professional sports teams who created COVID "bubbles", once Jake's students tested negative for COVID, and were quarantined in their rooms for the first five days, they would all be free to interact with each other and their instructors, even maskless, without a significant concern of infection. There would be no outside interaction with possible sources of infection because everyone, students and instructors alike, would be confined to the Academy grounds. The usual breaks to leave to visit family and friends were suspended at Jake's insistence. They had lost a couple of good recruits over this rule, but Jake thought it was worth it. Sports teams had used this "bubble" approach, and Jake thought it would work here as well.

Jake felt a lightness in his step as he grabbed his suitcases from the trunk of his car and headed up the steps to the building. He walked across the broad, two-tiered plaza in front of the main entrance before passing into the lobby. Surrounding him were the display cases holding historic memorabilia from the Bureau's past, such as Dillinger's handgun, Bonnie and Clyde's machine guns, and a framed portrait of J. Edgar Hoover. One display case held badges from the history of the Bureau, and another an array of the many weapons used in cases solved by the Bureau, from hatchets and garrotes, to guns and knives.

Jake took the elevator to his new office on the top floor of the administration building. From his vantage point, he could see the layout of what would be his main home for the next sixteen weeks, the usual length of the Academy training. Admin was the building furthest east. From there, the entire complex was a series of interconnected buildings. From the lobby two floors below him, Jake could walk west into the Hall of Honor where the fallen of the Bureau were memorialized. A right would take him to the library, and a left would lead to the main auditorium, where the graduation ceremonies would normally be held. Straight on led to the classroom building, where his charges would receive training from some of the best instructors the FBI could find. Many instructors were experienced agents like Jake, while some others were contracted from academia or the private sector due to their particular areas of expertise.

Beyond the classroom building was a state-of-the-art exercise facility, including cardio, a pool, an indoor running track, and classrooms where tactical combat techniques were taught and practiced.

But it was the living quarters where the personal relationships would be built that would sustain these new Agents in their careers. The two dormitory buildings, Washington and Madison, faced each other to the north of the library, connected by hallways to it. On the other end of the dormitories, hallways connected the students to the dining hall. Without ever going outside, his Agents could attend their classes, study, research, eat and sleep. Agents had individual rooms, with four rooms sharing a bathroom. One truly unique aspect of dormitory life at the Academy was the tradition of unlocked doors. The message was that you needed to trust your fellow agents, so no locks were ever even installed on the doors.

The sprawling grounds outside the main complex offered even more opportunities. Most famous was probably Hogan's Alley, a mock-up city street where the Academy taught techniques and strategies for surveillance, tactical assaults, arrests, and emergency responses. A separate building also housed one of the most sophisticated technical laboratory, computer, and evidence processing facilities available. Off to the west, Jake could see the paved track where the Emergency Vehicle Operator's Course (EVOC) was run, showing agents how to safely and effectively conduct high speed chases and operate their vehicles under all types of driving conditions. The firearms training facilities were off to the northwest, where Jake was sure Tony Chen was already setting up the rigorous standards Jake had asked him to establish for the new agents. Tony was one of several people he demanded to have as part of his team, and Steve Marks reluctantly gave in, complaining the whole time about costs and manpower.

One final part of the grounds was the "Yellow Brick Road", legendary in the Bureau. It was a beast of a military-style obstacle course, 6.1 miles of hell through rough and uneven terrain in the hills of the Marine Base. Graduation required that an Agent successfully complete the course. As a further reward, they each received a commemorative yellow brick, inscribed with their class number and date. Jake had his, and he had seen them proudly displayed on the desks of many of his fellow agents over the years. His Agents would be both well trained and fit. Despite his age, Jake was looking forward to running the "Road" with his charges.

Jake caught himself daydreaming and turned back to his work. He had learned the importance of delegation, and this assignment was no different. He had met with his team of instructors, set the parameters and expectations, and he would now trust them to be the professionals he knew they were. Micromanaging was not Jake's style, and his staff appreciated it.

One new component of the Academy that Jake had put in place was a high-level independent guided study for six select students. Jake himself would lead this elite class himself. The incoming class of just over 200 students was offered the opportunity to apply for his seminar, but were warned it would be rigorous, and would not be an excuse for relief from any of the other requirements of the Academy. Only a dozen had applied, probably knowing that even without the seminar, nearly ten percent of the students washed out. Jake was sorting through the files of the applicants and thought he had narrowed the list to the right six. He planned to meet with each of them personally over the next hour before making the final decision. What would help confirm his decision was the topic they chose for their focus. Each of them had a special area of interest, and this seminar could put them on a path to be an important part of the future of the Bureau.

Fritz Hemmer came into his office with a confident air. Tall and thin, with short-cropped blond hair, blue eyes, and the Germanic features one would expect from his name, Fritz had worked for the Chicago PD as an evidence tech for five years while getting his degree in Chemistry from Northwestern, no small feat. His grades, like all the applicants for the seminar, were outstanding, and his resume and background check were without blemish. After the formalities, Jake asked him about his proposed project for the seminar.

Fritz explained, "For the past five years, I've heard too much about the backlog on DNA testing, especially in rape cases. The Illinois State Crime Lab can't seem to keep up, and they are not unique. My goal is to develop testing systems that are more streamlined and efficient, so we get rid of the backlog, and keep ahead of the game in the future. I know we need to be careful, but I know we can do better."

"What if you can't?" Jake asked.

Fritz smiled. "You don't know me yet, but that is not an option. There are too many victims that have been denied justice to allow failure. We can and will do better."

Jake liked his confidence, and the victim-based focus. Fritz was in.

Next up was Frank Steele. Jake was especially intrigued by Steele's background. When he was fourteen, his mother had died of a heroin overdose. Six months later, his father was arrested for dealing drugs, and was still in prison in Kansas. Frank was a good student and managed to keep his grades up despite entering the foster care system. He enlisted in the Army, and after serving for four years, got his degree in psychology from the University of Nebraska on the GI Bill. Jake wondered how Frank would deal with drug crimes in light of his family history. He needn't have worried. Frank's project was the perfect blend of his education and personal history. He wanted to develop highly effective drug treatment programs for drug users as a bargaining chip in getting them to roll over on their dealers.

"The dealers are the real problem, just like my own father. He was my mother's supplier, and I'll never forgive him for her death." Frank explained.

Jake was impressed by Frank's willingness to reveal his personal feelings on such a sensitive subject. He would be a welcome part of the seminar.

The first of two women in the group came in next. Katie Arnold was fit and attractive, if a little bookish, with short blond hair cut into a severe bob, and the graceful poise of a long-distance swimmer or runner. But Jake's real interest was in her resume. She got her degree from Yale in Finance and Economics and earned her CPA at the same time. Jake's first question was one she'd likely have to answer many times. "Why the FBI? With your resume, you could write your own ticket on Wall Street."

Katie knew the question was coming. "Two reasons. First, my folks lost a big piece of their retirement nest-egg in the late 90's tech bubble and in the downturn in 2008. In my studies, I've come to realize that the average Joe can't possibly understand the complexities of how and why the market works. To use my education to make that system even more opaque just didn't seem right to me. Second, I like puzzles. The FBI is the place to be if you want to figure out how white-collar criminals are trying to game the system. That type of puzzle interests me. I would never be bored. That is more important to me than money or prestige."

Financial crimes had always been something of a mystery to Jake, so he might just learn something from her while she learned from him.

"Have you given any thought to your project?" Jake asked.

"Yes, I want to try to figure out the Nazi Gold Mystery that has stumped the Bureau all these years."

Jake knew it well. During World War II, the Nazis had paid their collaborators in eastern Europe in specially minted gold pieces imprinted with a swastika. Over the past two decades, someone had been selling one or two per year to a rare coin dealer here, a pawn shop there, or some other interested party. They were illegal to possess or sell, and the Bureau had been looking for the source for years. But no real pattern had ever emerged, so they were always one step behind, reacting to reports of sightings and confiscating one here and there. It was a source of frustration for the financial unit, so any new ideas might be welcome.

Jake's only comment was, "Boy you do like puzzles. It will be a pleasure to work with you."

Jake walked Katie out, and saw his next applicant was waiting patiently. "Come on in, Sean. I'm glad you're helping me stay on schedule."

As Sean King walked in the room, Jake was struck first by his appearance. Tall, well-muscled, with perfect posture, his curly black hair, deep-set dark eyes, and square chin would command the room in ways Jake knew he would never be able to do. Jake's first thought was the description of the biblical King David, as a boy, "he was ruddy, with a fine appearance and handsome features." But Sean was also one of the brightest applicants in his class. His IQ was off the charts, perhaps the result of being home-schooled in a small town in Idaho through the end of high school. His perfect ACT score earned him a scholarship to the University of Washington, where he received a dual major in psychology and public relations. His background check showed he was raised by a single mom, but never got in trouble with the local cops as so often happened in those situations. A "squared away" kid in all respects. He worked some campus jobs while in school, had excellent references, and now wanted to join the Bureau. Like Katie, Jake asked him why.

"Growing up in Idaho, there is a strong anti-government, anti-law enforcement attitude," Sean began, "lots of folks frustrated with the culture in California move to Idaho, and there is an overreaction to any limits on freedom. But I could see how important the Rule of Law is to maintaining order, so I began to think critically about the tension between freedom and regulation in a free society. My mom drilled it into me that I needed to think for myself using data, not emotion. So, in college, I began to study how public attitudes developed, especially attitudes towards law enforcement. Hence, the psychology/ public relations combination. My proposed project for your seminar is to figure out how the FBI can do a better job of selling itself, especially using social media, to improve its reputation in the public eye."

Jake was impressed, not only with his answer, but with how Sean looked Jake in the eye while speaking from the heart. He told him so. Sean would go far.

They chatted a bit more until there was a knock on Jake's door. When it opened, Jake's son, Charlie poked his head in, saying, "Sorry to interrupt, Dad, but I know you want to keep on schedule." Jake and Sean got up, and Jake introduced them. Sean smiled warmly, shook Charlie's hand, and excused himself, thanking Jake for his time.

"Charlie, I hear you are a runner. Let's go out for a run sometime so we can get to know each other better," Sean said.

Charlie said he'd like that.

This interview, Jake knew, would be both his easiest and hardest. Charlie had excellent grades and credentials, so there was no legitimate way anyone could claim he benefited from any undue influence from his dad. There was little to discuss, as Jake knew all there was to know about his son. Yet, Jake also sensed he hadn't always been the best father. Like so many of his generation, he spent too much time honing his work skills and furthering his career, leaving the child-rearing primarily to Kathy. Sure, he was there when needed to present a united front on matters of discipline, and they enjoyed family time and vacations together. But in retrospect, Jake felt he hadn't given his kids the day-to-day sharing that Kathy had given them. As a result, he wondered, did he really know his son as he should, or was Charlie really just another applicant to him?

"Well, Charlie, have you given your project any thought?" Jake asked. "Sure, Dad... er... I mean Mr. Mott." Charlie began. Jake had reminded him to address him as Mr. Mott in school to avoid exacerbating the potential nepotism perception problem. "I've heard you talk for years about how people in law enforcement are repeatedly exposed to horrific scenes of graphic violence, much like soldiers in war, but our legal system doesn't fully recognize the long-term effects of PTSD on them. Cops are notorious for having marital problems and alcohol addiction issues, but there is little help for them. In fact, the>macho' image they have often prevents cops from seeking help for fear of ridicule from their peers. That has to change. For my project, I'd like to analyze the current thinking of the medical experts and try to develop a system for addressing this problem."

Jake was pleased. His son had chosen to focus on helping others in need and had a sense of moral outrage about an injustice. How like his mother his son turned out to be.

"Charlie, I look forward to working with you on your project. I might add that Sean King, who you just met, had a degree in psychology, so he may be of some help with the technical aspects of your studies. I hope all of the people in my seminar will learn to help each other. The variety of interests was one of my criteria for selecting each of you. Now I need to see my last applicant, so get out of here and send her in."

Charlie gave his father a warm hug, said "Sorry Dad, this is your last hug before classes start tomorrow," winked at him, and headed for the door.

Jake's final selection timidly slid into his office and sat down. Lori Beam was, no doubt, a ›tech nerd' and all that that implied. Even her appearance—horn-rimmed glasses, rounded shoulders, slightly unkempt hair, and pasty complexion—screamed 'computer geek'. She had graduated with honors from MIT. Her parents both worked in law enforcement, her father as a Fish and Game Warden in Colorado, and her mother as a detective in the Denver Metro police department. Lori loved science. Her focus at MIT had been computers, but she took every class she could that would help her be the ‹best evidence technician ever'. At least that is what her application said, but Jake's review of her transcript showed she was right. Jake knew one challenge for Lori was to get her out of her shell. While evidence techs lived in the lab, they needed to work as part of a team, and had to be able to communicate effectively to a jury if their work was to actually help convict someone.

"So, Lori, are you ready to start classes tomorrow?" Jake asked, hoping to prompt a conversation.

Lori never looked up. "Sure, I guess," she replied.

"How is your dorm room, and your suitemates? Everything OK there?"

"Yes. Fine."

Oh boy, thought Jake, this should be fun. "Any idea what your project will be for my seminar?"

Lori immediately looked up and brightened. With an enthusiasm that surprised Jake, she said "I want to take another look at one of your old cases from Milwaukee. From a forensic point of view, it is unfortunate we were never able to locate the bank robber's accomplice. I'd like to see if there is anything we can do with some of our newer technology to pick up some new leads. Maybe it's a waste of time, but it would be an interesting way to hone my skills."

Jake had long ago given up on what he thought was a dead end. But he was pleased to see Lori show such enthusiasm, so he couldn't say no. "I can't wait. If there is anything you need from me by way of background, let me know. I'll put in a request right away for the evidence file, and you can see what you can do. Good luck. Now. Let's get you back to your dorm. Dinner is in an hour, and we don't want to miss out."

Jake had made the hard decision to stay in the dorms during the week, heading home on Friday night and returning on Sunday night. His contact on the weekends would be limited to Kathy, to maintain the COVID "bubble". Kathy was fine with that decision. Both knew that if he was going to be able to inspire dedication in these new agents, he would have to› walk the walk' with them. Besides, the food was good, and the gym would give him the chance to get in better shape before he retired at the end of the session. Just sixteen weeks away, but this seminar, and the quality people he chose, would make it a memorable sixteen weeks.

While Jake was locking his office and heading down the elevator, a cell phone rang in one of the rooms in the dorms across campus.

"Yes? Oh, hi, Mom. It went great, just as we had hoped. I was sincere and direct, like we practiced. No, I'm sure he has no idea. I'm already scoping out possibilities to carry out our plan. Rest assured I am going to make you very happy. We will talk again soon. Bye."

# Chapter 6

## 2002

Nadia's son was three years old now. It was time to start shaping him into the instrument, the tool, she would use to bring down both the FBI, and the man who had ruined her only hope for a good life. Nadia was aware that her decision to continue to breastfeed her son so late was uncommon. But she needed to send the clear message to his developing brain that she, and she alone, was the source of all life, all nourishment. As he grew, she would need to reinforce that message in other ways so he would be able to survive the task she would set before him.

So far, it looked like her efforts to cut all her ties between Bill and the tragic events in Milwaukee had worked. After getting back to their farm (she had thought of it as "theirs"), she started to erase any evidence that she had ever been there. She gathered up all her personal belongings, especially the heavy backpack she had carried with her since she left her father. She would need to rely on what was in that backpack, combined with her smoldering hatred towards those who had killed Bill, to make a new life for herself and her unborn child.

She looked around the farmhouse and thought about all the ways the detritus of her life could create an evidentiary connection back to her. Fingerprints everywhere, the odd scrap of paper with her name on it, the little notes she and Bill had written to each other, her DNA on the dirty dishes in the sink. She decided that erasing those connections quickly would require a desperate but necessary act. After moving everything of value she might need to the neighbor's borrowed car, she got the gas can from the barn and poured it throughout the house she had shared with Bill for nearly two years. Then, she turned on the gas in the stove, lit a candle, and ran to the car. As she looked in the rear-view mirror, she watched the windows from the kitchen blow out as the natural gas ignited. The flames spread quickly to the rest of the house, which was fully engulfed within minutes.

Wiping away a tear, Nadia drove away from the only place in her life she had ever felt safe. Turning left, she stopped at her neighbor's house a half mile down the road. Tom Oleson, who she and Bill just called "the Swede," was out on his porch, having heard the explosion. She walked from the car and hugged the Swede with more tears in her eyes. Oleson was widowed four years ago, about the same time as Bill's parents died, drawing them closer. Like Bill, he had been caught up in the bank proposal to go organic and was facing the same foreclosure as Bill. He knew about Bill's plan to get their money from the bank and was the one who had lent them his car for the day. "Oh, Swede, they killed him. They killed Bill. I'm so sorry!"

"Yeah, I heard on the radio. Why the fire?" the Swede asked.

Nadia replied, "They're going to want to find anyone who helped Bill or knew about this. If they catch me, I'll be arrested and charged as an accomplice. It was the only way I could think of to wipe out any connections to me. You are the only one who knows I'm having Bill's child, and I have to get away from here to protect this baby. I need your help."

The Swede assured her he would do anything he could to support her.

Nadia's brilliant mind continued to race. "First, the cops are going to want to talk to you. They will figure out this robbery was caused by the foreclosures by the bank, and you are one of the victims of their fraud. But I don't think there is any evidence you knew about Bill's plans, so just keep it that way. And I need you to keep my name out of it. I kept a pretty low profile around here, but you and a few others know about me. We can't hide that. But the less you tell them about me, the better. Just say I was an itinerant farm worker that was helping out for the last year or so and leave it at that. Can you do that?" Nadia asked.

"Sure. What else?"

"I'm hoping you would let me have your car. I can't use Bill's because the police will be looking for it. But they'd have no reason to look for yours. And even if they are clever enough to check for your car, I plan to be far away from here as soon as I can." Then, after an embarrassed pause, "Finally, if you have any cash, I'd be very grateful."

The Swede went inside and returned a few minutes later with a wad of bills. Nadia stuffed it in her jeans without counting it and said, "Thank you so much. You know how much you meant to Bill and me."

Finally, she handed the Swede an envelope. "Bill always knew this robbery could go bad. He and I talked about how to handle the farm after... you know... he was gone or in jail. You have been helping him, and his parents before him, for your whole life. With this foreclosure mess, neither of the farms may be worth much, but Bill wrote out a will giving everything to you. This is the will, the deed to the farm, and all the other paperwork you will need. Please take it."

The Swede paused. "This should go to you and to the little one. Bill was so happy you were expecting. I couldn't take it from you."

Nadia smiled with gratitude, but said, "No, that would do nobody any good. The minute I claimed the farm, I'd be arrested for being an accessory. It's a no-win situation. Please. Bill wanted a true farmer and a true friend to have it."

Reluctantly, the Swede took the envelope and gave Nadia another hug. "I'll protect you as best I can, and if you or the baby ever need anything, please call me. You deserve better. Now get going before the fire department gets here."

Nadia got in the car and drove west.

That was more than three years ago, thought Nadia. So much had happened since then. She had worried every day that the police would discover her, but so far, so good. She spent the first night sleeping in the car at a rest stop in southern Minnesota. During the long drive west from Madison, she listened to the radio coverage of the robbery, hearing Jake Mott's name for the first time, and learning that he was the one who had decided to take Bill's life. She also had time to think about her own future. In the two years she had been with Bill, she had been a voracious reader. She used his library card to check out books to expand her knowledge, but also read newspapers front to back. She had noticed a sense of rebellion and unrest from those who resented government intrusion in their lives. Stories about how the FBI and local law enforcement were at war with groups the press called 'radical separatists'. These groups tended to be found in rural areas like south Texas, Oklahoma, and Idaho. While she didn't care about their political agendas, these groups might provide a good place to give her cover for a while.

Nadia had been to Texas and Oklahoma and had no interest in going back. But Idaho. That might be a good place to disappear for a while. So, west it was. She continued her drive west all through Sunday and Monday. She had never seen the grandeur of the Rockies, the beauty of the Badlands, or the green valleys of western Montana, and found herself amazed every time she crested a hill or came around the side of a mountain. But also, as she drove, she made a mental checklist of all she needed to do to make a new life for herself. Step one was finding someplace to settle down.

During the long and sometimes tedious drive, Nadia looked often at the plain gold band on her finger. The night before the trip to Milwaukee, Bill had slipped it on her finger. "I don't know what will happen tomorrow, but I want you to know that I love you, and that I'm totally committed to living my life with you, no matter what," Bill told her. Nadia had been deeply touched by his gesture, but now, after all that had happened, the ring became, for her, not a symbol of his love, but rather a focal point for her anger and hatred.

During a brief stop at a mall in western South Dakota, Nadia bought an inexpensive chain necklace. Threading it through the ring, she wore it close to her heart. As she continued to drive, and for the next two decades, Nadia would often touch the ring, and remind herself of all she had lost. That constant and ever-present reminder allowed her hate and anger towards the FBI, and towards Jake Mott, to grow and fester, feelings she would somehow pass along to her unborn child.

Nadia got off the interstate in Boise and started driving north. State Highway 55 took her through small town after small town along the western slopes of a mountain ridge. Each looked as likely a place to stop as the next. But when she saw a hand-carved wooden sign reading ‹Freedom, Idaho. Pop.: None of Your Damn Business›, she had a good feeling. She took a right onto a winding dirt road for a mile and a half until she came to a settlement of sorts. Scattered along a slope on both sides of a creek were a motley collection of approximately seventy or eighty small ‘homes’, for lack of a better word. Some were old, run-down cabins, some trailer homes up on blocks with uneven porches looking out over the creek, and a few true houses in not much better shape than the rest. Near the creek, Nadia saw a larger building with a General Store sign, a newer log cabin that was obviously a bar, and behind the bar, a small, six-room motel that made the Bates Motel look positively cozy.

She pulled the car in front of the General Store, parked, and went in. As she expected, the shelves were lined with whatever one might need to live in rural Idaho, from food to clothes, hardware to pharmaceuticals, and everything in-between. It was like every other town's entire Main Street packed into one building. And watching her suspiciously was the likely owner, a balding, heavy-set man, behind the counter.

"What can I help you with on your way out of town?" was his opening line, not very encouraging to Nadia's ears. She knew from the sentiment on the sign that prying questions would bear little fruit. So, she decided to go slowly. "How do I get a room at the motel? I'm tired from driving, and I like the look of this town. I like the name, and especially the attitude. I don't want people poking in my business, and I suspect you don't either." Nadia didn't smile; she knew charm was a waste of time.

Baldy scowled. "Twenty-five dollars, cash. We don't use credit cards in this town. Too many ways for the government to fuck... I mean... mess with us. One night, and then you leave. We don't like strangers." Nadia said no more. She paid for the room, got a key, and settled in to a pretty standard, but she had to admit, clean room.

As Nadia expected, and frankly hoped, word got around fast that there was a stranger in town. She waited the few hours until the sun went down—which was pretty early in the mountains in November—and strolled over to the bar where she hoped they would serve food. They did. She took a stool at the end of the bar far away from the regulars, ordered a burger, fries, and a Coke from a fifty-something woman tending the bar, and waited for the inevitable approach. It didn't take long. A tall, older man, his face leathery from time in the sun and the wind, walked the length of the bar and sat next to her. He said nothing, and neither did Nadia.

He finally spoke. "You a Fed? Law says that if you are, you can't lie to me."

Nadia knew that wasn't true, but it told her a lot about him. "No, I am not a Fed, or any other kind of government asshole. How about you?"

He didn't smile but shouted to his buddies at the other end of the bar, "Hey, she wants to know if I am a Fed!" They all laughed. He turned back in all seriousness. "If you're just passing through, I'm sorry to bother you. Eat your burger and go. But if you are planning to hang around for a while, we need to know all about you. We'll check you out; we have sources. But if you want to stay, nobody pokes their nose in our business without us knowing why. So, I have two questions. Do you plan to stay for a while, and if so, what's your story?"

Nadia knew she was going to have to trust someone. "I need to settle somewhere, and this place looks like a good place to lay low. Like you, I want to be left alone. I've been kicked around for most of my life, and I want a fresh start. I hope I can get one here. My name is Nadia Trulenko, but you won't find me in any government database. I was born in a migrant worker camp to immigrants from Eastern Europe. No birth certificate, no driver's license, no Social Security card. Parents are both dead. I don't know much about anything but farming, but I'm smart, work hard, and can carry my own weight. I had some trouble out east, but nothing that can follow me here. Check out whatever you want, but I won't be any trouble. If I'm in the wrong place,

70

just say so and I'll move along. But Freedom, Idaho sounds like where I want to be. We all have one thing in common: the Federal Government is not to be trusted. I can be."

He looked at her. Hard. Then he seemed to relax. "My name is Matt Horn. Me and my buddies will check out your story, but it sounds like there won't be much to find. Go ahead and eat up, the food here is pretty good. Get a good night's sleep. I'll stop by your room in the morning and let you know." Matt stood up, touched the brim of his baseball cap, and walked out the door of the bar. Nadia did as she was told but didn't sleep much that night.

The sun was barely up when she heard the knock on her door. She was up and dressed in minutes and opened the door to Matt and another man holding a tray of coffee cups who Matt introduced as Steve. They had an extra cup of coffee for her, and asked to come in. They sat at the small table in her room, while she sat on the bed.

"We checked you out. The bad news is we didn't find anything useful. Your car is registered to a farmer in Wisconsin, but no report that it was stolen. No Nadia Trulenko in any system we could find. We even got your fingerprints from your glass at the bar last night and had a like-minded friend in law enforcement in Boise run them. Nothing came up."

Nadia was uneasy about the connections these guys obviously had.

"But the good news is that if we didn't find anything useful, the government won't either. So, for now, we are willing to let you stick around for a while. Steve here owns a vacant trailer about a quarter mile up the creek from here. It has a shed for wood and whatnot, a few tools for gardening, and a decent plot of land running up into the hills behind it. He'll rent it out to you for the winter until we get to know you a little better. Interested?"

Nadia was hopeful. "How much? I don't have much cash."

Steve spoke up. "In the winter, a lot of folks head south, including the waitress at the bar. I'm part owner of the bar, so if you are willing to tend bar three or four nights a week, I'd let you stay in the trailer for free, and you can keep the tips. Good?"

Nadia smiled. "Throw in a free meal on the nights I work, and we have a deal."

Matt said, "Remember, this is just until we get to know you better."

Nadia promised they wouldn't be disappointed.

The next few months were quite challenging for Nadia. The trailer was clean, and more space than she needed. She used her minimal sewing and handy-skills to make it nice. New curtains, repairs to a few of the cupboards, and a thorough scrubbing made it into the first true home she had ever had on her own. She cleaned out the woodshed and saw there was enough wood on hand to heat the place with the wood stove in the trailer, so she wouldn't need to run the electric backup. Her bartending skills were non-existent, but the patrons mostly ordered tap beer and shots, so she learned quickly. The food menu was simple, and the cook efficient, so she soon mastered that as well. Tips were small, but enough for her to grow the little roll of cash she had taken from the Swede. She bought what she needed from the General Store, and got to be friendly with Baldy, whose real name was Gino.

That first winter in Freedom brought three important developments for her. First, she started to experience the fatigue that comes with being pregnant. She calculated her due date as mid-May, so by January, she was four months along. She dressed to hide it but began to realize it was only a matter of time before the community learned her secret. She had no idea how they might react.

Nadia also realized she would need to figure out a way to make a living. She could grow some food for basic needs, and maybe even sell some, but she would need more. She was sure the waitress job wouldn't last. So, she tried her hand at baking. She had picked up some recipes for fresh muffins, scones, breads, and even bagels from some of the farm wives she had met on the migrant worker circuit. Bill and the Swede had told her how delicious they were. She bought some ingredients from Gino, made a few batches, and gave them away as free samples at the bar and at the General Store. She then asked Gino if he would mind if she sold them in the Store, and he agreed, later commenting that his coffee sales nearly doubled when her baked goods were available. It took her a while to figure out what sold best, and how much of each item to make, but soon had a system down for the winter crowd. She knew if this went on, the influx of summer residents, plus the business from those driving through, could be sustainable for her.

Last, the bakery business had a side benefit. The locals actually started to accept her as one of their own. They joked with her at the bar, warmly greeted her in the street, and shared their own life stories with her. They truly were an anti-government lot, many for good reason. Some had lost businesses from over-regulation, others had minor run-ins with law enforcement but didn't have good legal representation, so got in even worse trouble because of it. Some just had a deep-seated resentment of big government on purely philosophical grounds. Whatever the reason, they were unified in their dislike and distrust of what they collectively called "the Feds". As Nadia's own anger and desire for revenge against the FBI, and specifically Agent Mott, grew, her feeling of kinship with her neighbors grew as well.

In late January, Nadia made a short trip to Boise. She had read about a free pregnancy clinic there, and wanted to be sure everything was proceeding as it should. The staff didn't ask too many questions, and Nadia had no trouble getting to see the doctor. She left the clinic with a clean bill of health, and the happy knowledge that she was carrying a son.

In early February, her sense of kinship with her neighbors gave Nadia a solid foundation to begin her journey towards revenge. Matt Horn stopped by her trailer while she was baking. He told her how well she was fitting in, and how the whole community hoped she would stay on indefinitely. She was so pleased, she said, but then took a big chance.

With a heart-stopping mixture of hope and fear, Nadia quietly said to Matt, "I'm pregnant, and I'm going to need everyone's help."

Matt was shocked, at first asking who the father is. Nadia assured him it was nobody from town, and that she was due in mid-May, so he needn't worry.

Relieved at first, something paternal must have kicked in, because Matt told her, "We take care of our own here, and you are one of us. Don't worry. We have your back. Give me a few days to figure out how to help you."

Nadia had always been careful not to ask questions about the personal lives of her neighbors. But she listened and learned about Matt Horn's background. Ten years earlier, he and his wife had gone through a rough patch in their marriage. After an argument, Matt had made some loud threats as he stormed out of the house, overheard by the neighbors in their small California community. That night, there had been a break-in at the house, Matt's wife surprised the intruder, and was killed. The intruder fled. The police had investigated, talked to the neighbors, and wrongly concluded Matt had killed his wife.

Matt had no alibi other than stopping at a bar, drinking too much, and falling asleep in the park. It didn't help him that his in-laws, as a wedding present, had given the then-happy couple a sizable life insurance policy on each other, so Matt had motive, means, opportunity, and no verifiable alibi. A month later, the intruder tried to pawn some jewelry from the robbery, was arrested, charged and convicted. But by that time, Matt had seen first-hand the incredible power the government had to probe into every aspect of his life and didn't like it. So, once he was cleared, he quit his job, took the life insurance money, and looked for a safe haven. Like Nadia, he found Freedom, Idaho.

A few days after his reassuring words, Matt came back with another man. He looked bookish, with glasses and a pasty complexion, something you might get from working in an office all day. Matt cocked his head at his companion, saying, "You don't need to know his name, but he is going to help you. If you are going to have a baby, run your bakery business, and live here, eventually the Feds are going to want to take a closer look at you. That means paperwork. Credentials that will pass scrutiny. My friend here is going to fix you up with a complete identity. New name, a social security number, Idaho driver's license, even a passport if you want it. Now just follow his instructions. He has agreed to let you pay off his usual fee over time, so don't worry about the cost."

The man smiled at her. "I've got a daughter about your age. If she was pregnant, I'd want someone to help her. I'll need to take your picture, and have you sign some papers, but what I need to know first is this: What do you want your new name to be?"

Until that day, Nadia had only had a vague sense that she would get her revenge but had no idea how. A nameless nobody without a real identity had no chance. But with a new identity, she could mold her son into a credible weapon. He would have all the outward signs of social acceptability and success. An education, good manners, social skills, the works. But underneath it all would be the means to make Mott and his precious Bureau pay.

She thought a moment, and then sat up a little straighter. "My name will be Maria. Maria King."

# Chapter 7

## Week Three

Jake was proud of the team he had assembled for his seminar. Not only did they each have some mad skills in their own areas, but he hoped this class would also help them learn to work together. The first few weeks of the Academy had focused on the basics, so Jake didn't push his students very hard. But today he wanted to see what they might be capable of. They were all together in the small conference room Jake had commandeered as a permanent work room for the class. He looked at Lori Beam. "Lori, you've been taking a fresh look at my old Milwaukee bank robbery case. Please brief the class on where you are. The rest of you need to listen up, as I expect you all to help where you can."

Despite her usual reticence to talk in class, noted by Jake as well as some of the other instructors, Lori lit up when talking about a topic she knew well. She began, "As you all know, the investigation after the shooting incident hit mostly dead ends. The walkie-talkie used by the mysterious accomplice was found by a sanitation worker in a trash can three blocks away from the bank on Monday, two days after the shooting. The radio frequency matched the unit used by the perp, but there were no usable prints. The set was nearly fifteen years old per the manufacturer, so we couldn't trace the purchaser.

"The lead I've been focusing on came from the location of that trash can. I reviewed the video from the Command Post, which, as Mr. Mott could tell you, was mostly worthless. The crowd at the end of Water Street was on an oblique angle, and too far away. The best the investigators could conclude was that a taller, dark-haired woman turned away at the precise time everyone else in the crowd was craning their necks to see something after the shot was heard. Not much help at the time. But now, twenty years later, our technology is better. So, I downloaded the footage from that section of the video into the Bureau's computers to see if I could do anything with it."

Jake spoke up. "We enlarged that footage up as best we could, but it only got blurrier, so we eventually gave up."

Lori smiled. "At the time, you had no choice. But with all the computer power we now have, I tasked the system to "fill in" the blurry gaps based on several algorithms I've developed. Because the computer is guessing what to fill in between pixels, an ID based on what we see wouldn't hold up in court. But it could be a useful investigative tool to point us in a direction. Let me show you what I came up with."

Lori put the original footage up on the computer screen in the front of the room. Her fingers flew over the keyboard, and Jake saw the blurry images he had pored over more than twenty years earlier. Lori froze a single frame and blew up the shadow that Jake knew was the accomplice. After a few moments, and more tapping keys, the image became sharper, then sharper again. Soon, the face of a dark- haired woman emerged. She had high cheekbones, a broad face, with full lips and dark eyes.»

"That is amazing," Jake said.

Lori quickly responded. "Not so fast. As I said, this is only a computer-generated guess. Using other algorithms, we could be getting two or three different faces. Watch."

Soon, two other faces, sharing some similar characteristics, but clearly different people, appeared.

At this point, Fritz Hemmer spoke up. "I know my focus is on DNA matching, but I'm passingly familiar with facial recognition programs. They are not as reliable, but much simpler to run than DNA. Lori, can you forward your three pictures to my computer?" While she did so, Fritz went on to explain. "There are two big problems with facial recognition. First is that it merely matches head shapes, facial bone structures, lips, eyes, and the like. Unlike fingerprints and DNA, those characteristics are not unique, so we get a lot of false positives. Second, the system is only as good as the volume of faces you have to match. If your suspect isn't in the system, it will only spit out the faces closest to your target face, which can be very misleading to an investigator. However, like Lori said, if we are only looking for leads we otherwise don't have, it could help."

Now it was Fritz's turn to work the keyboard. While he typed, Sean King spoke up. Jake had noticed Sean was highly focused during the discussion, so he was interested in Sean's input.

"I'm a little concerned about the high likelihood of a false positive from either of these techniques. From a PR point of view, the Bureau could end up with a huge problem if we spend time and resources on leads based off of some very tenuous assumptions and technology the average Joe wouldn't understand."

Charlie responded, "I agree with Sean in the usual case. But when we are at an absolute dead end, any lead is better than none. We need to build in safeguards to protect the reputations of any person of interest we develop through these techniques, but that doesn't mean we shouldn't try."

Jake appreciated his son's support, but Sean's frown said he did not.

Suddenly, Fritz started to laugh. "Oh, well, I guess this sort of proves Sean's point." He put the results of his work up on the big screen. "I ran all three of Lori's pictures through the Bureau's database. As you know, our database includes everyone with a state or federal criminal record, plus all Federal Employees. We got only one hit. Here it is." They all looked up to see Sean King's photo on the screen. Jake saw Sean's face go white, while the rest of the class roared.

Jake broke into the laughter. "Ok, settle down. Let's learn from this. What happened here?"

Fritz explained. "All we really know is this. Of the faces scanned into the system, Sean's has the highest number of characteristics matching our artificially created face. This is exactly the problem Sean pointed out. At the time of the shooting, Sean hadn't even been born yet. And he is certainly not a woman. We also know the accomplice is not in our database, so has no prior record. Other than that, this is another dead end. Sorry Mr. Mott."

Jake didn't want this development to deter creativity. "This is exactly why I picked all of you for this seminar. This was a really good idea, and you worked well together to chase it down. The Milwaukee case is cold, so it is not surprising we can't crack it. But I want you all to keep plugging away. Got it?" Nods all around. "Good. Lori, please go on."

"Well, there wasn't much more to look at on the scene, so I reviewed the efforts to trace the motive as well as the accomplice at the perp's farm. As you all may recall, when our agent arrived at the farmhouse, the fire had done its work. The local fire department barely had time to save the basement. We sifted through the rubble for several days, but nearly everything had been destroyed."

Fritz spoke up again, "Was any DNA collected at the home?"

Lori checked the report. "They got some samples from the inside of the refrigerator that were protected from the fire, and a few from the outbuildings. Most matched the perp, but the rest did not." Fritz asked Lori to send him some of the samples so he could take another look. She said she would.

Lori continued, "It struck me as odd that we never were able to get anything from the neighbors. They were stuck in the same financial bind as the bank robber. During the robbery, the perp was only going to take the money he and his neighbors had coming from the bank. So, the neighbors had to be in on it. Mr. Mott, can you shed some light on that?"

Jake looked a little uncomfortable at first but decided to be honest. "We focused our investigation on the closest neighbor, known locally as 'the Swede'. He had been closest with Willie and ended up inheriting Willie's farm. We got a subpoena for his financial and banking records but found nothing hinky. Our investigators interviewed him twice, and I even went to talk to him personally. Despite all sorts of threats, and all the pressure we put on him, he remained a loyal friend. He told us about the itinerant farm worker who had been staying with Willie, and confirmed she was a woman, but claimed he didn't know much more. Not even her name. We suspected he was holding back, but we got nothing."

Katie Arnold, the financial crimes guru, piped up, "Can you send me the subpoena for his financial records?"

Lori located it on her laptop and sent it. Katie looked it over.

"Back then, the courts often didn't put a specific end date on their subpoenas. Technically, this one remains open as long as the case remains open. I'm going to poke around in the Swede's financial records and see what I can come up with. I'll let you know what I find. But I'm curious about something else, Mr. Mott. Why didn't the bankruptcy go through on all their farms?"

Jake saw another teaching moment. After a pause, he said, "In your careers, you will come across injustice. You may have the chance to fix that injustice rather than just doing your jobs. When I started digging into the motive issue, the Swede gave me copies of the documents the bank had given to Willie and his neighbors, encouraging them to move towards organic farming. I quickly saw the risk was all on the farmers, and none on the bank. So, when the farms started losing money while approval of their organic certifications from the USDA was delayed, the bank refused to cut them any slack. They pushed the bankruptcy threats that forced Willie and his neighbors into a corner they felt they couldn't get out of. When I then reviewed the bank records, there was no effort by the bank to work things out. The value of land for suburban development north of Madison had shot up, and the bank could make out very well on the resale of the confiscated land."

"I was bothered from the start by one question: Why rob a branch bank in Milwaukee when the loans were made by the Madison branch? I found my answer in the paperwork the Swede provided. The loan officer that sold the idea in the first place was a guy named George Varney. Sound familiar?" Heads shook around the table. "It should. Varney got a nice promotion from the Madison office to be the branch manager in the Milwaukee office. That is why Willie went to Milwaukee. Because that's where he could confront the architect of the loan scam that was going to cost him his family farm. I'm sure Varney knew that, and I hate being lied to."

Katie asked, "What did you do?"

"When it became clear to me that the Swede wasn't going to roll over on his friend, and the investigation was near an end, I asked to meet with Varney and his boss. I told them that Varney had lied to me in his office the day of the robbery. I had asked him point blank if he knew Willie or had any idea why he had tried to rob the bank, and Varney pled ignorance. His boss looked incredulous, and I thought Varney was going to piss his pants. I explained to them both that I was considering filing Obstruction of Justice charges against Varney, but appreciated how bad that might look: A man is killed by an FBI sharpshooter in their bank because he was talked into a bad loan deal by an agent of their bank. That same guy gets a promotion, and then lies to the FBI. Very bad press. Now they both looked sick.

"I told them I had no desire to be the cause of bad publicity for their bank. But unless they rewrote the loans on some very favorable terms for the farmers caught up in this deal, I wouldn't hesitate to do it. Varney's boss promised to do so and ended up true to his word. The farms were eventually certified as organic, they all paid back the loans. Except for Willie and his accomplice, things turned out okay."

Katie spoke up, a bit of outrage in her voice. "You had no right to do that. You used your authority to interfere in a private business deal. That's what lawyers are for. Private lawyers. We need to guard against misuse of our power, don't we?"

Jake gave her a wry smile. "You are mostly right. We do have to guard against misuse of our power. But we also serve the public. This job lets you see all sorts of injustice beyond what we can use the law to fix. I saw a chance to right a wrong and took it. Prosecution for Obstruction was a legitimate option I had. Varney handed it to me. I used it, the bank got its money, and some good people kept their farms. I'd do it again. Each of you will need to make similar judgment calls in your future careers. I hope you will think of this one when you have to make those judgments."

Sean was the next one to speak up. He seemed to have regained his composure after the facial recognition fiasco, and now looked thoughtful. "I had never heard that part of the story. I knew about the bad loans, of course, and the shooting. I always thought it was a black mark on the Bureau that a peaceful solution couldn't be found. But this aspect of the story could be a very positive spin that could help the Bureau's reputation. Why isn't it out there?"

Jake asked the group if anyone had an answer.

Katie replied, "Because of what I said. It isn't our job, even if it is a good result. People wouldn't like the meddling and would lose faith in the system. So, Jake's actions had to remain private. Right?"

Jake nodded. "Exactly."

After class was over, Jake's cell phone chirped. It was Kathy's ring, he knew, so he answered, "Hello beautiful, how are you?" Jake couldn't believe how strong their relationship had become since he had included her in the decision about whether to take this assignment or retire. As recent empty-nesters they took full advantage of the opportunity to establish new routines and habits they could sustain for many years to come. On the weekends when Jake was home from the Academy, Kathy had introduced him to yoga, and he learned to enjoy fixing little things for her around the house. They attended Sunday Mass together without fail, and they started to make friends at church, something Jake previously didn't have time to do. They would linger over coffee on Saturday mornings, talking more than they ever had, and spent some quality time in the bedroom that had been lacking for years. Whatever uncertainties either of them had harbored about their relationship had evaporated.

Kathy chuckled over the phone. "I know it's only Wednesday, but I was hoping you might join me for an early dinner tonight. I'm going to be doing some shopping near the Academy and thought you might like to get away for a few hours. How's your schedule?"

Jake glanced at his calendar but knew he could move things around. He was also concerned about the COVID bubble he had created at the Academy, but thought that if he limited contact to just Kathy, the risk would be low. "What good is being in charge if you can't have dinner with your wife? Of course, I can meet you. Where and when?"

Kathy said, "There is a nice restaurant and coffee shop in the Hilton Hotel just off I-95. How about 4:30?"

When he arrived, Kathy was already there in a booth near the back. When she stood to greet him, he was even more glad he had agreed to meet her. She was wearing a red, knee-length dress, cinched at the waist, with a scooped neck that was tasteful, but showed a little more cleavage than Jake was used to. Her face was perfectly made up, with lipstick to match her dress, and a new hair style. She looked gorgeous. When she kissed him, it lasted a bit longer than usual, and when she broke away, he first noticed an envelope on the table. Jake was mystified. "You look great! And a card? For me? What's the occasion?"

They sat down, and Kathy said, "Let's order first, then we'll talk."

They shared a wonderful meal. Jake had salmon with broccoli and garlic mashed potatoes, and Kathy chose a chopped salad with chicken and a cup of soup.

"I'm watching my figure, you know."

Jake replied, "So am I, and I like it!"

They talked about their upcoming cruise, small talk about the Academy, and news from their daughter, with Jake occasionally glancing at the envelope. Finally, as their waitress cleared their plates and brought coffee, he couldn't wait anymore.

"So, what's up?"

Taking her time sipping her coffee, Kathy started running her foot up and down Jake's calf before she finally relented. "You may not remember the exact date, but it was exactly three months ago today that you asked me about postponing your retirement. I can't emphasize enough how much that moment meant to me. After twenty years of you making your own decisions about your career, for you to seek out my opinion meant the world to me. I didn't want that to go unnoticed or unmarked. So, I planned this little get together. I bought this dress, got a new hairstyle, and got you a little gift. I hope you like it."

Jake reached for the envelope, but Kathy stopped him.

"Not so fast, big guy," Kathy slid out of the booth. "I need to go to the ladies' room. While I'm gone, you can open up your card."

Kathy then bent down to kiss her husband, intentionally giving him a nice view down the front of her dress when she did. Jake watched her walk towards the entrance, her hips swaying enticingly, before tearing open the envelope. Inside, Kathy had written, "To my husband: These past three months have been a joy for me. All the promises we made to each other when we were first married are coming true. Thank you for being the man I always wanted you to be." Jake certainly felt the same way and couldn't wait to tell Kathy that.

Tucked into the envelope was a hotel keycard, and a note, reading, "I'll be waiting in the hotel lobby for you. Please hurry!" Just then the waitress came by to offer more coffee. Jake quickly tucked the envelope and room key into his pocket and asked for the check. Minutes later, he entered the crowded hotel lobby to see Kathy sitting primly near the door with a coquettish smile on her face. She winked at him as he held out his hand to her.

As they walked to the elevators, he could only think about three things. First, what he was going to be doing with his wife in about four minutes, fewer if the elevators were fast. Second, he suspected that everyone in that lobby knew why guests checked in without any luggage. And third, how was he going to explain to his staff why he was wearing the same clothes on Thursday morning that he wore on Wednesday afternoon? But as the elevator doors opened, and he and Kathy stepped inside, Jake suddenly couldn't think of anything at all.

# Chapter 8

## 1992

Since her father had first laid his hands on her mother in anger when she was a small child, Nadia had watched the slow but inevitable unraveling of her family. Her only respite from the hopelessness that pervaded her daily life was through self-education, escaping into the many books she checked out of whatever local library she could find. She was a gifted and dedicated student despite the struggles she faced on a daily basis.

With Nadia's help, her mother recovered from that first beating at the hands of her father. Publicly, he blamed her bloody lip and black eye on walking into an open door, a story her mother didn't dare to contradict, but the rest of the itinerant farmers were not convinced by it. They all saw the way Nadia's father behaved when he had been drinking and knew her mother would stoically absorb the blows. What saddened Nadia was how her mother began to actually blame herself for her husband's behavior, apologizing for disappointing him after the next beating, and the one after that. Nadia felt powerless to do anything except comfort her mother as they cried themselves to sleep while her father had a few more drinks, and then fell asleep alone. The other farmers, recognizing the power he held as their boss, did nothing.

Nadia's life, then, from as far back as she could remember through this, her eighteenth birthday, was numbingly predictable. She and her mother would work in the fields all day, eat the meager food provided by the company for the workers, sleep in the dilapidated barracks-like housing the company provided, and hope her father didn't drink too much. On the days he did, Nadia and her mother did all they could to stay out of his way. When they couldn't avoid his anger, her mother would take the beating while doing all she could to protect her daughter. Then, when that crop was harvested, they would all move to the next stop on the circuit and start all over again.

When Nadia was eleven-years-old, she learned an important lesson about how the broader world viewed her and the other migrant workers. By then, her routine included attending whatever public school was nearby, this time in the Bremerton School District in rural Nebraska. She loved to learn. Sitting in class, soaking up information at a startling rate, and seeing her teachers smile at her whenever she knew the right answers, all gave her a sense of accomplishment she had never felt before. Her test scores were tops in the class. But best of all, she discovered she could take books home from the school library for free. At night in the barracks, she could escape from her life, her father, her hopelessness, and enter the world these books opened for her. Even though she might only be in a school for a few weeks at a time before moving on to a new one, she would still excel. In the summers, when school was not in session, she soon discovered the local public library, and continued to teach herself about a world she might never get to see.

Inevitably, for an eleven-year old girl, Nadia became so absorbed in her reading that she began to forget her obligations to help harvest the crops. Her mother tried to make excuses for her to her father, but by then her parents' relationship was virtually non-existent. On top of that, Nadia's academic successes stood as a constant reminder to her father that he would never escape the relentless cycle his life had become. One day Nadia's father caught her reading when she should have been working. He grabbed the book from her hands and screamed at her to get out into the fields. He tore the book in two, breaking her heart, and then ominously told her they were going to have 'a little talk' after dinner.

Dinner came and went, with Nadia and her mother dreading the confrontation. But her father was nowhere to be seen. When he showed up later that night, he had been drinking heavily. He told Nadia to come with him outside. Her mother insisted on coming as well, as the rest of the itinerant farmers cringed at what might happen.

Outside, Nico turned to Nadia and yelled, "I've had it with this fantasy world you live in! If you want to survive in this world, you need to learn to work hard, not waste your time reading a bunch of books. I had to learn the hard way, and you will too. No more school, no more books, and no more shirking your work. You are old enough now to pull your own weight, and you'll start working a full shift in the fields instead of all this silly schooling."

Nadia began to cry.

As much of a doormat as her mother had become, Nadia was shocked by what came next.

"No, Nico, you are wrong. Nadia will get as much education as she can, and I will not let you stand in her way. I have tolerated your abuse for years because I pity you for the way your life has turned out. When I took my vows, I meant them, though God knows I have every reason to walk away. But you will not destroy our daughter's life too."

Her father's face became red with anger as he came at both of them.

"You pity me? How dare you! Nadia will do as she is told, and you have nothing to say in the matter."

His fist drew back as he began to lunge at mother and daughter, but for the first time, Nadia's mother did not shrink in fear, or even flinch. She simply and stoically faced her red-faced husband. For a moment they all stood still, Nadia hoping beyond hope her father would back down.

No luck.

Her father screamed, "I'll kill you both!" and charged forward.

But her mother's knee came up hard, and her father gasped, dropped to the ground, and curled up in a ball. Before he could recover, her mother said to him, "Yes, you are bigger and stronger than me, and I know I will pay for this moment dearly someday, but you will not take away this opportunity from our daughter. You'll have to kill me first."

She took Nadia's hand, and they went back into the barracks. When they entered, Nadia saw the eyes of the other workers were on them. They had all heard what had happened and knew what it might mean. But Nadia knew that between her mother and these itinerant workers, somehow, she would continue her education.

The next day, Nadia's teacher asked her how the book she had borrowed from the library had been damaged. Perhaps feeling confident that last night's events represented a new chapter in her life, Nadia told her teacher about her father tearing up the book, his threats, and the fight with her mother. Her teacher asked her to come with her, and Nadia soon found herself in the principal's office with the school counselor and a Bremerton police officer. After she again recounted the night's events, she began to worry. Would her father be arrested? Would her mother get in trouble?

It turned out she needn't have worried. The police officer told the principal he would look into it. That evening, after dinner, the officer came to their barracks to talk to her father, who denied anything had happened. Her mother corroborated what Nadia had told them at school. The officer then met with all three of them.

"Look, I don't know what really happened here. You migrants come here for a few weeks a year, pay no taxes, contribute nothing to this town, and expect the locals to deal with your messes. The crop is almost in, and you will all be moving on in a few days. I'm not going to waste my time dealing with a domestic situation that will be someone else's problem in a week. So, I'm telling you there better not be any violence in my town. I'm going to file a report about this incident, so if anything should happen after you leave here the cops who have to deal with it will know you were warned. Do you think you can all put a lid on this for a few days?"

Her father promised there would be no further problems, but both Nadia and her mother knew that was an empty promise once they left Bremerton.

After that day, Nadia's life went on unchanged for a while. She still went to school. She still read every book she could. She tried to help with the harvest to bring in a few extra dollars, if only to take some of the pressure off her mother. And her father largely left her alone. But Nadia had to suffer through the knowledge of how her education changed her mother's life. Her father's drinking increased, as did the regularity and severity of the beatings. A few times, Nadia stepped between them before the fists flew, but her mother calmly ordered Nadia to go to her bunk as her father grabbed her mother's arm and roughly pulled her out into the night. Nadia later noticed her mother's face was untouched, but saw the bruises on her ribs and back, even if the other migrants did not. Still, Nadia saw no tears from her mother.

Nadia was also old enough to know about sex. So, when her mother came back into the barracks without any new bruises, but with torn clothes and tears streaking her face, she knew her father's abuses did not end with punches. This began to occur more frequently, and Nadia held her mother while she wept.

Once, her mother whispered to Nadia through her tears, "He makes me choose between this and his fists, and sometimes I just can't take another punch."

Nadia wept with her that night.

When Nadia was seventeen, her mother finally got the freedom she had longed for. They had returned to Texas at the end of the season. This was usually Nadia's favorite time of the year, as she was in the same school for two months, rather than a few weeks. Money was tighter, but there were no crops to be harvested, so Nadia could read to her heart's content. For her parents, though, there was no respite from their being together to face the reality of their failed lives. Her father drank more during these times, but Nadia and her mother had more options to stay out of his path, so confrontations were rare. But one night, everything fell apart.

Her father had started drinking at lunch, something he rarely did. It had been unseasonably warm, and he walked to the beach at the local lake with a six-pack of beer. The locals were out in force, especially the young college students, home on winter break. As he sat and drank, his eyes were drawn to the spectacle of dozens of young, bronzed women splashing in the water, playing volleyball, and seemingly taunting him, as if to say, 'Look at me. This is what you will never have.' His addled mind drifted, thinking how unfair it all was. He finished his beer, bought a bottle of whiskey, and started to drink it on the way back to the small trailer they shared. His return took Nadia and her mother by surprise. Nadia was reading as always, and her father took a long look at his daughters shapely tanned legs. How had he missed the fact that she had developed a woman's body? One so much better than her mother's?

«I'm supporting them both," he thought to himself. "And her mother disgusts me."

The fog in his brain brought about by years of frustration, alcohol, heat, and self-pity somehow convinced him Nadia should be his for the taking. But Nadia's mother was watching him carefully. She knew all too well how his eyes and his face revealed his thoughts. She had dreaded this possibility but knew it might come someday. Perhaps this was the day.

She quietly said to Nadia, "Why don't you go outside and read for a while. Your father and I need to talk." Perhaps reminding him that he was Nadia's father might bring him back to his senses.

He took a long pull on the whiskey bottle, and said, "No, I have a better idea. Maybe you should go outside so Nadia and I can have a little talk inside."

Her mother knew the time had come. She reached into a kitchen drawer for a knife, moved in front of her father, and in a low steely voice said, "Nadia, get up now and go outside like I said."

Nadia saw that her parent's eyes were locked on each other and knew something terrible was about to happen. She quickly did as she was told.

"Close the door behind you," were the last words she heard her mother say.

When the police car showed up an hour later, Officer Diaz spoke first to her father. "I had just come home from the beach. I'd been drinking but had no idea what I would come home to. My daughter was outside reading, and when I went inside, I found my wife on the floor with blood everywhere. I called you right away."

When they went inside, the two police officers found her mother on her back on the kitchen floor with a pool of drying blood soaking the back of her head.

Diaz said, "It looks like she must have fallen and hit her head on the edge of the stove. You can see the hair and blood stuck there, and I suspect the wound on her head will confirm that. Had she ever fallen before?"

Her father assured him she had not, and he was sure this was just a freak accident. He even pointed out the small puddle of water on the floor near her mother's feet, which Nadia was sure her father had put there before calling the police.

Diaz then turned to Nadia, "What do you think happened, young lady?"

Nadia did not miss the glowering look her father gave her. But the shock of seeing her beloved mother dead, never to hug or comfort Nadia again, gave her a courage she didn't know she had.

"My mother was alive when he came home! She sent me outside to protect me from him, and she was holding a knife when she did. Please, keep him away from me. He killed her!" Nadia began to cry.

The other officer looked questioningly at her father, who dismissively said, "My daughter lives in a fantasy world. She always has her nose in a book, and I'm afraid she may have picked up a little drama from something she must have read. She's a teenage girl, and they love melodrama. Look around. There is no knife, and no signs of any struggle. I love my wife. I know this accident must be quite a shock for her, but she will learn to deal with it in time."

Diaz told his partner to stay with Nadia's father and took her out behind the trailer. "Do you have any proof that your father has been abusive towards you or your mother in the past?"

Nadia thought for a moment. "A report was filed by the Bremerton, Nebraska police department a few months ago. Please read it. And talk to any one of the migrant workers in our caravan. They'll tell you. Please, you have to believe me!"

The officer escorted her to his squad car and spoke into his radio, "Jenny, could you check with the Bremerton, Nebraska PD about a report of abuse involving a Mr. Trulenko? His daughter says there should be something on file. Thanks."

They then drove the half mile or so to the old sheds where many of the migrant workers stayed during the winter break. Nadia pointed out two men she knew from their work crew, and the officer called them over.

"Do you two work with this girl and her father?"

They looked very uncomfortable. They said they did.

"Have you ever seen any physical abuse by Mr. Trulenko towards his wife or daughter?"

They looked sideways at Nadia, seeing the hopefulness in her face. But most of them were illegal and distrusted the police in all things. So, with shame in their downcast eyes, they said, "Sorry, señor, we have never seen anything like that."

Nadia was about to protest when the radio crackled to life, "Officer Diaz, it's Jenny. I just got off the phone with the Bremerton PD. No report on file about any abuse involving a Trulenko or any other similar name."

Diaz replied, "OK. Thanks for checking. And please send the coroner out to the Trulenko trailer. No need for an autopsy. Just a tragic accident."

Nadia could not believe her ears. Her mother was dead. Officer Diaz didn't believe her. There would be no serious investigation. The Bremerton officer had done nothing! Her fellow migrant workers were too afraid to tell the truth about her father. She now knew the ugly truth. Police didn't care. Even worse, they would either take the easy way out, or side with the person in charge. The victims didn't matter to them. The poor and powerless didn't matter to them. She was seventeen years old, alone, and living with a predator. Somehow, she would have to summon up the courage her mother had shown in protecting Nadia and figure out how to protect herself.

The next few days were a blur. Her father knew to give Nadia a wide berth. Whenever she saw fellow workers on the street, they would look away in shame and sadness. Once the coroner released her mother's body, Nadia arranged for a pauper's burial through the local church. The ceremony was simple. Her mother was now free of the abuse she had suffered. Nadia was sure her mother would have been pleased that so many of her fellow workers attended, but Nadia took no joy from it, knowing of their failure to help her. Her father was stoic throughout and shed no tears. But then again, neither did Nadia. She was past that. Once her mother's body was in the ground, Nadia could think of nothing other than her own safety.

The trailer she now shared with her father had two bedrooms. Nadia shoplifted a strong lock for her room from the local hardware store and used it whenever she was home. She would stay away from the trailer except to sleep. In the morning, if she knew her father had been drinking the night before, she would get up quietly, pack a quick lunch, and leave before he woke up. If he had been in early the night before, she would stay in her room until she heard him leave. She began to carry a backpack with her wherever she went, with a sharp kitchen knife easily accessible inside. The one time she and her father crossed paths in the trailer, she pulled out the knife. Without saying a word, he turned and left.

Nadia's thoughts turned to the future. She could no longer work or travel with her father. He would have too much power, and working all day in the fields, she would have neither the opportunity nor the energy to avoid him at night. She used her time talking to the other migrant workers to see if there was another group she could work and travel with, at least until she could figure out other options. She had no diploma, no birth certificate, no green card, no papers of any kind. She was non-existent for all anyone knew, so she felt the ‹normal' options, like going to college, applying for a job, or even getting a driver's license, were all out of the question. Fortunately, one of the two men who had refused to talk to Officer Diaz on her behalf, out of a sense of guilt, she knew, introduced her to Fernando. He was a pleasant man, working as an overseer on another migrant crew. When she was certain they would be following a different circuit than her father, she agreed to join them. She had only six more days before she would be free of her father, and hopefully her ugly past.

Her luck ran out the night before she was scheduled to leave. She had shared her good news with many of her old crew, and they were happy for her. So, with only one night left, she planned to tell her father. Everything she owned was sitting next to her in her backpack, and she waited in the living room with dread. She heard him coming up the steps, and when he came in the door, she knew immediately that he had been drinking. He was surprised to see her, but then an odd look of smug satisfaction came over his face as he plopped down in the chair across from her. She wasted no time. "

I'm joining another work crew. We leave tomorrow. I felt owed it to you to tell you out of respect for mom."

That smug look returned, "You may change your mind when you find out my good news. All my problems are over, and yours can be too if you play along."

His grin chilled her, and he went on, "We never shared much with you about our family history. It's time you learned where you came from. You know my parents, your grandparents, were farmers in Romania. During World War II, some of the most brutal and inhuman treatment of a local population ever seen occurred there. The Nazis needed access to the oil fields, as well as the fertile wheat fields to sustain their war efforts against Russia and the West. My parents told me of the horrific ways the Nazis would torture anyone who would not cooperate with them.

"But the Nazis also rewarded those who collaborated with them. Their early successes in the war, coupled with the seizure of the wealth of their Jewish citizens, made gold less valuable to them than loyalty, oil, and food. My parents were neither political nor greedy. But faced with the choice of being brutalized by the invading Nazis and losing their farm or being paid for the wheat they were growing and earning a little gold on the side by telling the Nazis about the activities of the local resistance, they made the easy choice. For the rest of the war, they were paid handsomely, while many of their neighbors quietly disappeared in the night. Some today might judge them as evil, but war makes people do things to survive that they might otherwise not do.

"When the Nazis began to lose, and the Red Army pushed them back west, my parents realized they could never spend the gold they had been given. If they were found out to have been collaborators, especially in Russian-controlled Communist Romania, after the war was over, they would likely have been jailed or hanged. So, they hid their gold, continued to farm, and eventually raised their family. So, my little 'head in the clouds' daughter, how does it feel to know you are the descendant of people like that?"

Nadia didn't rise to the taunt, "I am who I choose to be. I'm not defined by them, or by you. I'm just happy to get out of here."

Her father smirked. "We will see. So do you want to hear the good news?" He didn't wait for a reply. "Yesterday, I got a letter from a lawyer in Bulgaria, where my parents had been living since the breakup of Yugoslavia. My mother died two years ago, and my father recently passed away. The lawyer said everything had been sold, and after the taxes were paid, almost nothing remained. Except, the lawyer said, the contents of a safe deposit box. The will required the contents to remain sealed, and to be sent to me. It arrived today."

Her father got up and went to his room. When he returned, he was holding what was clearly a heavy metal box, which he placed on the table between them. When he opened it, the smug look returned. Stacked inside, row upon row, were shiny gold coins. Each was stamped with some words in German, which Nadia couldn't read, with a swastika on one side, and a likeness of Hitler on the other. Nadia picked one up, examined it, and put it back. Her father smiled.

"Each one weighs four ounces. There are eighty coins in this box. I checked the price of gold today. It is selling for over $300 an ounce. I'm sitting on over $10,000 of gold!" Nadia did some quick math in her head. He was wrong. It was actually nearly $100,000.

Her father went on. "I've been working all my life, supporting you and your ungrateful mother, and haven't been able to save a thing. Now this drops into my lap! It is time for me to celebrate a little."

He reached for the bottle he always had near at hand and took a big gulp. When he put it down, he stared at her. "You are eighteen now, or nearly that. I think it is time for you to pay me back for all the money I spent on you over the years."

He jumped up from the chair surprisingly fast and pinned Nadia to the couch. His hands were touching her in places that made her retch. His breath was sour, and she could feel his hardness pressing against her thigh. She tried to call out, but his calloused hand clamped down over her mouth.

Nadia began to panic. Then she saw her backpack lying next to her on the couch. While her father began to shift her body around and try to unzip her shorts, she reached down to the open pocket of the backpack where she kept the knife. Pulling it out, she planned to scare him with it. But when he saw it, he instead pulled his fist back for the kind of punch she had seen her mother take so many times. She didn't wait for it. She thrust the knife up under his exposed rib cage. She felt it slice through muscle and lodge deep in his chest. His body spasmed, and he fell to the ground twitching, face up, the knife handle sticking up and covered in blood. After a few moments, his bulging eyes closed, and his body went still.

At first, Nadia couldn't move. Drained of energy, emotion, even the ability to think, she could only stare at the dead, evil thing lying at her feet. After some minutes, she was able to sit up and begin to think again. Here she was, for the second time in a month, in her trailer with a dead body. Then the idea hit her. That was it! The lessons she had learned from her mother's death she would use to her advantage. If the police didn't care about one dead migrant, they certainly wouldn't care about another one. The other migrants wouldn't help the police when her mother was killed, so they certainly wouldn't help now. Nadia was a ghost at least as far as the legal system measured these things, with no credentials and no paper trail. She was supposed to leave tomorrow anyway, so her absence wouldn't raise any red flags, even in the unlikely event the police wanted to expend their resources to chase her down.

Nadia got to work. First, she dragged her father's body out the door and pushed it into the crawl space under the trailer. It was overgrown with weeds, and with any luck, nobody would even know it was there until the smell or the animals drew attention to it. She then went back into the trailer and grabbed the few possessions of her father, other than the gold coins, that might have value to a burglar. Those she wrapped up into a sheet, along with the bloody clothes she had been wearing, tying it off carefully so nothing would fall out. She then trashed the rest of the trailer to make it look as if her father had been robbed and had fought with the burglar. Finally, she dressed in clean clothes, and put the box of gold coins into her backpack. Taking one last look around, she left the trailer for the last time in her life.

She walked down towards the beach, careful to stay out of any well-lit areas. At the deserted end of the lake, she added several heavy rocks to the bundle of her father's belongings, and tossed it far out into the water. Then she walked down to the cluster of shacks where the other migrants lived. She knocked on Fernando's door and asked if she could sleep there just for the night. She explained she didn't want to have to confront her father, and as his abuse was well-known, she was welcomed in. As she lay down, she was surprised she experienced no fear, nervousness, or sense of guilt. Rather, she fell into a deep and satisfying sleep, and dreamed of a future with new opportunities.

# Chapter 9

## Week Five

Frank Steele shut down his computer for the night, crawled into bed, and slowly drifted off. The rigors of the usual Academy classes, plus his work in Jake Mott's Seminar, were taking a toll. Frank was passionate about developing a counseling regimen for drug addiction, and he was spending every extra hour he had working on his research. He always ended his night working on his diary, personally reflecting on how his mother could become addicted to heroin in the first place, and how his own father could participate in destroying the life of the woman he was supposed to love.

It had taken Frank and the other students a while to get used to the living conditions at the Academy. Each student had his or her own room in a four-room suite, with a shared bathroom. The hard part was the open-door policy. The Bureau thought that students eventually needed to be able to trust one another in the workplace, so there should be no locks on the doors at the Academy. The end of each hallway included a lounge for studying or socializing, but with the advent of live streaming and gaming, the lounge was usually empty, with most students retreating to their rooms. It could be an isolating existence, especially for an introvert like Frank. It had taken a few weeks before he could sleep comfortably.

When the damp cloth was suddenly clamped over his mouth and nose, Frank was still dazed from sleep. He remembered a powerful smell and a slight burning in his lungs as he inhaled. But then his body relaxed, and everything went dark. He was conscious of the passage of time but didn't know how much time. His eyes opened and closed at seemingly random intervals, and he could make no sense of what he saw. He caught a glimpse of Sean King bent over his computer and smelled the sulfur of a lit match, and the bubbling of heroin, a smell he recalled vividly from his childhood. He felt a rubber tube being tightened around his bicep.

When he looked up, he saw Sean again, slowly injecting something into his arm. Then he felt a euphoria like nothing he ever experienced before. Heat spread up his arm as the rubber tubing was released, and soon filled his entire body with first warmth, then uncomfortable heat, and then a painful burning. He felt his heart rate and breathing become frantic, then erratic, but couldn't move to do anything about it. He tried to speak, to shout for help, but Sean put his hand over Frank's mouth, whispering "just relax, it will all be over in a moment."

It was over in a moment. Sean King looked down at his first victim in the scheme he and his mother had conceived many years ago and had refined over the past few months. Frank Steele, star pupil of Jake Mott, was dead in his room at the FBI Academy of a heroin overdose. The planned embarrassment of the FBI, and Mott specifically, had begun.

Sean and his mother had initially merely planned to erode confidence in the Bureau from the inside. He attended university, duly took courses designed to get him into the FBI Academy and applied. His grades made him a shoo-in, and he had planned to continue to excel there until he was posted to his first local office before trying to make the Bureau look bad secretly from within. With access to the Bureau's computers, evidence rooms, and strategies for ongoing investigations, he could do great damage with little chance of being discovered for a long time. No immediate plan had formed about how to hurt Jake Mott personally.

But when it was announced that Agent Mott had been tapped to lead the Academy, everything changed. Sean and Nadia knew they had to move up their timeline so the harm to the Bureau's reputation would occur on Mott's watch, killing two birds with one stone. It would be more difficult for Sean to work in the insular environment of the Academy's closed COVID bubble, but with careful planning, it could be done. Sean liked the challenge. And when the Academy class was over, Nadia and Sean had decided Mott's life would end as well. Graduation Day would be the day, as Mick had said, "that the tree of liberty would be watered with the blood of martyrs."

With Frank, Sean had been very careful. Weeks earlier, he had put spyware on Frank's computer so he could monitor everything he was working on. He knew Frank was a loner, so he would be a good first victim. The irony of an FBI agent studying drug addiction, but then dying of an overdose, was delicious. But how to do it? Frank's diary gave Sean the idea. The diary was already full of musings about Frank's need to understand how any addiction started, and how drug use felt to the habitual user. Only then, he thought, could he have a better understanding how to fix it. Frank had read everything he could find about addiction, but there didn't seem to be any reliable consensus about the experience; it was as varied as the people who were addicted, and so the treatment regimens varied widely as well. Frank had openly expressed his frustration with that reality both in his diary, as well as in Jake's Seminar sessions with the "Gang of Six" as they had become known.

Spending a few days in D.C. before arriving at Quantico, Sean had no trouble buying the packet of heroin, syringe, and rubber hose ubiquitous in the inner city of the nation's capital. Some internet research, coupled with some of the chemistry classes he had taken at the U of Washington, taught Sean which chemicals dealers might inadvertently mix with the heroin to make it deadly. He had already purchased a small bottle of chloroform, pouring it carefully into an after-shave bottle so as not to attract notice by a curious visitor to his room. After reading Frank's diary, a credible plan started to form.

So, after everyone was asleep, Sean crept up the one flight of stairs in the dorms, and slipped into Frank's room with the chloroform-soaked cloth at the ready. Once Frank was rendered unconscious, Sean opened up Frank's computer, entered his password, and accessed the diary. There Sean wrote, ‹My inability to fully understand heroin addiction has led me to make a fateful choice. I'm going to inject myself with it so I can feel the high. Maybe then I can truly begin to deal with the curse that killed my mother, jailed my father, and left me wondering why.' Sean closed the entry, and in a few keystrokes, removed all trace of the spyware he had installed.

He then went about "cooking" the heroin, putting it into the syringe, applying the tourniquet, and injecting it into Frank's arm. He watched with fascination as Frank's eyes first fluttered, then opened, and then began to roll back into his head. Frank's entire body went limp at first, but then began to twitch as the poisons Sean had added to the heroin began to take effect. Within moments, Sean had to place his hand over Frank's mouth as his entire body went rigid and began to convulse. Sean had never watched anyone die, least of all by his own hand. To Sean's twisted mind, it was both terrifying and clinically fascinating at the same time. Somewhere deep down, Sean knew Frank's death was only collateral damage in the campaign to hurt Mott, and so Sean held Frank gently, and tried to get him to relax. As Frank's body went lifeless, Sean felt a little sadness, but no remorse. This was, after all, entirely Jake Mott's fault.

Sean wiped down the computer keys, the spoon and syringe, and the doorknob. He knew he had been in Frank's room many times, as had others, so wiping down the entire room would have raised suspicions if fingerprints were even taken. But Sean expected no serious investigation would ever be considered. This was a simple overdose, and the diary entries would confirm that. Sean then went to the lounge outside of Frank's room to grab the book he had 'forgotten' there in case he ran into someone, but the walk back to his own room was uneventful. He then picked up his cell phone and made the call his mother had been expecting.

"It's done! We are finally on our way," Sean whispered when his mother picked up.

Nadia felt a flush of excitement and satisfaction. "Any problems?" she asked her son.

"None. The chloroform knocked him out long enough for me to inject him and make the diary entry we planned. He died quietly, and nobody saw me coming or going. It was perfect. Now it's your turn. Do you remember what I told you about how to put the news out on the dark web? If you do as I showed you, nobody can trace it back to us."

Nadia assured him she was ready to do her part. "

"But be sure not to post anything until at least noon tomorrow," Sean continued, "We have a Seminar meeting at 8:30, and that will probably be the first time anyone knows he is dead. After that, word will spread here like wildfire. Anything before noon will narrow the source of the leak too much," Sean warned.

Nadia replied, "I understand." Then she added, "Oh Sean, I am so proud of you. Your father and I will finally begin to get the justice we deserve. Thank you. I can't wait for the next phase of the plan!"

The next morning, Jake was a little annoyed. His "Gang of Six" knew he valued punctuality, so when Frank Steele wasn't in the room at 8:30, it held up the class. The group was really starting to gel, and this was troubling. He asked his assistant, Paula, to go to Frank's room and tell him to get moving. Then he turned to the rest of the group and said, "We can't wait for him. Let's hear Katie's report on her search for the Nazi Gold."

Katie Arnold looked down at her notes and began, "First, here's what we know. The first gold coin was sold in a pawn shop in Omaha, Nebraska in 1992. Next, there was one coin sold in Des Moines, Minneapolis, Milwaukee, and Green Bay, Wisconsin, each one roughly once a year until 1998. Then the sales all moved to the Pacific Northwest, with one or two sales every year since. In 2018, a sale was made in Portland, Oregon, and the Bureau heard about it through a snitch the next day. When we questioned the owner of the coin shop, he described the seller as an attractive older woman with dark hair and high cheekbones. She gave a false name, on the paperwork, of course. As you might know, these types of businesses know they are often acting as a fence for stolen goods, and their sellers would dry up if they were too strict about checking IDs.

"Until now, the Bureau had been looking for patterns of people who may have been traveling on business to the various cities where the sales occurred. We've looked at travel records of salespeople, truckers, anyone with a need to travel for some other purpose. We kept coming up empty. We also tried to narrow down the search area to see where the seller might be living by drawing a circle on a map a predetermined distance from each city to see if there was any overlap. Whichever distance we chose only gave us too many options or none at all.

"So I decided to try something new. If you have used Google Maps or some other GPS system lately, you know miles don't matter, drive time does, right?" Jake nodded. "I was able to use a 'circle' of a fixed drive time rather than miles. This changed the potential search areas but still didn't narrow things enough. My next step was to assume, dangerous I know, that the seller didn't want to sell to the same place twice. That means she would have tolerated an ever-increasing driving distance, choosing pawn shops closer to home first, and being willing to drive farther later. Using those parameters, and an algorithm I developed with Lori's help, I thought we might be able to narrow our search."

Jake spoke up, "First, nice work. I think your efforts to think about the practical side of the sales and get inside the mind of our seller as a way to direct our investigative resources is smart. I also like how you worked with Lori. Teamwork is part of my goal with this seminar. Now, knowing that your answer is based on a lot of speculation and guesswork, what did you conclude?"

Katie hesitated, then said, "You are right, this is only useful as a way to direct scarce resources and proves nothing. But the only place that fits my parameters is in southwestern Idaho or far northeastern Oregon. But there is one other observation I'm sure you picked up on as well. I know coincidences do happen, but I think it is odd that sales shifted from the upper mid-west to the Pacific Northwest at the same time as your mystery accomplice in the Milwaukee Bank robbery case disappeared, and that the description from the pawn broker in Portland, while very general, could vaguely match your video of her. I just wonder if the cases aren't related somehow."

Jake scoffed at her suggestion, "I've been doing this for a long time, and the connections you are seeing are awfully tenuous. As they say in medicine 'when you hear hoofbeats, think horses, not zebras'. That usually applies to investigative work as well. You are already pretty far out on a limb with your assumptions; let's not go overboard. Stick to what you know is true." Jake then turned to Sean King, "Sean, you grew up in that area of the country. Do you have any insights to add?"

Sean didn't miss a beat, as he had been thinking through what he might say after Katie so accurately pegged his mother's actions over the years. "Katie's assumptions about that area of the country certainly wouldn't surprise me. There was a strong attitude of anti-government sentiment among my neighbors, which attracted some unsavory elements. I was just lucky my mother home-schooled me, or I might have been exposed to that attitude more than I was. If I wanted to stay below the radar of the government, that area is as good a place as any."

Jake was about to move on when Paula, his assistant, threw open the door, "Mr. Mott, please come quickly. Frank Steele is dead!" There were shocked expressions throughout the room, even on Sean King's face, well-planned though it was. Jake told the class to stay there, and he followed Paula over to the dorms. When he got to Frank's room, he saw the EMTs who worked at the hospital on the Marine base standing over Frank's body.

"What happened?" Jake asked.

A tall, uniformed Marine, with a classic military haircut, dark brown eyes, and distinctly Hispanic features stepped over to Jake. Jake noticed the gunnery sergeant's stripes and Military Police patch immediately. "Good morning, Mr. Mott. My name is Sgt. Luis Arroyo. I'm in charge of the MP unit here on the base," he began, "Sad to say, but this is a classic heroin overdose. We don't see many in the military, but my training took me to some seedy areas in Baltimore, and I've seen dozens just like this one. No doubt about it."

Jake was stunned. He knew Frank hated drugs because of what they had done to his parents, and through them, to his own life. It made no sense. But he couldn't deny the evidence: The glassine packet, the rubber hose, the spoon, and the syringe lying on the floor next to the bed. Jake spotted the open laptop next to the bed and touched the mouse to wake it up. There he read Frank's final diary entry, explaining his final, tragic act. What a waste, Jake thought. Frank had shown great promise, and his dedication to the issue of effective drug treatment could have helped so many people.

He turned to Sgt. Arroyo, "Could we seal off this room, please? I don't want anyone poking around in here. As this happened on military property, I know the Marines have jurisdiction. But I'd request a courtesy copy of the autopsy and anything else you dig up." Pausing a moment, Jake took Arroyo aside and spoke quietly, "Sergeant, the idea that one of my students, an FBI agent, died of a drug overdose here at the Academy is a sensitive issue. I'd appreciate you keeping all details of this matter confidential. Can you do that?"

Arroyo said he would, at least until the paperwork was completed. "After that, the Open Records laws tie my hands, but I'll do what I can."

Jake nodded his thanks, and they both watched somberly as the body was removed from the room, and the door was sealed with crime scene tape.

A few hours later, Jake stepped up to a microphone in the dining hall. He knew he had to address the issue with the student body, as rumors were already circulating. With few exceptions, all the students ate their meals together, so Jake felt lunchtime would be the best time to do it.

"I have some sad news to report. As some of you may have heard, one of our promising students, Frank Steele, died during the night in his room. No foul play is suspected. According to his diary entry, without our knowledge, and contrary to law, Frank was experimenting with heroin to try and better understand how to treat it. We believe he got hold of some tainted product and died before he could call for help. He will be missed.

"Out of respect for Frank, and so as not to disrupt your classes with a lot of outside inquiries, we are directing you all to refrain from communicating this news to anyone outside the Academy. The Marine unit conducting the autopsy has been cautioned about the importance of confidentiality as well. After we have the chance to explore this matter in more depth, and after we notify Frank's family, we will then decide how and when this matter will be communicated to the public. My condolences to those of you who knew Frank. If you have any questions, please see me in my office. Thank you."

As Jake was walking toward the exit, he heard a growing murmur in the hall. He saw a number of students looking at their phones and talking excitedly to others at their tables. Jake saw Fritz Hemmer, the former Chicago PD evidence tech in his Gang of Six and approached him. "

"What's going on, Fritz?" Jake asked.

"You're not going to like it, Mr. Mott. The word is already out on the street about Frank."

Fritz showed Jake the screen on his phone. The New York Times's on-line news service confirmed that, "Other news sources are reporting that an FBI agent-in-training at the FBI Academy in Quantico, Virginia died of a heroin overdose overnight. He was reportedly in his room at the Academy at the time of his death. It is unknown at this time whether the student was a habitual drug user, or how the victim was able to obtain the drugs while at the self-contained campus on the grounds of a Marine base. The Academy is under the direction of long-time FBI agent Jake

Mott, who has yet to comment on this story. The NYT has no independent information at this time, but is merely reporting what other news sources have said. More information will be made available as this story unfolds."

Jake was angry. How was this possible? The body was discovered only three hours ago! There were a few rumors among the students, but nothing that was reportable by any reputable news agency. And why would Jake be mentioned in the article? The only leak could have been by the EMTs. He stalked to his office, and a few moments later was talking to Sgt. Arroyo, although screaming was probably more accurate.

Arroyo patiently waited until Jake finished his tirade, and then said, "Jake, it wasn't us. I was with my guys the whole morning, transporting the body, preparing for the autopsy, and cataloguing the evidence. No paperwork has even been started on this thing yet. We have talked to nobody. Your leak isn't here. I guarantee it."

Jake thought highly of the integrity of the Marines. He believed Arroyo. So, he thought, it must have been a student. Damn! He called Julie and told her to have Lori Beam and Sean King meet him in his office ASAP. They arrived together a few minutes later.

"You two are my best tech experts. I need you to work together to find out where this report about Frank's death started. I'm going to find out where the leak came from and plug it...hard! Report back to me as soon as you know something."

Sean asked if they had carte blanche on FBI computer access, and Jake told him and Lori to do whatever it took to find the source of the leak.

Jake's next move was to go back to the dining hall, where the students were still finishing their lunch.

"Attention everyone. As many of you now know, the report of Frank Steele's death has been leaked to the press. This is unacceptable. I have been assured the source is someone from the Academy, not the Marine base. If you were the source, come and see me privately in my office. Until someone comes forward, we will be investigating this leak. We can examine all electronic messaging on department equipment, and we will. All students are directed to immediately surrender their personal electronic devices as well as their passwords to my assistant Paula within the hour so we can investigate where this leak came from. Your personal communications will be respected, but any communications with outside news agencies will be explored. If you have a problem with that, see me in my office as well." With that, Jake strode back to his office.

Moments after arriving, his phone rang. "Mott here," he angrily barked into the phone. Steve Marks matched Jake's heated tone. "What the hell is going on up there? Do you realize the PR problem this creates for the Bureau? Drug overdoses? A dead agent-in-training? All inside one of the most secure facilities in the country. I put you up there to do a job, and this is not acceptable!"

Jake had no patience for a dressing-down from someone he didn't respect in the first place. "Listen, this is exactly why I didn't want this out in the media yet. One of my best students is dead, and I really don't know how or why. And now you start bitching about how it looks? You do what you need to do to cover your own ass on this but leave me alone so I can deal with how this will affect this class of agents. When I know more, I'll let you know if I get anything useful, but for now, we need to 'no comment' this. Can you do that?"

Marks knew he was walking a thin line. He needed Jake to continue to run the Academy, and Marks was the one who talked

Jake out of retiring to do it. Marks also knew that with Jake there, the Bureau had a convenient scapegoat for whatever fallout would come. He decided to adopt a more conciliatory tone for now.

"Okay, Jake, I get it. I forgot how much you care about these students. This death must have hit you hard. I'm sorry for venting on you like that. Of course, we can sit on a response to the press for a while. Get things under control up there, and let's talk tomorrow morning about crafting a press strategy. Sound good?"

Jake curtly said that worked for him, and they hung up. He then called the Marine investigator, Sgt. Arroyo, back. Once again in control of his emotions, Jake began,

"I'm sorry about accusing your crew about the leak earlier. I was out of line." Arroyo said he understood. Jake then explained the Bureau was champing at the bit to get some information out in response to the leak. Could Arroyo rush the autopsy? Arroyo said he would and hoped to call Jake back before the day was out.

"Thanks, Sgt., I appreciate it." Jake said as he hung up.

Two hours later, Sean King and Lori Beam were in his office.

"We wanted to update you on the status of our search," Lori said, "The network here is pretty efficient. We have completed a pretty reliable search of all communications on the servers and from any device connected to the server over the last twelve hours. Nothing. Whoever leaked this information did it on a personal cellphone or laptop. All the students have been cooperative in turning in their personal devices and giving up their access codes. A few grumbled a bit about privacy, but everyone liked Frank, and they want to get to the bottom of this. The problem is the sheer volume of work to open and search each individual device from all 200-plus students and staff. Sean and I will keep at it, but we may not have an answer for a few days."

Jake thanked them, and suggested recruiting Katie Arnold to help them out, "She is pretty tech-savvy and might be able to share some of the load."

They said they would, and left. Jake sat back in his chair and took the brief silence to try to get his mind around these horrific events. How could he have missed something so fundamental as Frank's obsession with heroin? What would be the effect this has on the rest of the students here at the Academy? Should they suspend classes and send everyone home for a while? His head was swirling with questions, but he decided he might tap into the attitudes of his students by meeting with his son, Charlie. He quickly sent an email suggesting they meet in his office for dinner, and Charlie immediately responded saying he was tied up with work tonight, but tomorrow night was open. Jake told Charlie he'd get the food, and to stop by around 6:00.

Jake was just finishing up the mound of work on his desk around 6:30 that night when Sgt. Arroyo called. "Jake, we rushed the autopsy for you, and I'm ready to sign off on the death certificate. Because I know it would affect you to have either suicide or accidental drug overdose as the official cause of death, I wanted to give you a heads up before I signed off. Once it is final, I'll have no choice under FOIA to release it to the press. They are already hounding me for any information I have."

The reality of that decision hit Jake hard. He hated the idea of a suicide, not just because of the image of the Bureau, but because of his Catholic background and what that meant. But a drug overdose was even worse, especially in light of Frank's open disdain for drug abuse by his parents and his zealous campaign against it. Jake decided to ask a few questions that had been bothering him.

"Did you run a tox screen on the heroin he used?" Jake asked.

"Sure did. Normally, it would take a few days, but like I said, I rushed things along for you. It was heroin, cut with a form of chemical rat poison, as I suspected. I've seen it before in some inner-city cases, so I suspect Frank got it in downtown D.C. before reporting to the Academy."

Jake asked him, "How would the poison have affected Frank? Would it have been covered up by the euphoria of the heroin high?"

Arroyo's voice dropped, "Jake, this would have been a particularly painful and nasty way to die. The autopsy showed the poison started to eat away at several of Frank's internal organs as well as his nerve endings, especially his pain receptors and his brain stem. It was actually the convulsions from the pain that killed Frank. Very ugly."

Jake thought about that for a moment, "I'm trying to figure out why Frank never called out for help. No scream of pain. No effort to get out into the hallway. He was in the most excruciating pain, but simply laid in his bed and silently waited for death? That doesn't make sense to me. Any thoughts?"

Arroyo paused. "That is a stumper. I suppose someone with a huge amount of willpower who didn't want anyone to know he was using heroin might be able to keep silent, but based on the damage to his organs I saw in the autopsy, that is pretty unlikely."

Jake said, "So maybe he had a little help? Somebody in the room with him helping with his little experiment who tried to keep him quiet so neither of them was found out?" Jake never even considered the possibility of intentional harm by another in light of the notes found on Frank's computer diary.

"Sergeant, I'd like to ask you for another favor. Can you hold off on signing off on the cause of death for forty-eight hours? I'd like to investigate a bit further. If nothing else, knowing whether there was someone else in the room might help you choose accidental death over suicide. I'm not asking this to delay the records release. I just want to be sure we get it right, and this lack of any cry for help by Frank in light of the results of the tox screen really bothers me. Can you do that?"

Arroyo said, "The press is going to be pretty pissed off, but what good is living in the middle of a Marine base if you can't do the right thing every so often. I'll take care of it. Just be sure to let me know what you learn, okay?"

Jake assured him he would, thanked him, and hung up. He knew, as he crawled into bed that night that he wouldn't sleep much. He spoke briefly with Kathy, who was wonderfully supportive and concerned. He was trying to figure out how to investigate whether someone else had been with Frank when he died. He wondered what Sean and Lori's cell phone investigation would reveal. He tried to imagine the pain Frank had felt as his life was slipping away, and how he could have remained silent. He was looking forward to some quality time with Charlie, but dinner was a whole busy day away. Before drifting off to an uneasy sleep, Jake said a brief prayer for Frank and asked for guidance through what would be his most challenging assignment with the Bureau to date.

# Chapter 10

## The Crow

Sean was twelve-years-old when the crow first began to haunt his dreams. He'd grown up a generally happy child. For as long as he could remember, he and his mother were close. She had to work hard in her bakery business, and from the time he could walk, she taught him skills in the kitchen and included him in her work. He would help stir the ingredients, knead the dough for her much-in-demand scones, and even take a turn frosting her cinnamon rolls. When they dropped off the day's product at the General Store, Nadia would tell Gino that Sean had been her little helper, and Gino would always slip Sean a piece of chocolate from behind the counter. Sean enjoyed the work, the feeling of belonging, and the closeness to his mother.

She taught him to read. The library in Freedom took people's privacy seriously. When residents checked out books, the librarian knew not to create any record on the computer system for the Feds to monitor; everything was by hand records, which were destroyed when you returned the book. Once Sean could read on his own at the remarkable age of three, Nadia began checking out books for him, and books on psychology, the history and procedures of the FBI, communications and media, and computer science, for her. The two of them would curl up in the cozy living room of their trailer, Sean lost in the world of Dr. Suess, and later the Hardy Boys, while Nadia would be gathering the information she would need to plan her revenge for Bill's premature death at the hands of Jake Mott.

Sean and Nadia were inseparable, with one notable exception. Every few months, when money ran low, Nadia asked Matt Horn, the man who had first welcomed her to Freedom, if Sean could stay with him for the day while she ran an errand out of town. While Sean later understood this was necessary to allow Nadia to sell one of the gold coins she kept hidden in their trailer, the first time they were separated, he was inconsolable. He had cried until her car disappeared from sight and sat quietly in Matt's small living room reading until her return late that evening. When Matt told her about Sean's reaction to her absence when she returned, she outwardly expressed concern. But inside, she was pleased. She knew she needed to have Sean completely dependent on her if she was going to shape him into the weapon she required for Jake Mott's punishment. Even at this young age, her plans were on track. Sean was a model of obedience and dependence, just as she had hoped.

Sean was about eight-years-old when Nadia had to face the inevitable first act of rebellion that comes with having children. Freedom, Idaho was too small to have its own school, so at age five, Nadia had to decide between sending Sean thirty-five miles to the nearest public school just outside Boise, or learn how to home-school him. She had no doubt the public-school option would quickly unravel the bond she had formed with her son. She did some research on the internet, sent away for the necessary materials and applications, and found it was possible, with enough effort and patience, to educate her son in her own home. Many of the anti-government groups that Matt and Gino were connected with offered her support and guidance as well. So, by age eight, between his own natural talent, and Nadia's persistence, Sean was well ahead of his peers in all academic areas. He regularly scored in the top one percent of all the state-run standardized testing, and Nadia learned to tolerate the occasional visits to her home by the Idaho Department of Education regulators.

With this level of academic success, one day Sean decided he didn't have to study. Nadia said he would study anyway, and their first contest of wills began. But Nadia was ready for this. She had to send a strong message that Sean needed to obey her. She calmly ordered him to follow her to the shed behind the trailer. Intrigued, Sean did. Inside the shed, there was a large wooden box where they stored their firewood in the winter. Nadia had cleared out all the wood, and now ordered Sean to get into the box. Before she closed the lid, she calmly explained that if Sean did not do as he was told, he would not be allowed to enjoy the good things that come with being part of their family. No quiet time reading books, no helping with the bakery business, and most importantly, the loss of the love and support of his mother. Sean was stunned, and as he heard the padlock on the outside of the box snap shut, he began to cry.

Nearly an hour later, Sean began to call out to his mother. No response. Soon, his calls to her became pleading, then begging. He was sorry, he said. He would do whatever she wanted, he said. Still, no response. Sean softly began to cry again. What he did not know was that Nadia had never left the shed. Some part of her still loved and cared for her son, and that part would not let her leave him completely alone. But another part of her burned with the desire for revenge, and she was obsessed with the plan that had been forming in her mind. She needed Sean to carry out that plan, and his unquestioning obedience was going to be necessary for that to happen. This time in the box was, in her twisted mind, a necessary evil.

When Sean's crying finally subsided, Nadia unlocked the padlock and opened the lid. Sean squinted against the light through his teary eyes.

"I'm sorry, Mama. I'll study now. Please let me out."

Nadia gave him the most encouraging smile she could and reached for her son. As she hugged him, she asked, "Do you understand now? My love for you comes with expectations. Do not disappoint me again. You must do as I tell you, okay?"

Sean started crying again and promised he would. Of course, Sean was only eight-years-old. Over the next few years, he would stay late exploring the woods around their home instead of reading as Nadia had ordered him. He would throw a tantrum when he didn't want to get up early to help with the baking. Once, he even did poorly on a science test, even though Nadia knew he had mastered the material. Each time, she put him back in the box, leaving him for longer and longer periods. By the time he was twelve, his childish rebellious streak had been permanently broken.

On his twelfth birthday, Matt Horn came to visit their trailer, asking to talk to Nadia alone. Nadia sent Sean outside to read on the porch. Matt said to Nadia after Sean was outside, "I've been watching you raise your son, and you are doing a great job. Everyone in town loves him. You should be very proud."

Nadia saw the serious expression on Matt's face, and said, "Why do I sense there is a 'but' coming?"

Matt smiled. "I just want to help. Growing up without a father in the picture means there are some things a boy needs to learn that he just can't get from his mom. I don't care why his father isn't around, and it's none of my business. I know privacy is one of the things that drew you to settle in Freedom in the first place. But Sean needs to learn how to do manly things, too. How to shoot a gun. To hunt. To just hang out with the guys and talk stupid, you know? Not that he can't learn those things from some women, but I don't know if you can teach him. Can you?"

Nadia's mind was racing. If her plan to get Sean into the FBI would work, he would need to learn how to fit into a predominantly male workforce. He would need to be comfortable with guns and be able to speak intelligently about 'guy' things, like athletics, sports, even sex. Matt could do that for her without her needing to fear he would undermine the anti-government attitudes she was trying to instill in her son. Perfect.

"Matt, I really appreciate your thoughtful offer. Yes, I'd like that, and I'm sure Sean would as well. What did you have in mind?"

Matt replied. "I know today is Sean's birthday. I thought I could take him up the valley a ways to a little shooting range me and the boys use on occasion. Teach young Sean how to shoot a long gun, and maybe a few rounds with a pistol. I'll have him back by supper. Sound good?"

Nadia smiled and called to Sean. Turning to Matt, she said, "You tell him. He will be so excited."

Sean was excited. After thanking his mother profusely, he dropped his books in his room, and nearly ran to Matt's truck. That afternoon was a whole new experience for Sean. Not only did he learn about firearms, how to shoot them, safety protocols, and marksmanship, but he also learned that he was quite good at it. Under Matt's training, he was able to hit most of his targets with both the rifle and a pistol from distances of up to 100 yards by the end of the afternoon.

More important, though, Sean started to sense his own maleness. Matt, and the handful of other men using the range that afternoon, simply acted differently from his mother. They were gentle and encouraging towards him, but also showed a sense of confidence, a certain coarseness and swagger that Sean had not been exposed to before that day. They teased him when he missed the target, asked him about his interest in any of the girls in town, gave him an elbow in the ribs when they told a joke, and included him in their discussions of how the newly elected Obama was messing up the country. Sean didn't understand all of it, but he knew his relationship with these men was not something he could experience with his mother. He paid attention and learned. It was a truly great birthday.

Trips to the range to do 'guy stuff' as Sean put it, continued most weekends. Sean became even more proficient at shooting with practice and could outshoot most of the men there. Matt even let Sean try shooting a machine gun (too noisy and inaccurate), as well as a larger caliber handgun (too much recoil). Time permitting, Matt would take Sean into the woods around the range and show him how to be stealthy when stalking prey, and how to identify signs of animals. Each time, upon his return, he would tell Nadia all he had learned, and she would praise his accomplishments.

But back to the dreams about the crow. Two months later, Matt and Sean were stalking in the woods after target practice when Matt spotted a rabbit about fifty yards away. Matt motioned Sean to be silent, and then slowly handed him the rifle Matt had been carrying. Matt whispered, "Go ahead. Let's see if you can hit a live target."

Sean shouldered the weapon. He aimed carefully as Matt had taught him. When he had the rabbit in his sights, Sean stopped. The rabbit was chewing peacefully on some leaves. Sean wasn't hungry. The killing of the rabbit would serve no purpose. Something Sean couldn't explain made him lower the rifle, hand it back to Matt, and say, "Let's go shoot at some more targets, okay?"

Matt took back the rifle and shook his head sadly. Then he raised the rifle to his shoulder, took aim, and killed the rabbit himself.

"You need to learn how to do this," Matt said. "Killing is a part of life. You need to know about death, it's finality."

He took Sean over to the rabbit. It was truly dead, with the top of its head gone. Matt showed Sean how to cut open the skin, remove the entrails, peel away the skin, and store the meat for later. Sean was both shocked by the blood and attracted by the rawness of what Matt had shown him. Sean's emotions were spinning. He was silent the entire ride back home and continued his silence as Matt reported to his mother how Sean had refused to kill the rabbit. After Matt left, Sean sensed a storm was coming.

"Sean, your actions today with Mr. Horn were an embarrassment to me. To us. I thought you understood that when you are with Mr. Horn, you are to follow what he tells you to do," Nadia began, "I want you to be the best at everything you do, and hunting is a part of that. You need to learn that what Mr. Horn asked you to do, even killing, is expected of you. So, I'm going to lock you in your box for one hour to give you time to think about this. Then, next time, we will see if you have learned your lesson."

Sean started to protest, but the look in his mother's eyes told him that would be useless. Nadia, on her part, saw the flicker of rebellion in her son, and worried. While her lesson only related to killing small woodland creatures now, her true concern was about Sean killing much larger, human prey when the time came. She knew he could help her destroy Mott's reputation first, but after that, could he take his life? She had to know, and this was the first step to finding out.

Sean's time inside his punishment box gave him time to come to grips with his feelings about killing. He was gentle by nature, and seeing the blood, the entrails, and the finality of death, even just in a rabbit, had deeply disturbed him. Yet, he wanted to please his mother, and had come to truly hate his time in the box.

So, he did what he could to rationalize the killing. "We eat cows, and chickens, and pigs, don't we?" he thought. "This is really no different. Those animals were all alive at one point. I guess I can be the one doing the killing if I have to". He resolved to do what he needed to do and told his mother that an hour later when she returned to unlock the lid of the box.

"I hope so" was all she said.

The next weekend found Sean at the range with Matt. After the target practice Sean so loved, Matt said it was time to hunt again. Sean braced himself, nodded his head somberly, and they set out with their rifles. Sean knew Matt was watching him carefully and was determined to make Matt and his mother proud of him. Sean saw that Matt took a different route into the woods than last week, so he did not know if it was just luck or by Matt's design that they came across a small mule deer about twenty minutes into their hike. The beautiful animal was grazing peacefully, unaware of Sean and Matt, downwind and hidden in the brush a mere seventy-five yards away.

Matt whispered to Sean, "Your target is just behind the front shoulder. The bullet will hit his heart and lungs and deliver a quick kill. He's all yours. Take him down."

Sean took aim. His mind raced. This deer was so much different from the rabbit somehow. Bigger, smarter, more beautiful. But Sean knew he had no choice. Shaking just a bit, he tried to get himself under control, and then slowly squeezed the trigger. From that distance, Sean should have hit his target with no problem. But this time, his shot caught the deer mid-torso, missing the quick kill shot Matt had described. Instead, Sean saw the deer's hind legs drop, and dark blood flowed from the wound. The deer began to drag itself forward, pulling its now useless hindquarters, clearly paralyzed by Sean's errant shot. After struggling for a few steps, it turned its head towards Sean, seeming to plead for its life. Matt shouted to Sean to take another shot and put the deer out of its misery. Sean didn't miss this time, and the poor animal stopped its struggles.

As they approached the now inert form, Sean was in a daze. He was numb as he helped Matt field dress the deer and bury the entrails. Matt showed Sean where each bullet had entered the deer's body, what damage each had done, and again stressed the importance of a single, accurate kill shot. But the lesson barely registered in Sean's spinning head. They then slung their rifles over their shoulders and carried the deer back to the shooting range. The men at the range hooted and hollered, congratulating Sean on his first kill. They patted him on the back, told him how impressed they were, and even kidded him about how he had missed on the first shot. Sean didn't think the suffering he had caused the poor animal was something to joke about, but he kept his feelings deep inside. Outwardly, he smiled, accepted their praise, and looked forward to telling his mother and win back her approval.

Upon their return to Nadia's trailer, Matt was effusive with his praise of Sean's performance. He explained that Sean's kill would be butchered by one of Matt's buddies and delivered to their trailer in a few days. They would have fresh venison to last throughout the winter, all thanks to Sean. He also promised to have the deer's skin tanned and delivered as well so she and Sean could enjoy its warmth. Nadia was so very pleased, showered Sean with praise, and thanked Matt for helping her son through this ‹rite of passage' as she called it. While her words were focused on killing a deer, inside, she was ecstatic that Sean had gotten over his aversion to killing. She had passed another important milestone in her quest for revenge.

But Sean was another story altogether. After Matt left, Sean told his mother how tired he was, and went to his room. As he tried to fall asleep, he struggled with his emotions about the events of the day. Of course, he had basked in the outpouring of praise and camaraderie from Matt and the rest of the men at the range. And his mother's reactions warmed his heart as well. But that small voice deep inside of him kept telling him that killing the deer was, simply put, wrong. And not just the way the deer had died as a result of Sean's poor first shot, but the death itself. Sean hadn't yet studied philosophy or theology, but he sensed notions of right and wrong were universal, and came from a small, quiet voice inside of him. That voice that was telling him that killing was wrong as sleep overtook him.

It was in his dreams that night the crow first came to him. He was back in the woods, stalking the deer, but this time he was alone. Spotting his prey, he took aim. As he began to squeeze the trigger, he felt a sharp pain in his chest. Lowering the rifle, Sean looked down and saw an immense crow, pecking at him. He was powerless to move and watched in horror as the pecking continued until the crow had torn through muscle and bone, reached inside his chest, tore out his heart, and flew away.

Sean shrieked in pain and fear and felt his mother shaking him awake.

"What is it, Sean?" she asked, concern in her eyes, "You were screaming, 'please make it stop' over and over. What happened?"

Sean regained his composure. He couldn't let his mother know how emotionally conflicted he was over the hunting incident, nor the fact the horrible dream was connected to the decision to kill."

"I'm sorry, Mom. I just had a bad dream. It's nothing. Please, let's both go back to sleep. I'm sure I'll be fine in the morning. I guess the excitement of the day just caught up with me."

Nadia looked a little skeptical, but kissed he son on the forehead, and returned to her bed. She would have to watch him carefully as his hunting excursions continued. She knew killing wasn't easy for a young man, but she hoped repetition would solve the problem.

On one level, Nadia was right. In the months and years ahead, Sean became very proficient at killing. His marksmanship improved until he became known as the best shot around. He routinely shot rabbits, turkeys, and the occasional wild pigs that roamed the forest. And most importantly, he and Matt continued to go on longer hunts for deer, elk, mountain sheep, and other larger prey. Sean learned to shoot accurately and to kill without hesitation. Their freezer was always well-stocked with meat, and the array of animal hides grew. Nadia's fears were put to rest, knowing that when the time came to kill, Sean would not hesitate.

But on another level, one Nadia did not know about, there was a problem. Surrounded by the constant reminders of his kills in the form of meat and hides, Sean dreaded sleep. He might go for weeks or months without nightmares, but inevitably, usually right after a kill, the crow would return. Seeing his own heart plucked from his chest led to Sean waking up in a sweat, heart pounding. And while he had learned not to cry out in the night, he would then lay awake, pondering the struggle inside of him between his desire for his mother's love, and that insistent, tiny voice inside, trying to tell him that what he was doing was wrong.

# Chapter 11

## The Obstacle Course

Years later, Sean still truly enjoyed the outdoors. He especially enjoyed running the Yellow Brick Road at the FBI Academy. He loved the feel of his pounding feet as he ran the hills and valleys on the well-worn path. He enjoyed the various obstacles placed in his path, climbing the wall, the cargo netting, the ladder, and the balance beam. He enjoyed filling his lungs with the late summer air, and the warm feeling of his muscles as they strained to improve his time. It also gave him time to think. And today, he was thinking about how well things were working out. Frank Steele's death, and the ensuing publicity were embarrassing to the FBI as a whole, and as the man in charge, especially disturbing to Mr. Mott. Good.

Sean thought he was going to have to be very careful during the next few weeks of classes if the rest of their plans for Mr. Mott were going to work. Scrutiny on all the students was ramping up, and the use of any electronic communications was going to be especially risky. The public stain on the FBI's reputation from Frank Steele's drug overdose was a good start, but the plan he and his mother had mapped out included one more embarrassing death in the closed environment of the Academy grounds before the big event at graduation. Sean's pulse quickened at the thought of meeting this complex challenge.

Sean had developed a reputation among the students and teachers for having an obsession with running the obstacle course. The fitness instructor, a retired Marine named Bob "Bullet" Davis, practically lived at the gym. The students all had fitness classes with him in both self-defense and general fitness concepts, but also consulted with him on their individual goals. Because the students had workout habits at all hours of the day and night, Bullet was always around to accommodate them. He was universally well-liked and respected. Sean had developed a special rapport with the smiling former warrior with the shaved head that was the basis for his nickname. When he told Bullet he wanted to improve his times on the Yellow Brick Road, Sean got an enthusiastic response. Since then, the former Marine had given Sean lots of tips about how to improve his times, and even more encouragement for his goal.

While he enjoyed the physical challenge, Sean's true reason for having developed that reputation was to give himself an opportunity to contact his mother. All cell phones had been confiscated, as Sean suspected they would, so trying to hide one in the buildings would be dangerous. On one of his runs, Sean had scoped out possible hiding places, and returned later to the most promising spot at a point just past the half-way point of the course. There, the course crossed a small stream, which Sean followed for about 100 yards into the underbrush, where it drained into a culvert lined with large, flat stones. Sean pried up one of the stones, hollowed out the ground beneath, and placed his personal cell phone in a Ziplock baggie into the hole. When he replaced the stone, the presence of the phone was undetectable.

Since then, whenever Sean wanted to make contact with his mother, he would run the course particularly hard until he got to the stream, veer off into the underbrush, make his call, and return to the course. Once, upon his return, Bullet was in the gym where the obstacle course began and ended. He asked Sean why his time that day was a little slower than normal. This was alarming to Sean, as he had no idea Bullet or anyone else was noticing his workout regimen or keeping an eye on his times.

"I've been working on my technique on the obstacles, so I repeated a few of them several times. It looks like the cargo net obstacle is easiest when you dive over head-first rather than climbing to the top and throwing your leg over first. Is that what you found as well?"

The instructor looked impressed, and said, "yes, it is faster, but be careful so you don't get caught up in the ropes when you go over. We've had some nasty injuries using that technique."

Sean thanked him, but was more thankful he was able to think on his feet to avoid suspicion.

It was one of Sean's scheduled days to speak with his mother so he pushed himself hard, skipped the obstacles on the first half of the run, and checking behind him first, veered off the path at the stream. Satisfied he was alone; Sean retrieved his phone and pressed speed dial for the only number programmed into it. She answered on the first ring, expecting his call.

"The mainstream press is having a field day with Steele's drug overdose!" she said, excitement and satisfaction clear in her voice. "They are even raising questions about Mott directly, wondering if he is to blame. Son, our plan is working well so far. I'm so very happy. Thank you!"

Inwardly, Sean felt reassured. He had begun to struggle with the idea that a good man like Frank had died at his hand. Just last night he had the dream about the crow again, something that hadn't happened for over a year. He knew in his head the goal of avenging his father's death might generate some collateral damage, but his heart sometimes made him doubt whether it was worth it. His mother's words quieted those doubts. He knew she had sacrificed much to raise him, care for him, and teach him, and that pleasing her was only right, no matter how it made him feel.

Sean spoke quietly, "Thank you, Mom, that means so much to me. Now we're ready for the next step. And I have some good news. I was outside of Mr. Mott's office before our seminar yesterday and heard him plan to have dinner with his son, Charlie, on Tuesday. So that is the day I'll be going forward with the next step in the plan. Once that happens, security will get even tighter here, so I may not be able to contact you until just before graduation. And I don't think you will need to get out any information to the press this time. The news of this next death just won't be able to be contained now that the spotlight is on the Academy. If I need something, I'll call you, but for now, let's not talk again until the week of graduation. Classes will be over by noon on Thursday of that week, so I'll plan a farewell run on the obstacle course, and call you at 2:00 my time on Wednesday, okay?"

Nadia said, "That plan works for me. I'll be on my way to D.C. to attend the graduation by then, but I'll leave the phone on. Son, please be careful. And please know how happy you have made me already." Sean smiled, powered down his phone, and replaced it under the stone.

"What are you doing back there, Sean?" Sean froze as he recognized Bullet Davis' voice.

What was he doing out here? Even if he hadn't seen the phone, Davis could raise questions Sean didn't want to have to answer. Think fast. Be decisive. Solve the problem. Sean's brilliant mind chewed through the options, and after only a moment's hesitation, said eagerly, "Bullet, you've got to see this. Come over here!"

Davis started picking his way through the brush, as Sean continued. "When I was running, I spotted a small feral pig run in here. I was curious and decided to investigate. I found a den with the mother pig and three or four babies. Come and look".

Davis emerged from the bushes, where Sean was pointing towards the culvert.

"I can't see anything," he said.

"You need to crouch down over here and look just past that small shrub at the entrance to the culvert. See?"

Sean crouched down just behind Davis, who said he still couldn't see anything.

"Here, tilt your head over this way a bit," Sean said, as he placed one hand under Davis' chin, and the other on the back of his head. Then, with a sudden violent twist, Sean snapped the unsuspecting Marine's neck with a sickening crack of bone. The big man's body slid out of Sean's grasp and slumped to the ground, face up. Sean stared into the eyes of a man who had cared for him, coached him, and encouraged him. He watched that face show first incomprehension, then anger, then sadness, before death finally took over, and the former warrior's face went slack.

Sean's immediate reaction was shock, and an immense sense of regret. This was not part of their plan. He could only sit in stunned silence on the ground next to the body. He began to shake, and tears welled in his eyes. But after a few deep breaths, Sean got himself under control again, and began to think through his next steps. He formed a plan, thought it through one more time, and then acted.

Using a fireman's carry so as to avoid dragging the body, Sean returned to the obstacle course. Satisfied nobody was likely to be out running in the middle of the day, Sean walked the hundred yards or so down the trail to the cargo net obstacle. Remembering Davis' warning to him about the dangers of going over the netting headfirst, Sean placed Davis' head into one of the squares of the netting near the top on the far side of the obstacle, facing outward, allowing the rest of his body to hang down from there. It looked grotesque and was an ignominious end for a soldier. Sean was hoping that whoever came upon the body would see it as an accidental death from Davis getting tangled in the cargo net after a head-first flip over the top.

Looking back with sadness for just a moment, Sean began running the rest of the course at the fastest speed he could manage, while skipping the remaining obstacles. He knew he needed to return to the gym as soon as possible so nobody would question why he did not see Davis' body. To further divert suspicion, his first stop upon finishing the course was Davis' office, where Davis' assistant and a few students were having coffee.

"Where's Bullet?" Sean asked. "I wanted to tell him I shaved fifteen seconds off my time today thanks to his advice to go over the cargo net head-first. It really helped!"

The students just shrugged, but Davis' assistant said he had gone out for a run about fifteen minutes ago.

"Ask him to call me when he gets in, would you? I want to thank him for the tip." More nervous than he showed, Sean showered and returned to his dorm room, knowing the call from his former instructor would never come.

# Chapter 12

## Tuesday, Two Weeks Until Graduation

Jake swore he wouldn't let anything interfere with his enjoyment of the night's dinner with Charlie. It had been postponed several times during the hectic semester, so on Friday, when they scheduled it for the following Tuesday, Jake told Charlie nothing would cause him to cancel dinner this time. That promise was tested later, on Friday, with the sad news of Bullet Davis' death, and further by the very disturbing development he had just heard from Sgt. Arroyo a few hours ago. But Jake knew it was going to be difficult to focus on his son.

Graduation was a little over two short weeks away. Charlie had been doing very well in all his classes and was making friends with his fellow agents-to-be that Jake hoped would last a lifetime. As Jake reflected on his past relationship with his son, he knew how poorly he had performed as a father. Jake had convinced himself that his career was his highest calling, and that creating a safe and secure financial future for Kathy and his two children was his primary role in the family. He knew what a great mother his wife had been, and thought, rightly or wrongly, that staying out of her way was best for the kids. She was the one who fed them, picked out their clothes, checked their homework, nursed them when they were sick, and saw to their religious upbringing.

Jake, on the other hand, like his father before him, thought his role at home was only to support any decision Kathy made, be the disciplinarian when necessary, and go back to work. He had convinced himself that demonstrating a serious work ethic was what his kids, especially his son, most needed to see, and if he did that, he was doing his job as a father. Lately, however, Jake was starting to question that attitude. He saw a new generation of fathers who were more intimately involved in their children's lives, sharing in their interests, hobbies, schoolwork, and even helping to shape their views on politics and religion. He'd missed those opportunities, and now hoped to have the kind of open dialogue with Charlie he should have been cultivating for the past twenty years. Maybe this was a case of too little, too late, but he had to try.

It was last thing on Friday, only a few hours after he had set the date for his dinner with Charlie, that Davis' assistant came to Jake with the news. One of the other students, while doing a training run on the obstacle course, came upon the lifeless body of one of the Academy's favorite instructors, Bullet Davis, tangled in the cargo netting, with his neck obviously broken. She wanted to know what to do. Jake immediately picked up the phone and called the Marine base, and as luck would have it, reached Sgt. Arroyo. Jake explained what he knew, and the two agreed to meet at the site with Arroyo's medical team. Both knew the location well, having run the course many times.

Jake arrived first. Several students and faculty were already there, a few of them visibly shaken by the knowledge their friend was gone. He saw Tony Chen, who worked in the shooting facility adjacent to the fitness facility, and who Jake knew had been good friends with Davis.

"How are you holding up, Tony?" Jake asked as he put his arm around his oldest friend in the Bureau.

Tony's face was a mixture of grief and anger. "This just isn't right, Jake. He was the fittest, strongest, most agile man I know. For him to die in a freak accident like this, doing what he was best at, it makes me, ... I don't know... start to question God. Is He sadistic, or does He just love irony? It's just wrong, and I don't understand."

Jake tightened his grip on Tony's shoulder. "I hear you, buddy. Maybe we won't ever understand it. But we need to move on. That was what Bullet would have done if it had been you or me."

Jake looked around at the students, spotting Sean King. He walked over to him, and said, "Were you the one who found him? I know you are out here running all the time."

Sean's reaction was oddly defensive. "No, it wasn't me," he said a bit too loudly. "I ran earlier in the day, and even asked to see him when I got back. How was I supposed to know this would happen while I was in the shower?"

Chalking it up to Sean being upset by the death of his instructor, Jake didn't respond, other than to tell Sean "It'll be okay. We all will miss him."


Just then, Sgt. Arroyo arrived with an ambulance and two Marine medics. "We have to stop meeting like this, Jake," was all Arroyo said.

Jake knew well the dark sense of humor shared by soldiers and law enforcement types everywhere, so Arroyo's glib comment didn't bother him. He gave Arroyo a wry smile, and they both approached the body.

"Who found him?" Arroyo asked, and one of the students timidly stepped forward. Jake recognized him, but only vaguely, a 'Walter' something-or-other.

"I did. But I was careful not to touch anything and ran straight back to the gym to report it. Then I ran back here. Couldn't have been gone more than twenty-five minutes. I hope that is okay."

Jake nodded. "You did fine, son. I'll need you to type up a report of everything you can remember and get it to Sgt. Arroyo here. Sergeant, do you need anything from... is it Walter...?"

Walter nodded.

Arroyo said "No, thanks. And the rest of you should clear out of here so I can do my job."

The onlookers slowly and respectfully drifted down the trail towards the Academy. Arroyo was a true professional. He photographed the body from every angle and distance, including the marks on his neck from the cargo net rope. He collected trace evidence samples from Davis' hands, neck, and running shoes. Then he carefully lifted the body into a body bag to further preserve evidence, and zipped it closed, but not before he gently moved Davis' head from side-to-side; it moved without any resistance. "Jake, this looks like as clear a case of an accidental broken neck as I've seen. But you know we always collect evidence as if foul play was involved until we know for sure otherwise. I'll get my medical examiner to conduct the autopsy as soon as possible, and we can get this case closed. I know you asked me to hold off on the cause of death for Frank Steele, but this one looks easy. I'll let you know when we're done."

The ambulance slowly drove away, leaving Jake to take the long walk back to his office alone. He was not looking forward to making the call to Davis' wife and hoped Tony might join him for that call as the Chens and the Davises often socialized. He'd have to get a notice out to the students and staff as well. That would be hard, as Bullet was well-liked. A bit annoyed, Jake also dreaded his conversation with Steve Marks, who would, no doubt, blame Jake for this incident.

"Ah, well," thought Jake, "only a few more weeks until I'm fully retired and can tell Marks to... well... never mind."

In light of both tragic deaths so close to one another, Jake decided to break with his usual schedule and stay on campus over the weekend. His normal schedule had consisted of driving home each Friday night in time for a late dinner with Kathy. They could then spend the day together on Saturday, with Jake doing the mindless chores around the house that took his mind off the Academy, while Kathy enjoyed thinking about what their life as retirees would be like in a few short months. They might see friends on Saturday evening, or just have a quiet dinner alone. On Sunday, they would attend Mass together, something Jake hadn't always taken the time to do. Jake would then drive back to the Academy, giving himself enough time to prepare for the week.

But this weekend would be different. Jake wanted to be seen on the Academy grounds and help any students struggling with the reality of death that had come to their own. And he was glad he stayed. Several students, individually and in small groups, wanted to talk to Jake about his experiences with death in the Bureau. Everyone knew about the Milwaukee bank robbery shooting that Jake had ordered, but Jake was also able to talk about fellow agents, some friends of his, who had died too young. Jake shared his feelings about people who had died in the line of duty, and those who were taken by disease or accidents. In every case, his message was simple: Death is a constant companion in law enforcement, and you need to learn to deal with it, it was no different than any other aspect of the job. Jake took time to listen to the thoughts and fears of the students, tried to reassure them, and encouraged them to turn to their faith if it would help. Like all grief, Jake knew, it takes time and patience.

On Saturday night, Jake was sound asleep on the makeshift cot he had set up in one of the empty dorm rooms. Suddenly he heard someone screaming, and Jake ran into the hall, following the terrified sounds. He saw a student come out in the hall from one of the suites and yell for help.

When he spotted Jake, he yelled, "Come quick, it's Sean!"

Jake ran past the student into the suite and opened the door to the room where Jake could now hear sobbing. Inside, Jake saw Sean King curled into a ball. His blankets were tangled around him, and Sean was shaking and covered in a sheen of sweat, tears running down his face. Jake sat on the bed, helped Sean to sit up, and put his arms around him. Sean gripped him tight and continued to cry.

Jake told the handful of students, "Get back to bed, the show is over."

He closed the door, pulled the desk chair over to the bed, and sat down.

"Sean, what's going on?" Sean looked at Jake, still dazed and confused.

"Is it gone? Please tell me it's gone!" Sean blurted out, then began to cry again.

Jake decided to just sit quietly to give Sean a chance to settle down. When the crying stopped, Jake asked, "Is what gone? Sean appeared confused, so Jake explained "When you woke up, you asked if it was gone. What were you talking about?"

By now, Sean had realized what had happened, and needed to come up with an explanation. He decided a story close to the truth would be the most credible.

"I'm not proud of this, but years ago, I started having a dream where a black crow would attack me in my sleep. I'd try to push the crow away, but eventually, it would peck at my chest until it pulled out my heart. It was terrifying for a ten-year-old boy. I told my mom, and she stayed in my room with me for a few nights, and the dreams stopped."

Jake was concerned. "Did the dream ever come back?"

Sean looked down. "My first time away from home at college, I had the same dream once or twice. My roommate was dating a psych grad student, so I talked to her about it. She told me it was common, probably brought on by anxiety from being away from home and told me to see her again if they didn't stop. That seemed to help. I've had the dream once or twice since then, but knowing it is no big deal, I just learned to live with it."

What Sean didn't tell Jake was that the dreams had continued off and on for years. He didn't see a pattern, but always wondered if the time he spent dwelling on his mother's plans for revenge on Jake might not be part of the cause. In any event, they were terrifying, but there was nothing he could do about them. Anyone getting psychiatric help for stress was going to have a problem getting into the Academy, and that was not an option for Sean and his mother.

Jake looked at Sean sympathetically.

"To be honest with you, I know what you are going through. As a young agent, I had to make the awful decision to end a man's life in Milwaukee. You know the story. But what you don't know is that I had nightmares for weeks afterward, wondering if I had made the right decision. And, like you, I felt seeking counseling could hurt my career, so I just tried to deal with it alone. The good news is that the Bureau now is much better at helping agents deal with job-related stress, including confidential counseling. So, I'll make a deal with you. I won't say anything about this incident, but right after graduation, you need to promise me you will get some help, either through the Bureau's Help Line, or privately. Do we have a deal?"

Sean just nodded his agreement. But he thought about two things. First, he was surprised to hear Jake had felt any remorse after giving the order to kill Sean's father. Was it true, he wondered? Did Sean's mother hate Jake so much that she couldn't judge the situation rationally? Or was Jake just trying to appear sympathetic so other people wouldn't know that he was an unfeeling killer? Second, Sean knew he'd never have to fulfill his promise. Come graduation day in only two weeks, their plans would come to fruition, and Sean's days with the FBI, one way or another, would be over. He could only hope the nightmares wouldn't return until then.

By Tuesday morning, the students and staff had absorbed the news about Bullet and seemed to be dealing with it. Still reeling from the loss of Frank Steele, they were a resilient bunch. Classes were continuing, and chatter about both deaths had almost ended. Davis' wife Cyndi had been devastated, but Jake had given Tony a couple days off for Tony and his wife to be with her and help with funeral arrangements. Of course, they needed the body released, which was why Jake was calling Sgt. Arroyo. As he was dialing, Jake's door opened, and Arroyo stepped in. Looking serious, as he always did, Arroyo closed the door behind him.

"I was just calling you about releasing Davis' body to the widow. What's up?" Jake asked, surprised by Arroyo's presence.

"Sit down, Jake. We need to talk," Arroyo said as he pulled a chair over to Jake's desk. "We finished the autopsy yesterday morning, which prompted a few questions."

Intrigued, Jake just nodded.

"Go on."

"How familiar are you with the hyoid bone?"

Jake shrugged. "I know it sits in the throat in front of the cervical spine. I've had a few death investigations where it was found broken, showing the victim was strangled to death. Why?"

Arroyo replied, "There are other things we can learn from it. In Davis' case, it was cracked vertically. Also, there was a spiral fracture in the C-2 vertebrae, the likely cause of death."

Jake looked confused. "So? It was no surprise Bullet died from a broken neck. We could all see that."

Arroyo shook his head. "Think about what Bullet was supposedly doing when he died. He was climbing the cargo net face forward. When his body was halfway over the top crossbar, he dove over the top headfirst, swinging his lower body over and, in essence doing a flip so his body would be facing forward again, with his feet on the ground, right? That is the most efficient way to attack the obstacle, and how we were all trained."

Jake replied, "Right, but we were also trained to be careful not to let our head get tangled in the ropes or what happened to Bullet could happen to us. He just didn't take his own advice."

"That is where the bone fractures come into play. It struck me as unlikely one of our best instructors would be so careless, which made me want to be even more vigilant in the autopsy. So, I sat in when the ME did his examination. When examining the neck bones, the ME and I both were surprised to see the spiral fracture and the vertical break in the hyoid bone. If the fatal injury happened the way we just described, the hyoid bone wouldn't have been affected at all, and Davis' spinal cord would have been severed by a lateral bone break, not a spiral."

Jake was incredulous. "You think he was killed? That's nuts. Maybe his head was just turned the wrong way as he went over, or he was just tired or lazy."

Arroyo looked annoyed but held his emotions in check. "Jake, come on. Bullet Davis was 'just tired or lazy'? You know better than that. But you also know I'm not one to jump to conclusions. We went on to check Davis' neck. We saw some light abrasions, but no series rope burns or indentations, which you would expect if the entire weight of his body was suspended by his neck. We also checked for rope fibers on his hands. Nothing. If he had gotten tangled in the netting as he went over, surely he would have tried to grip the ropes to relieve the pressure on his neck. I'm sorry, Jake, but I can't see any other conclusion from what we know. Davis was killed, his neck snapped with a hard left-to-right twist, and he was then hung on the netting to make it look like an accident. This is now a homicide case."

Jake went silent, as his mind chewed on the implications. The universe of possible suspects was relatively finite. Barring a civilian managing to breach the perimeter of the Marine base surrounding the Academy, the perp could only be a Marine, an Academy instructor, or a student. It would also have to be someone either very strong, strong enough to overpower a very powerful man and break his neck, or someone very trusted, who could get Davis into a position where he or she could snap his neck without being suspected. It would also take someone strong enough to lift Davis' body onto the cargo netting. Then a new thought hit him. Frank Steele. Could his death scene also have been manipulated? Was Davis' death the second murder at the Academy? These were scary thoughts.

"OK, Sergeant. I understand. Now what?"

Arroyo could see Jake grasped the implications. "I suggest we move slowly, and treat both the Steele and Davis cases as open for more investigation. I won't issue any paperwork or documentation until we look into this further. I'm not quite ready to rule the Steele case as a homicide, but the Davis case certainly makes me wonder. I'd like you to continue your analysis of the phone records on the Steele case. Whoever leaked that death to the outside world may know more once we get a name. I'm going to look into any past conflicts any of my Marines might have had with Davis from his days with us, and I'd like you to look through your files for any similar connections between any of your students and Davis. Let's plan to meet on Thursday to update one another. Until then, be careful. The cases might not be linked, but I hate coincidences."

Jake stuck out his hand. "Thanks, Sarge, you're a true professional. I appreciate how you've handled this. Let's keep working together until we get to the bottom of this."

The two men shook hands, and Arroyo left Jake's office. Jake glanced at the clock. Damn! Only forty-five minutes until Charlie arrived for their dinner together. What a day this was turning out to be.

# Chapter 13

## 2013

Nadia knew there was one last potential problem with Sean's reliability to carry out her plans. Everything she had done up until now was designed to ensure he would be fully compliant with her objectives. She'd nursed him until he was almost three years old. She'd home-schooled him to fully control the information and attitudes he was exposed to. She'd chosen to live in a social environment that fostered resistance to government control, especially law enforcement. She had used the wood box for punishment sparingly but was sure the message of total loyalty and obedience to her and her alone had been received loud and clear. She had exposed him to a male 'macho' environment to prepare him for his infiltration behind enemy lines in the FBI. But was it enough?

Since he was a small child, Nadia had been reading books about psychology whenever Sean was busy reading Dr. Suess, the Hardy Boys, and later, his textbooks. Her strategies of control and discipline were consistent with traditional thinking about child psychology. But now, puberty loomed. Hormones. Textbooks and every scholarly article she had read consistently warned that the human sex drive was incredibly strong, and that young men would break from their mothers in pursuit of relationships with other women. If that happened with Sean, all her careful planning and grooming could be wasted by the wrong relationship at the wrong time.

So, Nadia dug deeper into the literature surrounding this separation from the mother and found some causes for hope. She learned Freud, and later Carl Jung, had studied the issue in depth, writing about the normal sexual development of male children. At a young age, four or five years old, the male child develops a sexual attraction towards his mother and begins to resent the father's close relationship with the mother. In a healthy situation, the young boy gradually begins to view the father as a role model, begins to idolize him, then emulate him. This results in the maternal attraction waning, and the boy pursuing his own relationships with women outside the family unit, generally by the onset of puberty. In an unhealthy relationship, however, the young man continues to find the mother sexually desirable, and as Oedipus did in Sophocles's famous drama 'Oedipus Rex', actually kills his own father and marries his mother.

Nadia feared losing her son to another woman, and thereby losing her own chance at revenge. Nonetheless, as time passed, and as she read more about the sexual development process, she began to understand how she might be able to use Sean's normal attachment to his own mother to her benefit without any long-term harm to Sean. While Freud had focused on the normal family unit, Nadia had also researched what happened when there is no father figure in the home for the boy to eventually idolize and emulate. In some cases of early divorce, death of the father, or an absent father, the male child retains the bond with the mother, and never develops healthy romantic attractions with other women. Nadia just needed to strike a delicate balance between her being the sole object of Sean's sexual attraction for now, delaying any attachment Sean might develop with another male father figure. Then, when her revenge on Jake Mott was complete, Sean would be free to pursue any female companionship he desired. Nadia would let him go.

And there was one final piece of the Oedipal drama that Nadia could use to her advantage as well: In Oedipus Rex, the son kills the father to prove he is the better man, and therefore the better mate, for the mother. If that principle held true in Sean's case, and deep down he wanted to prove himself better than his father, what better way to prove it than by killing the very person who had killed his own father? Nadia had already planted the seeds of revenge in Sean's mind, but now that he was starting puberty, that urge to prove himself worthy in her eyes would be even stronger.

So, when she was sure Sean was well into the onset of puberty, around his fourteenth birthday, she started laying the groundwork for keeping Sean even more under her control in the face of his soon-to-be raging hormones. First, she made a point of leaving her bedroom door open slightly whenever she was getting ready for bed at night. In the small trailer they shared, Sean's bed was only a few feet from her door. She didn't know how often Sean might have caught a glimpse of her while she was changing into her nightgown, but she knew it wouldn't take much to pique his imagination. During the day, she would often casually touch his shoulder or thigh, not enough to even be noticeable to others, but more than enough for a young boy becoming a man. She would compliment his schoolwork (always an easy thing to do in light of his success in school), and also his appearance and his physique.

At the same time, she knew she had to temper Sean's relationship with Matt Horn. This was tricky, because she wanted Sean to continue his proficiency with weapons and hunting, but not if it meant Sean would see Matt as the paternal role model to replace Nadia. It took her several weeks to consider the best strategy and settle on a plan that would use Sean's budding desires for his mother to her advantage.

One night when Matt dropped Sean off after hunting, Nadia asked to talk to Matt alone. After Sean went to bed, Matt and Nadia went out to his truck. As she went around to the passenger side, she secretly unbuttoned two more buttons on her blouse before climbing in.

"I'm so appreciative of all the attention you've given to Sean, but I'm worried we are imposing on you," she said as she settled in her seat. "I hope you don't think we are taking advantage of you."

Matt was looking straight ahead, "Sean is a great kid. I only wish I could have had kids. I would have wanted someone like him, so don't worry about imposing. He is a joy to have around."

As he said this, he turned towards Nadia, and first noticed the now open neckline, the dusky cleavage, and the lacy edges of Nadia's bra that framed it. Nadia tentatively reached over and ran her right hand up Matt's leg while placing her left hand behind his neck, gently pulling his face down to hers. Matt, taken by surprise, resisted at first, while staring into Nadia's eyes. He saw passion, and invitation, and curiosity. They began to kiss, and Matt placed one hand slowly Nadia's breast, while pulling her shirt out of her waistband. It had been many years since Nadia had been with a man, but she remembered what they liked. It didn't take long for her to get Matt aroused, and for him to urgently open the top of her jeans. But then she stopped him, much to his surprise.

"This is so wrong," she told Matt. Looking into his questioning eyes, she explained, "I appreciate all you do for us, but I need to be a good role model for Sean. If you and I go down this path, I don't know how Sean might react. Can we please stop?"

Matt was stunned. He had never thought of Nadia in a romantic or sexual way, but now that she initiated this, how could he 'unthink' these new desires? He let go of her, and slowly and reluctantly put his hands firmly on the steering wheel.

"Nadia, I think the world of you and the great job you are doing with Sean. I'd be lying if I told you I didn't want more with you. But I respect you, so if this is what you want, then we will just continue to be friends. But don't think this won't make it harder for me and Sean. I'm going to have to back off with him a bit personally. I'll be sure he still joins us up at the shooting range and keeps up his hunting because he seems to love it so much, but I'm going to ask some of the other men to take turns teaching him. Hell, he's already learned everything I can teach him anyway."

Nadia was pleased. She caressed Matt's cheek and kissed him there.

"Thank you, Matt. You truly are a good man."

Then, she climbed down from his truck and walked into the trailer, knowing that Sean was almost certainly still secretly awake. Nadia intentionally left her pants unsnapped, her shirt unbuttoned and disheveled, and her lipstick smeared. She wanted Sean to see.

And he did see her as she walked slowly into her own bedroom. His mind was racing. "I thought Matt was my friend. I looked up to him! And now he starts making out with my mom?" Tears started to stream down his cheeks. A few minutes later, having changed her clothes, his mother came in and sat on the edge of his bed.

"Sean, Matt and I had a talk. He thinks it is time for you to spend a little less time with him and more time with the other men at the shooting range. What do you think of that?"

Nadia thought it a bit of irony that she could blame Matt for the idea as a further way to drive them apart. But she needn't have worried. By now, Sean was fully infatuated with Nadia, and the evidence of Matt's advances on his mother that she had "accidentally" shown to Sean were more than enough for Sean to start resenting Matt. It didn't matter that Nadia had planned the whole event. In Sean's mind, Matt was no longer to be trusted. And as an added bonus, Nadia knew Sean's firearms training would continue uninterrupted.

Nadia's late-night conversation with Sean continued. "Sean, I'm sorry things turned out the way they did with Matt. I know you were starting to look up to him. But I learned something a long time ago, and that is that all men are deeply flawed. You know all about Jake Mott and what he did. I've also told you about that bastard of a loan officer that sold your dad a bad loan and then wouldn't help your dad when he needed it. Well, you're also old enough now to know that your grandfather was a mean drunk. He beat your grandmother and tried to beat me until she stepped between us. For all my life, men have done nothing but take advantage of me.

"The one exception to that was your father. He was kind and gentle, and there was nothing he wouldn't do for me. You are already so much like him. If you really want to show the world what a man you are, you can help me bring down the man that killed your father. Can you do that for your mother?"

Sean looked trustingly into his mother's eyes. Between his devoted relationship with his mother becoming twisted into something sexual, and tonight's betrayal by the one man he had looked up to, something had broken deep inside of him.

"Yes, mother. It's just you and me now."

When Nadia went to bed that night, if she had believed in a God, that is the moment she would have begged for forgiveness. Until now, she could rationalize the way she had raised her son. But no longer. The die had been cast, and whatever happened in the future would be her doing. Her son was just a pawn.

If Nadia had doubts about her decision to separate Sean from Matt Horn as a role model, she needn't have worried. Freedom, Idaho, and the men's hunting club, was rife with able substitutes who consistently reinforced Nadia's preaching. Wherever Sean turned, he heard the men and women around him explain that law enforcement, especially federal law enforcement agencies like the FBI, were out of control.

"They have too much power, and don't respect the legitimate rights of law-abiding citizens," was a constant refrain. With the upbringing he'd already had, how could Sean have even begun to critically challenge this constant drumbeat? Most influential of these voices was Mick. When Matt Horn had stepped away from his mentorship of Sean, a burly Irishman named Michael Dugan—Mick to his friends—took Sean under his wing. Mick had many of the same attitudes as the rest of the residents of Freedom, but with a virulence that was unmatched. Mick's parents had been radicals in the turbulent 60's, advocating the use of violence to "transform" society. They had been convicted of participating in a failed plot to blow up a recruiting center for the military and were jailed in California when Mick was only four years old. He'd bounced around some group homes and the occasional foster placement until he turned eighteen, when he enlisted in the army, primarily to take advantage of the GI Bill. It was there that he learned to shoot and to resent being told what to do. After he left the army, he drifted from job to job, eventually finding himself in Freedom.

Despite having little to do with his parents, he idolized their philosophy that violence was sometimes necessary to force society to change. To them, and to Mick, blood, sometimes innocent blood, had to be shed to 'wake people up'. Mick was quick to tell his neighbors and friends about his philosophy, and that included Sean.

Nadia would reinforce that theme. At this stage, a plan was beginning to form in her mind about how she and Sean might proceed. As a child, Nadia had read prolifically, and had enjoyed the tale of the siege of Troy. Perhaps her son could be the FBI's Trojan horse, who would attend the FBI Academy, become an agent, and slowly and secretly work to destroy the monolith of the Bureau from within. And to do that, innocent people might get hurt. Mick's message, that "the tree of liberty must occasionally be watered with the blood of martyrs" could come in useful.

As if the influences of Nadia, Matt, and now Mick, were not enough, when Sean was sixteen years old, Mick's nephew Thomas came to live with him in Freedom. Tom's story was tragic. He had lived in a suburb of Chicago with Mick's older brother and his wife. The local police departments had faced a wave of carjackings by inner-city gangs, resulting in car chases that often ended in crashes, injuries, and even one death. Worried about liability for what was essentially a property crime, Tom's local police chief announced they would not conduct chases in carjacking cases.

Predictably, the gangs were drawn to Tom's community like bees to honey. Frustrated by the lack of police support, Tom's parents bought a gun. When they were later confronted by two men trying to steal their car, they refused to turn over the keys. In the ensuing gunfight, both Tom's parents were killed. At age fourteen, Tom came to Freedom to live with his only living relative, Uncle Mick, and soon became fast friends with Sean. They hunted together, and because Nadia agreed to homeschool Tom with Sean, they studied together as well. But most importantly, they learned together that law enforcement officials don't really care about the safety of law-abiding citizens like Tom's parents, and according to Mick, "something has to be done!"

And so, upon graduation from high school, Sean knew what he wanted to do with his life. Attend college, go through the FBI Academy, and from inside, begin to tear down the institution that had killed his father, and the system that cost his good friend Tom his parents.

# Chapter 14

## Tuesday, Ten Days Until Graduation

"Come on in, Charlie, dinner is served!" It was 5:30 on Tuesday afternoon. Classes were over for the day, and Jake somehow had put the tumultuous events of the day aside. For the next several hours, he and his son were going to have quiet dinner in Jake's office and talk about many things Jake felt he had neglected while Charlie was growing up. Jake had pulled some strings with the cafeteria staff, and the smell of a couple of medium-rare New York strips, baked potatoes with lots of butter and sour cream, and grilled green beans filled his otherwise sterile office.

Jake had come out of his office just a few minutes earlier to send his assistant home for the day. She was just finishing up talking with Sean King about his research paper.

Jake said hello, and then asked Sean, "Can I get an update on your search for who leaked the news of Frank Steele's death?"

Sean said, "Sorry, but it is taking loads of time. I'll keep working on it tonight and let you know what I've come up with tomorrow in class, if that's OK."

Jake nodded. "Of course. Right now, I'm just looking forward to some alone time with Charlie. Thanks for working on this. I know you have a full schedule, and graduation is almost here. I'll let you go."

That is when Charlie showed up. Father and son went in, and Jake closed the door. Their conversation started light as they began to eat with gusto. Progress of Charlie's classes. News from Kathy and from Charlie's sister, now beginning her freshman year at college. The Washington National's prospects for the baseball playoffs.

When the meal was almost over, Jake asked, "So, tell me why you joined the FBI. I know I should have asked you that a long time ago, or maybe even known you well enough not to have to ask, but I'm asking you now."

Charlie thought for a moment. "Dad, I don't know why you think you don't know me very well. And I'm going to answer your question. But before I do, or maybe even as part of my answer, I want to give you a little gift to thank you for everything you've done for me." Charlie reached into his briefcase, produced a small, wrapped package, and handed it to his father. "Go ahead, open it."

Jake was mystified. Tearing open the wrapping, he saw a small wooden plaque mounted on an easel.

"It's for your desk," Charlie explained.

Jake read the words inscribed on the gift: "To my father. He didn't tell me how to live. He lived and let me watch him do it." Jake carefully set it on his desk, then rose and hugged his son, at a loss for words. Charlie went on. "So here is my answer. You showed me the value of a lifetime committed to maintaining order in society. You showed me how a man can lift up those around him by exercising self-discipline, honest and caring leadership, and dedication to family. I know from your example that I can do all of those things in any career I choose. But I've been immersed in law enforcement all my life. Of course, I would choose to continue your legacy. That should come as no surprise to you."

Jake sat back down and continued to pick at the remains of his dinner. "That is very flattering, son, but I hope you don't feel any pressure by making the choice you did. I've done well in my career, but it's a different Bureau now, and it demands different skills. There would be no problem on my end if you decided to do something else."

Charlie nodded. "That the FBI has changed is clear, but it is also a benefit for me. I have more choices in how I can best serve the law enforcement community than you ever did. I plan to figure out where my skill set lies, but I will always be your son, and always try to live the values you passed on to me."

Satisfied, Jake decided to try to go even deeper with Charlie. "Speaking of those values, where would you say you are in terms of your Catholic faith?"

Jake always felt he had failed to espouse the importance of faith in his own life in front of both of his kids. Frankly, Jake recognized he spent years simply going through the motions of his Catholic upbringing, leaving the religious formation of the kids to Kathy. Now, Jake was beginning to see not only how important his faith would be to him in the future, but moreover how failing to openly live his faith in the past sent the wrong message to his kids. If Charlie's plaque was correct, Jake hadn't modeled the religious habits he now wished he had passed on.

Charlie was clearly uncomfortable with the direction the conversation had taken. Like most young men his age, religion was not even a peripheral concern. He had done all the "required" Catholic rituals of baptism, confession, First Communion, and Confirmation. But the old joke about how young Catholics were happy at their confirmation because it meant they didn't have to go to Mass anymore seemed to apply to Charlie. Sure, he went to Mass every Sunday until he left for Georgetown, but while away, went only rarely, despite the Jesuit influence there. Couple that with the constant allure of secular society, the clergy abuse scandals, and the waning of the role of religion in society generally, it was no surprise that Charlie was somewhere between "I don't know" and "I don't care" when it came to religion.

"Well, Dad, I must admit my faith life is probably not what you or Mom want it to be. But I never thought it was important to you. Sure, Mom always made sure we went to Mass and to religious education, but you were often working, and just didn't seem that interested in what we were learning. I don't want to criticize you, but did something happen recently that makes you ask me about this?"

Jake was not surprised by Charlie's answer but was certainly saddened by it. But he was hopeful it was not too late to change that. He smiled at his son. "Nothing specific has happened, other than getting older, and hopefully wiser. When I was young, and strong, and having lots of success in my career and in my family life, I thought I didn't need to have faith. I thought that I had it all figured out. I suspect you do, too. But with the perspective of hindsight, I now see all the ways my life could have gone badly, but didn't. Sure, living right, and making good choices helps improve the odds that your life will turn out well. But I know a lot of good men who have faced tragedies not of their own making that I somehow avoided. I believe now that God was helping me, and I plan to continue to explore that belief in the time I have left. I guess my message to you is this: Keep nurturing your faith. Ask yourself the big questions about whether God exists and what he asks of you. That search ought to be part of your growth as a person. I don't recall who said it, but I've heard that the two most important days of your life are the day you are born, and the day you figure out why."

Charlie assured his dad he would try. Trying to move to a lighter topic, Charlie asked Jake about his plans after retirement. Jake was happy to move on as well, and they started to discuss the planned Mediterranean Cruise Kathy wanted, a possible move back to Florida, consulting opportunities for Jake, and even taking some golf lessons, a sport Jake never had the patience for when he was working all the time. They then meandered through Charlie's dating prospects, more baseball talk, and reminisced about family trips they'd taken in the past. It was as pleasant a conversation Jake had ever had with Charlie, and was immensely satisfying. So, to bring it to an end, Jake went into his desk drawer and pulled out bottle of eighteen-year-old port, Jake's favorite drink. He poured them each a glass and handed one to Charlie. Raising his own, Jake said, "To my son, who makes his father a very proud man."

After sipping their drinks in silence, Jake was surprised to see how much time had passed. It was now nearly 10:30, and both Jake and Charlie had busy schedules the next day. Sadly, it was time to part.

"Well, son, thanks for a great evening. Tomorrow, it is back to calling me Mr. Mott, but tonight was special. I hope you thought so, too."

Charlie smiled at his dad, reaching out his hand. Jake looked at it, then took up his son in a hug they both wished wouldn't end. When they separated, they both were a little teary, but like most men, neither would say a word. Charlie picked up his briefcase, and silently left the office. They could not have guessed the storm that would engulf them the next morning.

As Sean heard Jake's office door close for the dinner with Charlie, he knew he would have to work both quickly and carefully to take advantage of this golden opportunity. Not even his own mother could have planned what Sean was about to undertake. She would be so pleased!

In the past few days, since learning of the planned private dinner, Sean had laid the groundwork for this evening. Jake's decision to assign Sean the task of searching for evidence of the leak about Frank Steele's death had given Sean unprecedented access to explore the FBI's database. Part of that exploration had led Sean to the Automated Fingerprint Identification System, or AFIS, a computerized system maintained by the FBI since 1999. Law enforcement agencies all over the country could enter a fingerprint from a crime scene, and within minutes determine if there was a name to go with that print. The system not only kept the fingerprints of known criminals on file, but those of many classes of non-criminals, including all federal employees. Sean, and every other student at the Academy, had been fingerprinted as a condition of hire by the FBI. Sean discovered that with a few keystrokes, he could manipulate the data in the AFIS system in ways that might eventually be uncovered, but in the short term, could be very useful.

Sean also studied the various weapons contained in the historical display cases in the lobby of the admin building. He wanted to use one of them for this next kill, because the investigators wouldn't be able to trace who the weapon belonged to. It could have been used by anyone at the Academy. He also knew he couldn't use a firearm, as the noise would draw other students to the scene too quickly and ruin the fun. A knife was not an option either, as the blood spatter would be too difficult to control. Sean finally settled on a garrote used by one of the members of the Capone gang to eliminate a rival in 1930. The two sturdy oak dowels attached to a thick length of piano wire should be just perfect for what Sean had in mind.

Finally, Sean had meticulously walked off the distances between Jake's office, Fritz Hemmer's room on the second floor of the Madison dormitory, Charlie's room on the third floor of Madison, and his own room across the way in the Washington dorm. He knew how much time he had to walk the route and knew where he could duck out of sight if he unexpectedly encountered someone on his route. He knew his excursion would be taking place at a time when most students were hard at work either in the library or in their rooms. The Academy was winding down, and nearly every student had papers to write, projects to finish, and tests to prepare for, with not nearly enough time to do it. When test-walking his route the previous three days at 8:30 each evening, Sean had only seen one other student, and was able to move quickly to a stairwell before being seen himself.

With his heart beating fast, Sean walked down the stairs to the lobby of the admin building. Satisfied the place was deserted, he used a letter opener to slip the flimsy lock on the display case and lifted the garrote from its place. Coiling it and sliding it into his pocket, he closed the case and calmly walked towards the cafeteria. He couldn't arrive in Fritz's room too early, as it would disrupt the timing of his plan. Sean enjoyed a quiet dinner, reading his notes for one of the final exams he would be taking on Friday, but keenly aware of the slow ticking of the clock. Finally, at 8:00, Sean rose and began his casual walk to the Madison dorm and Fritz Hemmer's room.

Fritz was hunched over his laptop when he heard a quiet knock on his door. Realizing he needed a break, he rubbed his eyes as he said, "Come in."

Sean King appeared, and asked, "Do you have a couple minutes to talk about Mott's seminar? I'm struggling a bit with my final paper and wanted to bounce some ideas off of you."

Fritz was under a lot of pressure himself, but was also a decent man willing to help whenever he could, so he gestured towards the bed, saying, "Sure, but let's make it quick. I'm a bit backed up myself. What's on your mind?"

Sean said, "For my final paper, for Mott's class, I'm focused on the public profile of the FBI, and ways we might use social media better. I'm trying to figure out if Mott is looking for one specific recommendation, or if he just wants us to offer some alternatives with pros and cons. You take pretty good notes. Do you know what he told us?"

Fritz replied, "I'm coming up with one specific, concrete recommendation, and supporting it with my research. I think that is what he wants."

"But is that the only option? Can you check your notes on the assignment? I'd appreciate it."

Fritz looked annoyed but nodded.

"Sure, I have them on my laptop. Just let me check, but then I need to get back to work, okay?"

Fritz turned away from Sean and moved his chair back to his desk. Sean watched him carefully as he withdrew the garrote and held the wooden dowels in each hand. Then, before Fritz could react, Sean slipped the piano wire over his unsuspecting victim's neck and pulled back hard, placing his knee firmly on the back of Fritz's neck. Sean recalled the lessons he had been taught by Matt many years ago when he had killed his first deer with that sloppy missed shot. He knew not to let any animal suffer any more than necessary, so he jerked hard on the wooden handles. The piano wire dug deeply into Fritz's windpipe, sawing through the skin, muscle and cartilage while choking off any air to his lungs. At the same time, the wire dug into his carotid arteries, cutting off blood flow to Fritz's brain. While his body feebly resisted, it was only a matter of time before Fritz would pass out, and then die. Sean only hoped it would be relatively quick, so he pulled even harder, feeling Fritz's body go limp just as a spray of blood gushed out of the thin line slicing across his throat, landing on the desk, the laptop, and the floor at Fritz's feet.

As Sean had expected when he chose this weapon, by remaining behind his victim he had avoided any blood spatter. But now that

Fritz was dead, he could take advantage of all he had learned here at the Academy about evidence collection to further his plans. Sean pulled out a Ziplock baggie with several Q-tips. Being careful to avoid the blood now pooling on the floor at Fritz's feet, Sean soaked two of the cotton swabs in the blood, and slid them into the baggie, sealing it tight. Satisfied, he then slowly opened Fritz's door, checked to be sure the hall was empty, and slipped down the hall to the nearest stairwell.

Quietly ascending one flight, Sean again checked the hallway before walking to Charlie's room. Once inside, Sean saw what he expected. Charlie was as neat as you would expect from the son of a squared-away FBI agent. Clothes carefully hung up, pants on one side, shirts on another, and Charlie's standard-issue black rubber-soled shoes properly in the closet. The students had all joked about how you could always tell a "fed" by his shoes, but nevertheless they each had bought two pair of nearly identical shoes. Charlie was wearing one pair at the dinner with his father, and the other pair was waiting neatly in his closet.

Sean withdrew the baggie with the blood-soaked Q-tips and dabbed several drops of Fritz's blood on the tips and top of the soles of Charlie's shoes. Returning the swabs to the baggie, and the baggie to his pocket, Sean then withdrew from Charlie's room, returning to the cafeteria, where he wrapped the baggie in several napkins and disposed of it in one of the un-emptied garbage cans, pushing it deep into the messy trash. His heart rate back to normal, and privately elated that all his preparations had apparently been successful, he returned to his room. While he was not visited by the crow that night, he still slept fitfully, eagerly anticipating what the next day would bring, and the pride his mother would feel for all his hard work.

# Chapter 15

## Wednesday, Nine Days Until Graduation

Jake woke up late, a little groggy, but in good spirits. The quality food, the alcohol, the late hour, and some wonderful conversation with his son all combined to make him upbeat about the coming day. His first meeting wasn't until 10:00, so he allowed himself the luxury a sleeping until after 9:00, and after a shower and shave, walked briskly to his office. When he saw Sgt. Arroyo waiting for him, and took in the serious look on his face, Jake knew this day was not going to be the good one he had hoped for.

"Jake, I need to talk to you in your office right away. It's bad," Arroyo said. Jake unlocked the door, noticing the shocked expression on his assistant's face, and the curious looks from the students in the vicinity of Jake's office. Taking a seat, and pointing to one for Arroyo, Jake was concerned,

"What is it? Is it, Kathy? Charlie? What?"

Arroyo's reaction when Jake said Charlie's name made Jake's heart leap into his throat. "Dammit, Arroyo, spit it out. What's going on?"

Arroyo paused and gathered his thoughts. "First, Charlie is safe. But another student was found dead this morning. Charlie is involved, and it is ugly."

Jake was stunned, and very confused. "Who was the student? And how is Charlie involved?"

Arroyo opened his notebook, looked at Jake, and started to explain. "At 6:30 this morning, Bill Hood knocked on the door of his suite mate, Fritz Hemmer, looking to borrow some toothpaste. Not getting an answer, Bill opened the door and found Fritz slumped in his desk chair, dead. Hood says he didn't disturb anything as Hemmer was clearly dead, and immediately tried to call your office, but there was no answer. He then called my office. He told me he knew I had been working on the Steele case, so figured I should be notified. I grabbed a couple of my guys, and we rushed right over to the scene.

"When we entered the room, it was clear Fritz had been murdered. There was an old-fashioned garrote still wrapped around his neck, and copious amounts of blood on the table in front of the body as well as on the floor at his feet. No other signs of a struggle, suggesting the killer was known to Hemmer, allowing the killer to get behind him without a problem. We carefully dusted the murder weapon for prints, lifted a very clean set, and sent them into AFIS for identification. Frankly, I didn't expect any luck on the prints because anyone in our system would know enough to wear gloves, but we sent them in anyway. After taking evidence samples, we removed the body for an autopsy. The ME took body temperature readings and based on that and the blood pooling inside the body, put the time of death between 8:30 and 9:30 last night. We secured the room, and I went back to my office."

Jake was still both stunned and confused. "Fritz was a really promising student. He was doing excellent work on some cutting-edge evidence techniques. His murder is a real loss to the Bureau. Personally, I really liked him, as did the other students. I can't believe anyone from the Academy would have anything to do with this. After Frank Steele, and then Bullet's death, this year's class couldn't get worse. But you said Charlie was involved somehow. What is his connection?"

Arroyo put away his notebook and shook his head sadly. "Jake, they were Charlie's prints."

At first, the words didn't even register. Then they sank in, and Jake stood up with tears in his eyes, and began moving around his desk to the door.

"Wait. My Charlie? Charlie Mott? That just isn't possible. Charlie would never do something like this. It's just crazy. Let's go talk to him and get this straightened out."

Arroyo stood and blocked Jake's exit. "Jake, you can't see him right now. A few minutes ago, my guys took him into custody. You know the drill. A suspect doesn't get to see anyone except his lawyer until we are done questioning him. We are going to treat him right, but we need to do this by the book, especially because he's your son. So, calm down and take a seat. Let's talk this through like professionals. okay?"

Arroyo had been reading people under stress for his whole career. He could tell Jake was teetering between fear, anger and confusion, and was ready to throw a punch if necessary. Much to Arroyo's relief, Jake's shoulders slumped as he slowly made his way back to his desk.

"Okay, you're right. If anyone should trust the system, it should be me. So, what now?" Jake asked.

Arroyo replied, "We do what we always do: we gather the facts. We secured Charlie's room when we took him into custody. We are processing his room for evidence. We are talking to the other students and instructors to see if anyone saw or heard anything, but we aren't getting much. Most everyone was cramming to finish their work before graduation either in their rooms, or in the library. We found a couple students who were in the gym, but nobody saw anything remotely helpful. The hallways were a ghost town.

"And finally, we tried to retrace Charlie's and Fritz's steps yesterday. We know from his instructors and several students that Fritz attended all his usual classes yesterday, ending at 3:00. He then went for a run, showered at the gym, and told several classmates he was planning on finishing up his seminar paper for you in his room all night. We couldn't find any instances of Fritz crossing paths with Charlie at any time during the day."

Jake processed this information, and then suddenly brightened. "It couldn't have been Charlie! You said the ME put the time of death at around 9:00, right? Well, Charlie was with me from 6:30 until 10:30! He's off the hook!"

Arroyo looked interested. "What were you two doing? Where were you, exactly?" Jake replied, "We had dinner together, right here in this office. We talked late into the evening, but he didn't leave until 10:30. I specifically looked at the clock when he left."

Arroyo looked thoughtful. After a few moments, he said, "We will need to get a written statement from you about Charlie's alibi. I'll send one of my guys over here to nail it down. But we are still gathering all the evidence, and I'm not going to reach any conclusions here until I have all the facts."

Jake looked at Arroyo coldly. "What other facts do you need? I just told you Charlie was with me all last night. He didn't do it. Now I expect you to let him go, and I mean now!"

Arroyo held up his hands in an effort to calm Jake down. "Now Jake, just take it easy. Another few hours in custody won't hurt your boy. And I appreciate how upsetting this is. But look at it from my point of view. How many fathers wouldn't say they were with their son all night just to get them out of trouble?" Seeing Jake's anger about to erupt, Arroyo continued, "I'm not saying you're not being straight with me. But think about how much trouble

I would be in if I shut down an investigation based solely on an unsubstantiated alibi from the suspect's loving father. If you were thinking straight, you'd see that. Now if you really want to help your son, help me. If what you say is true, I'll need two things from you. First, get me a witness that can say Charlie was with you until 10:30. And second, help me figure out how Charlie's fingerprints got on the murder weapon when, according to you, he wasn't even there. Are you starting to see the problem?"

Jake nodded. "I do. Let me give the fingerprint problem some thought. And you should add questions about Charlie's whereabouts last night when you canvass the students and staff. I suspect everyone was in their rooms by 10:30, but maybe you'll get lucky. I know you have work to do, but I'd appreciate you keeping me in the loop if anything else comes up. Thanks."

Arroyo demurred. "I'm not sure I can do any more than I already have. You are the father of the main suspect in a murder investigation, and you have connections in law enforcement that could be manipulated to the suspect's benefit. You need to be passive and let me do my job. If you come up with any ideas, my door is open, but I need to go by the book from here on out. If there is anything I can tell you, I will, but don't expect any special favors. I'm sorry, but that's how it has to be."

As Arroyo left the office, Jake's assistant told him he had a call. Picking up, Jake was not pleased to hear Steve Marks' high-pitched, whiney voice.

"Jake, I just heard about Charlie being arrested for murder. How do you want to handle this in terms of your leadership of the Academy. The Bureau was having a problem with its reputation before this, but to now have a third death at the Academy, with the Academy Director's son as the killer is intolerable."

This was almost too much for Jake to handle. His first instinct was to tell Marks to go to hell, quit his job, and go home. But Jake would not let this petty bureaucrat get the best of him. Jake had been the consummate professional too long to go out this way. So, he took a deep breath, let it out, and replied, "If you are asking me to quit, I refuse. I was asked to do a job, and I intend to do it. And as for firing me, you know that with my longevity with the Bureau, and all the procedural hoops you need to jump through to protect my Due Process rights, it would take weeks before I was off the job, and graduation is only nine days away. And you don't have the authority to fire a Bureau employee anyway. Only the Director can do that."

Jake could hear the snark in Marks' voice over the phone.

"You always despised me because I'm a 'paper-pusher' to you. But I also know how the system works. You see, Jake, I can fire you. Today. Now. And do you know why? When I asked you to take this job, I gave you papers to sign formally withdrawing your retirement request. I warned you that if you didn't sign them, your retirement would take effect, and your status at the Academy would be as a contractor with the Bureau. And as the chief 'paper-pusher," I do have the authority to terminate independent contractors. So, let's get back to my original question. What do you think we should do about this situation?"

Jake was getting pretty steamed at the idea of someone he didn't respect having any power over him. But he also wanted to stay in control of the situation and knew he couldn't do that from home. Knowing that weak men respond to strength, Jake replied, "First, let's get a few things straight. Charlie was not arrested. He was taken into custody for questioning, a distinction a real cop would appreciate. Second, he is no killer, and he had nothing to do with this murder. A good investigation will prove that, something else a real cop would understand. So don't ever refer to my son as a killer again. I want you to tell me you understand. Do you?"

Marks said he did.

"Furthermore, while I care about the Bureau's reputation, probably more than you do, that is not my primary responsibility here. My job is to graduate as many good future FBI agents as I can, and that includes Charlie. So, it is my intention to continue doing my job until the end of the graduation ceremonies next week. If you want to stop me, I guess that may be your call. But now I have a job to do, and I'd appreciate you letting me get on with it."

Marks knew that practically speaking, he couldn't fire Jake. First, there were too many powerful people in the Bureau that liked and respected him. Second, as troubled as the Academy seemed in the public eye right now, the black eye would be even worse if the Director of the Academy was to be removed only nine days before graduation. But Marks couldn't just back down either.

"OK, Jake, but this is how it's going to be. I can't have you interfering in this current investigation in any shape, manner or form. And until Charlie is fully cleared of any wrongdoing, I don't care if he is in custody, a suspect, or only a witness. He is not to be in attendance on the grounds. If you can get him his instruction remotely, I'll allow it. But I want him away from Quantico completely. Those are my terms. Do we have a deal?"

Jake asked Marks, "What about graduation? Can he attend?"

Marks replied, "I can't answer that right now. Let's see what his status is by then. If he's arrested, charged, and out on bail, no way he comes to graduation. But if he's cleared, we can talk."

Jake knew it was the best he could do. "Okay, thanks. You've got a deal. Now if there is nothing else, I have work to do. I'll let you know as things develop."

After Jake hung up, he knew his next call would be the worst. He would have to break the news to his wife, and then ask her to come down to the Academy to pick up their son and take him home, likely never to return to the Academy. Twelve hours earlier, Jake felt like his world was golden. Now, he faced his greatest challenge to his faith in himself, his family, and his profession that he had ever known.

Later that afternoon, Jake got through the first of many stacks of papers he needed to grade before graduation. The work helped take his mind off Charlie, and also let him reset his thought process. At 3:00, Jake decided to put aside his work, turn off his phone, close his door, and try to think through the murder of Fritz Hemmer. All his life, Jake had tried to look for patterns. The Academy had experienced three untimely deaths in only a few weeks. Frank Steele could have been an accidental overdose, but the fact that he didn't call out for help while experiencing an excruciatingly painful death certainly raised questions. And Bullet Davis' death appeared to be an accident, but Sgt. Arroyo suggested the way the neck bones were broken, coupled with the unlikelihood of an experienced instructor accidentally breaking his neck also raised questions.

Now, Fritz Hemmer had clearly been killed. What if the three deaths are all connected? If all three victims were intentionally killed, what do we know? Motive, means, and opportunity are the Holy Grail of all investigations. Opportunity first. All three murders, if that's what they were, could have been done by anyone on campus, either students or instructors. The dorm rooms are all unlocked, and the Yellow Brick Road is open to everyone. No help there.

Means. Same thing. By the time of Frank Steele's death, everyone on campus would have had classes in drug interdiction, the ways chemicals were used to enhance certain drugs, and how evidence was collected at crime scenes. Ditto for the Davis and Hemmer killings. No murder weapon was needed for Davis, and the drugs used on Steele could have been brought in by any student. No help there. The use of the garrote as a murder weapon was new, so they would need to figure out where that came from. It might help narrow down the suspect pool.

As for motive, Jake was completely befuddled. Every student and instructor went through a battery of psychological tests as well as detailed background checks before setting foot on the Academy grounds. Nothing seemed to connect the three victims in terms of any one person having a personal motive against all three. Jake could only conclude somebody was using these deaths as a way to attack the Academy, and thereby the Bureau, itself. But again, who, and why?

The single difference between the Hemmer murder and the two others was the presence of physical evidence identifying a single suspect. While others might be skeptical, at least Jake knew Charlie didn't do it. So, Jake concluded, the killer who was smart enough not to leave any evidence in the first two murders has now decided to frame Charlie. Was Charlie a random patsy or did this tie into the yet-to-be-determined motive? Instead of trying to embarrass the Bureau, was the killer trying to embarrass me personally? That might be a useful line of inquiry, but given Jake's long and productive career, the list of people who would want to attack him or his family was too long to contemplate.

Then Jake turned to the physical evidence itself. If we know Charlie didn't do it, how did his prints get on the murder weapon? Maybe Charlie handled the murder weapon earlier, and the killer then wore gloves when he used it? No, Arroyo said the prints were clear, not smudged, as they surely would be if the killer used gloves and applied the kind of force necessary to cut Hemmer's throat.

Jake had heard stories and seen movies where the killer lifted someone's prints from a glass or other object with tape and transferred them elsewhere. But those were movie fantasies, and even if it could work on a clean and smooth surface, the wooden handles of the garrote would not take transferred fingerprints so cleanly. That theory did not hold water. Or maybe the real killer somehow switched Charlie's prints with his own after they were lifted from the murder weapon but before they were sent into the AFIS system. But Arroyo was in charge of the crime scene, and he'd never let that happen.

But then Jake had an idea. Maybe the real killer's prints were on the murder weapon. And maybe they were properly sent into AFIS for analysis. But what if the computer system had been compromised? That is the only explanation Jake could think of. He decided to call Arroyo.

"Sergeant, it's Jake. Now, I'm not trying to pry into your investigation, but you asked me to call if I had any ideas about the fingerprints. I know it's a long shot, but what if the AFIS system was wrong? When you get right down to it, the database has millions of fingerprints, each one tied electronically to one name. Wouldn't it be easy for someone with computer skills and access to the system to tie one set of prints to a different name? If I'm telling you the truth that Charlie was nowhere near Hemming's room last night at the time of death, then his fingerprints must be wrong. We have an entire student body and most of our instructors who have both the knowledge and the access that would allow manipulation of AFIS. What do you think?"

Arroyo replied, "Jake, before I get to that question, you have a bigger problem now. I need to ask you a question. What shoes was Charlie wearing when he had dinner with you last night?"

Jake thought a moment. "His shoes? Why do you want to know? That's a crazy question."

Arroyo said, "I know, but I'm asking it anyway."

Jake thought about it, and then said, "I remember noticing how much he looked like an FBI agent. Blue button-down shirt, khaki pants, and his standard black rubber-soled shoes. Why?"

Arroyo paused, then said, "I was going to give you a courtesy call once I had the written report, but my evidence tech just called me. When they searched Charlie's room, they found a drop of blood on the top of one of his shoes, the same shoes you just described. It was Hemmer's blood. The lab just confirmed it. And we also found where the murder weapon came from. It was in the display case in the lobby of the admin building. And Charlie would have walked right past that case when he left your office after your dinner. Jake, I'm sorry, but the evidence just keeps adding up. I'm thinking I need to formally arrest Charlie. I'd appreciate his, and your, cooperation."

Jake's heart sank. He had been so hopeful to have found a plausible explanation for the fingerprint, but this new evidence was overwhelming. Hemmer's blood? How did that get on Charlie's shoes?

"Sergeant, I appreciate the heads up. It will help me prepare my wife and me for the inevitable. Kathy picked Charlie up today. Can I call her and have her drive him down here for the formal arrest? It would avoid the embarrassment of having the arrest in our neighborhood. And once he's arrested, I'm going to have to resign. How about if Charlie and I show up at your office in an hour?"

Arroyo agreed.

At 5:30 that afternoon, Jake, Kathy, and Charlie were in Arroyo's office at the Marine Base in Quantico. Kathy was crying, and Jake was doing what he could to hold himself together. He had written his resignation letter and called Steve Marks to tell him his plans. Charlie just looked dazed. Arroyo, for his part, was his usual professional self. Once he closed his office door, he said,

"The booking area has too many eyes, so we are going to do everything we can right here. I'd like to start with the fingerprinting process."

Jake thanked him for the courtesy.

Arroyo produced the fingerprint card and ink pad from his top desk drawer. He made sure Charlie pressed each finger firmly on the pad, and then rolled each one onto the card. He handed Charlie a wet cloth, and said, "This will take a few minutes. Sit tight. I'll be back as soon as I can."

In his absence, none of them knew what to say. Jake thought about telling his son to stay positive and to trust the system, but in his head, those words sounded empty. So, he sat quietly, one arm around his tearful wife, and the other resting on his son's knee.

Arroyo was gone longer than Jake had expected. When he came in, he had his administrative assistant, a Marine corporal, with him.

"Jake, everything just went sideways. I wanted the corporal in here as a witness. On a hunch, before I entered Charlie's fingerprint card into the arrest record, I decided to run it through AFIS again. Those prints I took from Charlie thirty minutes ago? They belong to Mario Grendel. But our friend Mario died in prison ten months ago. I'm going to have the corporal here fingerprint Charlie again, and rerun them through AFIS just to be sure, but this is a game-changer."

Jake was having difficulty processing what this meant. He turned to Arroyo. "I'm confused. What are you saying? That this dead convict killed Hemmer? I don't understand."

Arroyo smiled at Jake. "After your phone call this afternoon, I started to think about how easy it would be to compromise the AFIS system. I wondered how we could ever figure out how to correct the problem. Since Charlie was going to be here anyway,

I figured if his fingerprints were on the murder weapon, and I ran these fresh ones through again, they should still come back as Charlie's. But they didn't. Charlie's prints are not on the murder weapon!"

Jake began to have hope. But he still had questions. "So, what next? Whose prints are on the garrote? And what about the blood on Charlie's shoes?"

Arroyo nodded. "I agree, we have a lot of work to do. First, we are definitely not arresting Charlie. And Jake, you are definitely not resigning. I'm going to need your help if we are going to get to the bottom of this. Based on everything that has happened, I think we have a serial killer here at the Academy. I'm now officially considering both Frank Steele's and Bullet Davis' deaths to be homicides. And we have about 250 suspects, between the students, instructors, and staff.

"Here is my game plan. I don't want to tip off the killer, so I'd like to ask that Charlie stay off campus. Now that you and Kathy know he's not a suspect, I need you to let him still be considered a suspect by the outside world. When this is over, we can clear his name in the public eye, but for now, I want the killer to think his frame is still working. I know it's asking a lot, but do I have your support?"

Jake looked at his family. They both nodded. "Okay, sergeant, understood. What else?"

"I've got a tech geek here on my staff, PFC Bill Williams. He'll be assigned to dig into AFIS to see if we can find any evidence of tampering. I'm not sure what he will find, but he's pretty good. Next, I think you and I should independently go over all three files. Now that we have a working theory that they are all connected, maybe a fresh look will open some new ideas. I'll have copies of everything I have sent over to your office first thing tomorrow. And finally, we need to do what we can to protect possible future victims. Without tipping our hand on the Steele and Davis cases, I think you should warn the student body that even though Charlie is off campus 'pending further investigation', all students should remain cautious, protect themselves, and look out for each other. I know the dorm rooms don't lock, but hopefully vigilance alone will keep this guy from acting again."

Jake, Kathy, and Charlie stood up. Jake shook Arroyo's hand. "Thank you for believing me. We owe you."

Kathy first extended her hand, but then hugged the rather embarrassed Marine, tears running down her cheeks. Charlie, like his father, thanked Arroyo, and shook his hand as well.

Arroyo replied, "This is the job. We do it right, or not at all. Charlie, don't forget, you need to be fingerprinted again by the corporal just to make it official, but congratulations. We are going to find the guy who put you through this."

As Charlie, Kathy, and the corporal left the office, Jake paused. "Sergeant, the only thing I can see connecting these murders is the black eye it gives the Academy and the Bureau. We need to consider motive, but what has me worried is that the motive may be personal to me. Was Charlie's ordeal specific to him to get at me, or was it random? I'm looking forward to what your tech geek finds."

Arroyo replied, "That has me stumped as well. I went over all the files of your students after Steele's death and could find no motive. I'm going to take a second look for motive as it relates to Davis and Hemmer, but I'm not hopeful. Whatever motive there is may be buried deeply into our killer's psyche or his past. Who knows if we will ever figure it all out. And we only have nine days until graduation. After that, we lose control over our suspect pool."

As Jake left the building, the fresh air felt good. His heart was lighter, but the prospect of trying to find a serial killer among his students was disturbing. But at least his family was safe. When Kathy dropped Jake off at the admin building, he kissed her, and hugged his son.

"Keep up your homework. I have every expectation that you will be walking across that stage with a proud father watching next Friday. I'll see you then. I love you."

Charlie smiled for the first time since this all happened.

"Thanks, Dad, I love you too."

# Chapter 16

## Monday, Five Days Until Graduation

The initial euphoria and hopefulness that Jake had felt the prior week soon faded. He knew in his head that all investigations were driven by slow, painstaking work, with long dry spells punctuated by small victories. But in his heart, triggered by the fact that this case had become so personal by involving his family, Jake wanted it solved, and solved fast!

Jake and Arroyo spoke frequently by phone, but they had met in person this morning to cover the progress, or more accurately, lack of progress, on the case. Jake reviewed the steps he was taking. He had spent the weekend reviewing the personnel jackets, background checks, references, and pre-hire polygraph tests of every student at the Academy. But he'd come across nothing promising. A few students had gotten in a little trouble in high school, but nothing that would indicate a deep-seated resentment against law enforcement. Besides, their polygraph results showed sincere remorse for these minor run-ins, with no indication of deception.

Jake further reported to Arroyo that the team of students from his seminar, specifically Sean King and Katie Arnold, were still working on opening each cell phones of over 200 students and searching for any indication of who might have sent out the information about Frank Steele's death. Between their own studies, and the end-of-semester rush to finish their research papers, they had still found time to complete nearly 185 of them, with no tangible results. It had been Katie who devised a way to open the individual phone, link it to the Academy computer system, and then run a search program for specific words within the narrow time frame between when Steele's death had been discovered and the time it hit the media. Even with those limitations, it was mind-numbing work to read the hundreds of text messages and emails. Arroyo didn't help matters by pointing out that the killer could easily have a hidden phone, making the search unnecessary and a waste of time.

Arroyo didn't have any helpful information either. His first line of investigation was to figure out how the blood got onto Charlie's shoes. After talking to Charlie as well as several other students, he learned that nearly all the male students had brought more than one pair of black shoes to the Academy. While Charlie was wearing one pair, the killer could have simply slipped into Charlie's unlocked room, planted the evidence, and walked out. But the disturbing part of that reality is that it was looking more and more that Charlie was specifically targeted. It was his name that was tied to the false fingerprint in the AFIS system, and his shoes that had the planted blood. If the killer was simply trying to hurt the Academy, he didn't need to offer up a patsy. The murder alone would have been enough. When Arroyo related his thoughts on that, Jake agreed. As further evidence that Jake was being specifically targeted, he reminded Arroyo that the initial press coverage of Steele's death had mentioned Jake's name, which had struck Jake as odd at the time. It now made more sense.

Jake then asked whether Arroyo had learned anything about the tampering with the AFIS system. Arroyo said he'd had no luck there, again, because they were dealing with a needle in a haystack. Arroyo had brought his tech guy, Private Williams, to the meeting, who explained that thousands of federal, state, and local law enforcement agencies accessed the database every week. Any one of them could have switched Charlie's prints with those of the now-departed Mario Grendel. To try and retrace millions of keystrokes to find who had done it was too big a task.

Williams went on, "Many times, these agencies are simply sending in a print for analysis, but they can also send in new prints not previously in the system. For some, it is in the form of a fingerprint card like the one we used for Charlie. There, they know the identity of the arrestee, and enter his or her name into the system, connecting that specific print to that name. But they also take prints from a crime scene and send them in hoping for a match. When they don't get one, that fingerprint stays in the system without a name attached. If we get a match from a print at a later crime, we get to solve both cases."

Listening carefully to this explanation, Jake had an idea.

"So, if I have this right, there is a universe of fingerprints in the system that have already been identified as belonging to one specific person, right?"

Williams nodded.

"And there is a different universe of prints that have not yet been tied to a specific name. Also true?"

Again, Williams nodded.

"But we know that every one of the students and instructors on this campus have a fingerprint in the system that is tied to their name. If the killer's prints are on that garrote, and that killer is one of our students or instructors, we have his prints in our system. We just need to match them."

Arroyo and Private Williams shook their heads.

"I don't follow. What are you thinking? Now that we have broken the link between Charlie's name and the prints on the garrote, all we have is an unidentified print. How does that help us?"

Jake remained thoughtful. "Well, the killer somehow got into the system and disconnected his own name from his prints and connected Charlie's name to them. But now he had to do something with Charlie's own prints, so he linked them to Mr. Grindel's name." Still puzzled, Arroyo said, "So?" Jake continued. "So, whose name is now attached to Grindel's prints? It would have to be our killer's, right?"

Private Williams spoke up. "Not necessarily, but you are on to something. If a new set of prints without a corresponding name were introduced into the system, we'd know it. The system keeps track of new, unmatched prints. But if names and their matching prints were only swapped, like we seem to have here, we wouldn't be able to trace the changes. And there is no guarantee the killer only used a three-way switch of names. He could have shuffled dozens of names and have us chasing our tails for days or weeks. We don't have that kind of time. But we do know one thing. The killer is on this campus. And we have his prints. All we need to do is re-fingerprint everyone on the campus, compare them to the fingerprint on the murder weapon, and we've got him!"

Jake and Arroyo were excited. It would take some time, but they'd certainly be able to complete the process before graduation.

"Let's get the ball rolling on this," Jake said. "Sergeant, can you devote some of your manpower to setting up a fingerprint station here at the Academy? I'll get a directive out to the students and instructors."

Arroyo said he'd send a team over that afternoon, and he and Private Williams left with a bounce in their step that wasn't there when they'd walked into the meeting. Jake drafted a memo to everyone at the Academy requiring them all to report to the lobby of the admin building, following an alphabetical schedule he laid out in the memo, beginning at 3:00 that afternoon, and ending at 5:00 pm on Tuesday. He sent it out electronically just before lunch.

For the first time in weeks, Jake was feeling pretty good. He didn't even mind when, an hour later, his assistant told him Steve Marks was on the line and needed to talk to him right away.

Jake picked up the phone and said, "Steve, to what do I owe the pleasure?"

"Jake, help me understand what you think you are doing with this fingerprint thing. Are you nuts?"

Jake was surprised Marks even knew about it, but explained what he and Arroyo had discussed earlier, what Private Williams had told them, and why this was the solution to their investigatory stalemate.

Marks listened intently, and said, "I'm sorry, Jake, but you need to withdraw your directive immediately."

Jake was stunned.

"Why would I do that when it is the easiest way to catch someone who has proven to be quite adept at covering his tracks, and who has killed at least one, if not three people here? This makes no sense!"

Marks' condescending tone was really starting to get under Jake's skin.

"There is a very simple explanation. And it is laid out in a formal union grievance I just received from the FBI Agents Association. They claim, and I quote, 'the directive imposes burdens on current and future agents of the FBI and subjects them to ridicule without any specific individualized suspicion of wrongdoing' end of quote. In short, they say you are on a fishing expedition, and they don't want their members getting caught up in it."

Jake replied, "Well that's too bad. Once they give us their fingerprints, all of them will be cleared of any suspicion, and they'll help us catch the bad guy. Isn't that what their members want?"

Marks paused to consider his answer. While Jake had spent his career focused on investigatory techniques, evidence, and arrests, Marks had studied the Bureau as an institution. How it worked. Who the players were, and what motivated them. There was a simple explanation, but Marks suspected Jake wouldn't really understand it. But he needed to try.

"Jake, the Agent's Association does not see their job as primarily one of law enforcement. They are simply looking to get everything they believe their members can get. We are starting up negotiations for a new labor contract. The Association needs to flex their muscle to show the management team, and their own members, that they are powerful. They don't really care about this particular case, but worry that if management can force their members to give fingerprints without specific evidence, why not random locker searches, or surprise drug tests? You are so focused on your immediate problem that you may not understand their concerns. But at the end of the day, the FBI Director has already made his decision. The fingerprint order is to be cancelled immediately."

Marks heard Jake mutter something like 'effing bureaucrats' under his breath, but let it slide.

"Jake, we can finesse this problem, but I need a few days. Once I get a chance to meet with the Association reps and make them feel important and respected, we can work out a deal that allows you to do your fingerprinting on a non-precedential basis while still protecting their members from the other types of intrusions they really care about. But I need you to be patient."

Jake replied, "We don't have that luxury. Graduation is on Friday. Once the students and instructors all leave Quantico, the killer could take off."

But Marks would not be deterred. "We know who they are, and we can find them to be fingerprinted even after they leave the Academy. Jake, we will get this guy. Just not the way you want, or in the time frame you want. So, get out a new memo cancelling the fingerprint order ASAP, and I'll try to get a meeting with the Association as soon as I can. That's the best I can do. Sorry."

Pausing, Marks went on, "On a positive note, I told the Director about your son when he and I met about this grievance. At my request, he agreed to allow Charlie to attend the graduation ceremony on Friday. That's a bit of good news, don't you think?"

Jake had already decided he was going to allow Charlie to attend the graduation ceremony. The idea that Marks thought he had some sort of say in that decision, or that Jake somehow 'owed him' for it, was galling. But Jake knew which battles to fight, so he bit back the reply he wanted to make, and just said,

"Thanks. I'm sure Charlie will be pleased," and ended the call.

As Jake was typing up the memo cancelling the fingerprint order, Todd Chen stopped in his office.

"Todd, what a pleasant surprise! It is great to see you."

Jake truly was pleased. Todd's office and classroom at the firearms range were far removed from the admin building. Todd had set up a sleeping area there as well, surrounded by the tools of a marksman's trade, and his beloved books. Todd had always been a voracious reader of history, and like many former snipers, preferred solitude. As a result, Todd's path rarely crossed Jake's. Todd noticed the lines of worry on his friend's face, as well as the beat-down body language.

"You look like hell, Jake. I thought you'd be excited to be narrowing your suspect list once the fingerprints were all in. I heard about your plan from Arroyo, and it's a good one."

Jake gave his oldest friend and colleague a wry smile.

"Gee, thanks for telling me how nice I look. I guess just sitting on your ass waiting to shoot somebody is a lot less stressful than what I do," Jake joked.

Todd responded, "Are you kidding me? It's a lot more stressful than sitting on your ass waiting for someone else to shoot somebody, like you do all day!' They both laughed. It had been a running joke between them for over twenty years, ever since Milwaukee.

"Seriously, though," Jake said, "the fingerprinting is cancelled. The union pitched a fit about the directive, and that weenie Marks is giving in to them. He says we might get to fingerprint eventually, but not today. I'm drafting the memo now."

Todd thought for a minute. "You know, the students and staff here are all behind you. If you can't order the fingerprinting, why not make it voluntary? You may still get a few people to opt out on principle or in support of the Association grievance, but at least you'll narrow your suspect pool further."

Jake smiled.

"Great suggestion. Plus, it'll really piss off Marks. I like it. Thanks. But what brought you up here? You certainly weren't just checking on me."

"Well, I know how you have this need to know everything that goes on around here," Chen began. "The students wanted to get you something to thank you for your leadership, but they need to leave Quantico to pick it up. One of them asked me for permission to leave campus on Thursday afternoon for a few hours, and I said it would be OK. Classes end on Wednesday, and Thursday is more of a free day for those who have all their projects turned in anyway. I just thought you should know. Is that okay?"

With all the turmoil he had been going through, Jake had forgotten the Academy was still an excellent training experience for the future agents and would help shape their careers for many years to come. That they might want to honor him for his role in that experience is something Jake hadn't had time to consider.

"Of course, it's okay. Thanks for telling me. By the way, who is the student?"

"Sean. Sean King"

# Chapter 17

## Wednesday, Two Days to Graduation

It was the last day of formal classes, including the final meeting of Jake's now depleted seminar. As he called the class to order, he was saddened by the acute losses this group had suffered. Frank Steele was dead. Fritz Hemmer was dead as well. Charlie was banned from campus, at least until Friday. Only Katie Arnold, the financial guru, Sean King, and mousy Lori Beam remained. Despite their losses, Jake still wanted to finish up their education as best he could. The teamwork he'd hoped to instill hadn't developed, but each of them had turned in excellent papers on their separate subjects of interest. Today, he planned to hold a group discussion of those papers, and then dismiss class early. Jake had a ton of work to do before Friday.

"Before we start our discussion of your work, I'd like an update on your search of the cell phones we collected. Were you able to find any evidence showing who leaked the news of Frank's overdose to the outside world?"

Lori spoke up first. "Mr. Mott, we tried everything we could think of. We examined the call logs, text messages, and emails both sent and received by every phone turned in to us. Our search parameters started the morning Frank's body was found and ended the time the news release hit the public airwaves.

We did it manually, and then through a search program Sean and Katie developed on the FBI computer system. There was nothing. Maybe the leak didn't come from one of us. Have you thought about looking at one of the Marines who responded to the medical call?"

Jake asked, "What conclusions do you all reach from the information you just cited? That it wasn't one of us? Are there other possibilities? Remember, you are suggesting a United States Marine did something wrong. We probably shouldn't do that unless that is the only possibility. Think critically! What do we really know?"

Katie said, "One possibility is the source of the leak hid the phone he used."

Jake nodded. "Any other possibilities?"

Sean stared at his shoes. Jake prompted him.

"Sean, any creative ideas? This is the time when you need to speak up with any idea, no matter how farfetched. That is how cases sometimes are solved. Use that brain of yours!"

Sean looked startled. "Well, if Frank was intentionally killed, the information could have been leaked by the killer well before the body was found. That would suggest our search parameters were too narrow."

That had not occurred to Jake. He had stuck with his original assumption that Frank had overdosed, so thought the leak had to have occurred after the body was discovered. But in light of Hemmer's clear murder, Jake had failed to re-think that assumption about Frank. He was amazed Sean had come up with that scenario.

"Well done, Sean. You certainly have shown an ability to get inside a killer's head. Any thoughts about motive, though? Just because the killer could have leaked the news before the body was discovered, why would he do it?"

Lori jumped in again, not wanting to be outdone by Sean.

"Well, Occam's Razor tells us the simplest explanation is usually the right one. The killer's motive for the leak is the same as the reason the Bureau didn't like the leak. It was an embarrassment to them. Perhaps the motive for the leak also reveals the motive for the killing itself."

Again, Jake was impressed, and a bit sad. This team would have been an incredible asset to the Bureau.

"All right. Good work, all of you. Let's move on to your papers."

Katie interrupted. "Mr. Mott, I have a request. Early this morning I was on the FBI's internal crime information system. You know my paper was on the Nazi Gold problem. Well, we've been able to account for thirty-six gold coins since they first surfaced a little over twenty years ago, each one being sold one at a time. On Monday morning, four of them were sold at a collector's shop in Salt Lake City. The owner called local law enforcement right after the seller left, but they had other priorities at the time. The seller was a dark-haired tall woman, about forty years of age, but there were no cameras at the collector's shop. This morning, as soon as a pawn shop in downtown Indianapolis opened at 8:00 am, there was another sale, this time of twenty coins! The owner's father was killed at Auschwitz and can't stand the thought of someone making money from the Nazis. The owner called the Bureau first, and our agents were there within twenty minutes of the seller leaving. The owner said the seller was desperate, willing to sell them at a deep discount. Same description of the seller, but this time there were cameras.

"Mr. Mott, you know how much this case has meant to me. Indianapolis is only an eight hour drive from here. I'd like your permission to drive there right now and work with the locals. Maybe I can see something they miss. Worst case scenario, I'm back here by graduation with some field experience. Mr. Mott, something is going on here. One or two coins were sold per year for over twenty years, and now twenty-four coins were sold in two days, well below market value. And the locations are strange. A few coins sold in the Midwest years ago, followed by every sale in the Pacific Northwest. But now, Salt Lake City and Indianapolis? The seller is moving east, and I'd say by car. Let me go have a look, please?"

Jake was intrigued. The case itself was not a high priority for the Bureau. More of an itch that needed to be scratched. But Katie's passion was something to be encouraged, and there wasn't much to lose.

"Okay, I'll let you drive out there and look around. But don't get in the way, and be sure you are back here Friday morning. The ceremony starts at 11:00 sharp, and I want you there. Have my assistant fill out the paperwork authorizing your travel and I'll sign it so you can hit the road. Good luck."

Katie scooped up her papers and nearly ran for the door.

Turning to the other two students, Jake said, "Well, I guess class is dismissed. I'll give you my feedback on your papers in writing later. But I wanted you both to know how impressed I've been with your work here at the Academy. You both have promising law enforcement careers ahead of you. It has been a pleasure." With that, he shook their hands warmly. The normally shy Lori glowed and smiled, while Sean seemed distracted. Jake asked him why.

"Oh, I don't know. I'm going to take one last run on the Yellow Brick Road to clear my head. After Mr. Davis died out there, it lost its attraction for me. But I think I need to run it one last time." Jake said, "Do you want some company?" Sean was abrupt. "No! I mean, no thank you. I need to be alone for a while, if that's okay with you."

Jake waited until Lori left the room, and then turned to Sean.

"Are you doing all right? You seem a little distracted and testy today."

Sean wouldn't look Jake in the eye, and just shrugged.

"I'm fine," was all he said.

"Any repeats of the dream with the crow?" Jake asked.

Sean shook his head.

"I said I'm fine! Can't you just leave it at that?"

Worried about one of his more promising students, Jake said, "Just don't forget your promise to me. After graduation, you'll get some counseling?"

Sean stared at Jake, then looked down, nodded his agreement, packed up his things, and left without another word.

"Well, that was weird," Jake said to nobody in particular.

Alone again, Jake started to go through the mountain of work on his desk. First was an update on the voluntary fingerprinting process. As Tony Chen had predicted, there was a very positive response from the students and instructors. As of 9:00 this morning, 164 out of the 208 remaining students had been fingerprinted, processed, and cleared. Initial compliance had been slower, but once peer pressure kicked in, the numbers had risen dramatically. Response among the instructors was not as robust, just over fifty percent, but they were all long-time members of the Agent's Association. The Association had allowed the voluntary process to go forward without a legal challenge, but they had discouraged their members from complying. Jake saw the fifty percent rate to be a victory of sorts. Nonetheless, that still left over forty students and nearly twenty instructors on the potential suspect list, and less than forty-eight hours to go before they all left Quantico.

Next, Jake needed to get out a memo to the Academy about the graduation ceremony. The big news was that he'd decided to move it outdoors, onto the open plaza in front of the entrance to the administration building. The plaza had two levels, with five concrete steps leading up to the top level. The instructors and graduates would sit on risers on the upper level rather than on the raised stage in the auditorium. The maintenance staff would then set up chairs for the family and friends of the graduates on the lower level. On the upper level, the graduates would be facing due west, with the classroom building behind them to block any wind, and the administration building on their left to keep them and the audience in the shade.

The decision to move the ceremony outdoors was ostensibly due to COVID. While the pandemic continued to linger longer than anyone had hoped, outdoor settings seemed to be more acceptable for larger gatherings.. Masks would still be encouraged, but not required. But Jake had another reason for his decision. Someone had killed three people in the past month. The only motive seems to be a direct attack on the reputation of either the Academy as a whole, or on Jake in particular. Jake was worried the killer wasn't done. If something was going to happen at the ceremony, the enclosed nature of the auditorium would be an advantage for the killer. At least outdoors, graduates and audience members had more options for escape.

Jake was saddened that instead of focusing on the joy and sense of accomplishment the graduates and instructors would be feeling, he had to deal with securing a perimeter. This thought reminded Jake of another phone call he needed to make. Tony Chen answered on the first ring.

"What's up, Jake? I just dismissed my last class."

Jake informed Tony of his plans to hold graduation outdoors, and of his concerns about security.

"Tony, my friend, I have a favor to ask," and went on to explain what he needed from Tony.

Tony listened intently, and said, "You can count on me, Jake. Don't worry about a thing." Satisfied, Jake thanked him, and ended the call.

After putting the finishing touches on his memo describing the details of the ceremony, Jake sent it out to all students and staff. The ceremony would start at 10:30 am, with a welcome reception on the plaza for all students, guests, and instructors. At 11:15, everyone would be in their seats for the formal program. Jake would give the welcoming remarks, followed by comments by an instructor selected by the students. Then, each student would be called by name in alphabetical order, proceed to the front of the risers, receive their Certificate of Completion, shake hands with the Director of the FBI, and return to their seat. Jake would then give some closing remarks, and everyone would be free to leave. Jake knew that most of the students, long separated from their families, would be in a hurry to leave for lunch reservations off-campus, or to parties held in their honor. It was an exciting time for them, something Jake was glad about. They had all earned it.

Jake walked over to the coffee pot in his office and poured himself another cup. Standing by his window, he recalled the day he first arrived in his office a few months ago, staring out this same window. He had been excited about the opportunities, the new students, and his anticipated retirement. Now, the deaths of two students and a beloved instructor overshadowed all that. He hoped the events of graduation would help him put his assignment here at Quantico into a better light.

Looking out past the library, classrooms and the dorms, Jake could just make out a solitary figure leaving the gym, stretching, and then beginning a slow but steady run on the Yellow Brick Road. It was Sean King, Jake could tell.

"I sure hope he can get his head on straight," thought Jake, as Sean disappeared into the woods.

Before tucking his things into the locker at the gym, Sean checked his emails. He read, and then re-read, Jake's email detailing the graduation ceremony. He and his mother had planned things as well as possible, but these new details need to be considered before finalizing how they would finish things with Mott. Sean then stepped outside, did some brief stretching, and headed down the path to the obstacle course. The sense of serenity he had while running, the smooth, effortless strides, the sense of pushing himself still soothed Sean's mind. For a few minutes, he was able to push aside the inevitable turmoil of the next few days, and just be.

As Sean rounded the bend at the far end of the course, he stopped short. This was where Mr. Davis had discovered Sean. Where Sean had lured him into the underbrush and snapped his neck. Where he had hung his lifeless body on the cargo netting. Sean felt an overwhelming sense of sadness and loss. Buried deep inside of him, Sean felt, rather than heard, a voice asking, "Is this worth it?" Either unwilling or incapable of answering the question, Sean shook off the feeling, steeled himself to his task, and turned off the path. Lifting up the flat rock by the creek for the last time, Sean powered up his cell phone, and dialed his dear loving mother.

"Son, it's so good to hear your voice!" Nadia said with true emotion. "I think this is the longest we've ever gone without talking. Are you doing okay?"

Whatever unease Sean had been feeling melted away when he heard her voice. He was enthused once again to bring their careful planning to fruition.

"Yes, mother, everything is fine on my end, but we have a lot to talk about. I don't have much time. First things first. Where are you?"

"As we planned, I booked a small hotel about an hour from you in Quantico. I should arrive there in a few hours. I plan to stay there two nights and check out on Friday morning," Nadia told him.

"I was able to get the pass to leave campus tomorrow afternoon. I really look forward to seeing you. The gift we ordered for our instructor is at a store just up the I-95 from here at the Potomac Mills Mall. Can you meet me there at 3:00? There's a Cheesecake Factory. We can have a bite to eat and finalize our plans. Sound good?"

Nadia agreed.

"Mom, you need to be very careful. They know you sold more of the gold coins in Indianapolis this morning, and there were cameras. You need to assume they will have pictures of your face, and maybe your license plate by now."

Nadia was worried. "Thanks, son. With this COVID pandemic, I'll be able to wear a mask that covers my face pretty well. I knew there was a camera, and I always turned my head to avoid a clear shot, but I hadn't thought about cameras in the parking lot. When I arrive at the hotel, I'll back in so a nosy cop can't read my plate easily. I'll think about other options once I'm checked in."

"Another thing. I also know the schedule for Friday," Sean said. "They're having an outdoor reception at 10:30, followed by the ceremony at 11:15. They should be calling my name right around noon if they stick to the schedule. Let's think about it and we can talk about details when we meet tomorrow. Now, I really need to go. Do we need to talk about anything else right now?"

Nadia replied, "No, except to tell you how proud I am. You have been by my side every minute, helping me to make sure your poor father's tragic death is avenged. We are almost done. Thank you so much!"

Sean flushed upon hearing her praise for him.

"Okay. I'll see you tomorrow. Again, be very careful."

After Sean ended the call, he saw the battery power was down to nothing. He placed the phone he knew he would never need again under the rock, returned to the obstacle course, and completed his last run at the Academy.

# Chapter 18

## Thursday, One Day Until Graduation

As Sean pulled into his parking place at the mall, he was confident that this meeting with his mother wouldn't be noticed. All the students and staff at the Academy were still confined to the COVID "bubble". The mall was a sprawling mass of stores, restaurants, theaters, and services, with thousands of people coming and going throughout the day. There would be nothing remarkable about a young man having a bite to eat with his mother.

He remained concerned, however, about the risk his mother had taken by selling the gold coins. He knew they would need ready cash if either of them had a chance of getting away, but Sean wondered if the risk of getting caught before graduation was worth it. As he walked into the mall entrance nearest the Cheesecake Factory, he was nervously vigilant. But he had made an important decision, and he knew he needed to be face-to-face with his mother if he had any hope to convince her, so the risk of being noticed, however small, was necessary.

Sean was a bit early, so he sat down in one of the clusters of casual chairs outside the entrance to the restaurant and waited for his mother to arrive. As he scanned the faces of the stream of both masked and unmasked shoppers filing past his vantage point, he was surprised how similar they all looked. So, when a woman wearing a mask with long blonde hair approached him, he didn't recognize her right away. But when she lowered the mask, he saw the smiling face of his mother! He quickly jumped up and hugged her, and she returned the embrace with a forcefulness and enthusiasm that matched her son's.

Sliding the mask back into place, she took his arm and said, "Shall we get something to eat?"

They turned and went into the Cheesecake Factory. Because it was mid-afternoon, they were seated immediately in a booth along the windows. Sean looked around and saw there was nobody in the booths or tables immediately adjacent to theirs. They would be able to talk safely.

"Mom, you look so different. Tell me about the hair!"

She looked around quickly, and then removed her mask.

"I think we're safe enough to dispense with the mask for a while, don't you? I figured that between the mask and the dye job, I should be able to avoid discovery if pictures from Indianapolis should surface. What do you think?"

Sean cocked his head, and said, "It's strange for me to see you this way, but you look pretty good in blonde hair. But I'm still worried about the plates on your car."

Nadia replied, "I've taken care of that. On the way to the hotel after we talked yesterday, I stopped at a Park and Ride lot off the highway and switched plates with another car there. I know the owner will report them stolen, but how often do people really check their own license plates? And even when the owner does report the theft, the police will just be looking for a different plate than the one they are looking for now. We're no worse off than we were before, but we may have bought a little time. And a little time is all we need, right Sean? This is it! We are finally on the verge of seeing all our plans come together."

Sean paused, thought about what he had decided, and started. "Mom, there's something I want to talk to you about. Something important. But first, I want to go over the details for tomorrow. It ties into what I have to say."

Nadia looked at her son quizzically, and said, "I don't know what you are talking about, but I have some changes to the plans that we need to talk about too. I'll get to my change in a minute, but let's go over our original plan. You have done a wonderful job of setting the stage. The FBI looks inept. Three deaths in their own backyard, and no idea how they happened! The public criticism is mounting, and pinning the last death on Mott's own son was priceless. And tomorrow we will finish it.

"As you and I had discussed, after the ceremony is over, and the graduates, staff, and families are socializing, I will approach Mott. I brought one of the handguns from our trailer, small enough to fit in my purse. I shoot Mott, and in the confusion that follows, I'll be arrested, while you sneak away in my rental car. I know you will have to live on the run, but with the cash from the gold coins I've sold, you should be able to get far enough away and start a life of your own. As for me, I will be in jail, but oh so happy that Mott has gotten what he has coming."

Sean nodded. "Okay, that was the original plan. What is this change you are talking about?"

His mother stared out the window.

"As I was driving across the country, I thought about what we, you and I, have suffered as a result of Jake Mott murdering your father. We have been deprived of your father's presence, his goodness, and his love. I know we had planned to kill Mott to avenge your father's death. I realize now that is a mistake. What he needs to feel is the same loss that we have suffered. His son, Sean. His son. To really suffer, he has to lose Charlie."

Sean's eyes went wide.

"Mom, that is crazy. Mr. Mott's son had nothing to do with Dad's death. Why take yet another innocent life?"

Nadia looked sternly at Sean. "Now you listen to me, son. You weren't there the day your father was needlessly shot down in cold blood. You talk about innocent life, but what about your father's innocent life? He was trying to right a wrong, and Mott killed him for it. And so, I suffered. And you suffered. So now Mott has to suffer. We lost someone we loved, and tomorrow, Mott will lose someone he loves. I know I'll spend the rest of my life in prison, but it will be worth it to me. So don't tell me my plan is crazy. It is the sanest thing I've done in my life!"

Sean was shocked, both by the viciousness of his mother's new plan, as well as the vehemence with which she defended it. His hopes fell, but he still felt he needed to try his own change in plans.

"Mom, I heard you out. Now you need to let me talk. I've given this a lot of thought, and I think we should just stop this."

Nadia started to interrupt, but Sean put up his hand.

"I asked you to listen to me. Please let me say what I need to say."

"Go ahead."

"What Mott did to my father was a terrible thing. You're right. It hurt us in profound ways. We can't fix that, and he has to pay. But I have seen how badly he has already suffered. First a promising student dies of an overdose on his watch. Then his friend dies of a broken neck. And then another student is brutally murdered, and his own son is arrested for the crime. I have watched him age ten years in the last ten weeks. The optimism and excitement he once projected is gone, replaced by stoicism and sadness. I'm telling you, Mom, he is a broken, tired, and disillusioned man. He has suffered, and will continue to suffer.

"I've also thought about the rest of my own life. You are right. Either way, I'll be on the run. The money will last for a while, but I have to believe that at some point, maybe months from now, maybe years, the Bureau will catch up to me, and I'll have to pay for what I've done. I can accept that. But if I only have a limited amount of freedom left, I want to spend it with you. Remember baking scones together? Sitting and reading books on the front porch? Gardening together and selling what we grew? We were truly happy. So, I'm begging you, Mom, let's not punish Mott any more than we already have. Let's leave right now. Go on the run together. You figured out how to live under the radar for the past twenty-two years. Together, maybe we can do it for another twenty-two years. Just us."

The desperate and wistful look on Sean's face as he made his plea was painful for Nadia to watch. She had always known that despite her best efforts, Sean might someday hesitate when it counted the most. That day had come.

"Sean, my son, I'm sorry. I know that from where you stand, everything you say makes sense. But you never even met your father. And you did not feel the sense of loss I did. I've told you the story of my life. I was a hopeless child of migrant workers. I watched my father become a mean drunk, who beat and eventually killed my own mother. To stop him from abusing me the same way, I killed him and ran, until I found hope. Hope in a good man who loved me. His death didn't just end a life. It robbed me of hope. And created an insatiable need for revenge. I simply cannot be at peace until I know that Mott has suffered at my hands. And he will. Tomorrow. Now let's put this nonsense aside. Your role is done. It is time for me to complete what I started, and I will not be talked out of it. Got it?"

Sean knew he had no choice. His shoulders slumped. He had tried and failed.

"All right mother, I'll respect your wishes. But it makes me so sad to think this is the last time we will be alone together. Let's talk of happier things, okay?" And so they did.

As they left the restaurant, Sean walked his mother to her car. Hugging her close, he told her he loved her for the last time. They both had tears in their eyes.

Nadia said, "I'm proud of you, son. How I wish things could have been different."

Sean nodded, and said, "Mom, no matter how carefully we planned things, the unexpected could happen tomorrow. If it does, promise me you will try to get away, okay?"

Nadia replied, "Nonsense. It is a perfect plan."

As Sean walked away, he knew he had one final choice to make. One last act of free will that could allow some good to come out of this whole mess. He only hoped he had the courage to go through with it. Tomorrow.

# Chapter 19

## Graduation Day

When Jake woke up in his small dorm room, he was happy about so many things. This was the last time he'd sleep in this sterile room instead of in his big comfy bed at home with Kathy by his side. He would see his son graduate from the Academy today. As of 5:00 today, he would be officially retired from the Bureau. And to top it off, the weather had cooperated. They were predicting beautiful sunny skies, low humidity for the usually muggy D.C. area, and a gentle breeze. Jake didn't pray as much as he should, but he said a quick prayer of thanksgiving as he prepared for the big day.

After a shower and shave, Jake dressed in his standard FBI agent outfit: Khaki slacks, white button-down shirt, striped tie, and navy blazer. He then packed the rest of his clothes for the last time before checking his emails. Sorting through the junk, Jake opened one from Katie Arnold sent at 12:30 in the morning, and read:

*Thank you for giving me the opportunity to make this run into Indianapolis. I made some great contacts with the Bureau Office here, and with local law enforcement. I wanted to update you on what we found. First, the photo wasn't ideal, but it is the best we've been able to come up with so far. I used Fritz Hemmer's experimental facial recognition software, and with some legitimate modifications, we have what I think is a pretty good image. The original and enhanced photos are attached to this email. We also were able to do a screen grab from the camera feed in the parking lot, and we got her license plate. We put out a BOLO, and got a hit on a vehicle about 30 miles from D. C. It turns out to belong to a grandmother from Maryland visiting her son. Our perp must have switched plates, so we have put out a new alert for the plate we believe is now on her vehicle. Nothing on that yet.*

*Mr. Mott, I know I shouldn't speculate without facts, but I'm a little concerned. Immediately after your Milwaukee shooting case, the gold sales switched from Wisconsin to the Pacific Northwest. Under my theory, the seller probably was in the western Idaho or eastern Oregon area. Now there's one new sale in Salt Lake City, a big one in Indianapolis, and her car was thirty miles from Quantico only two days before our graduation.*

*Couple that with the deaths we have been dealing with and... well, I just don't know. You taught us that when we hear hoofbeats, think horses, not zebras, but I don't like these coincidences piling up. Please be careful.*

*I'm leaving for Quantico now and expect to be at the graduation ceremony on time. Thanks again for everything you've done for me.*

Jake opened up the attachments. The original photo was grainy, but usable. The enhanced version was clearly the same person, but much easier to see. Jake studied her face, turned slightly to the left in profile in an apparent effort to avoid the cameras. Long black hair, parted down the middle, with a bit of curl to it. High cheekbones, full lips, and dark eyes with high arched eyebrows. She had an oval face, with a strong jawline and a soft chin. Eastern European, Jake thought, but hard to tell without skin tone. Katie had done a nice job, and he hoped her work would pay off. As for her speculation, there were so many possible reasons for the seller's change of location that he didn't give it another thought. Right now, he had plenty else to worry about.

Jake took the notes for his welcome speech out of his jacket pocket and went over them one last time. Satisfied, he trundled his suitcase out to his car, and walked to the plaza to be sure everything was prepared. The chairs for the guests on the lower level were all set, and maintenance was still setting up chairs on the three-tiered risers on the upper level. Various officials, including Jake, the FBI Director, and Kyle Gulya, the Law and Ethics instructor selected by the students to speak, would occupy the front row on the left side of the podium as you faced the audience. To Jake's displeasure, they would be joined by Steve Marks, who never seemed to miss an opportunity to ingratiate himself with the Director. Name tags were placed on each seat, and Jake noted the front row was filled. Calling over one of the maintenance staff, Jake asked them to add one chair to the front row immediately to Jake's left. As his last official act, Jake would be sure to sit proudly next to his son.

Seeing that everything was in place, Jake went up to his office. His loyal assistant, Julie, was working as always.

"Don't you ever stop working, Julie?" he asked. "Not when my boss takes on more than he can handle. When he looks bad, I look bad, so, no, I don't ever stop working. At least, not until you do." Julie smiled at him, and started to tear up. "I'm really going to miss you, boss. This sure has been a tough three months for you. I just hope it's all over now, and you can enjoy the retirement you so richly deserve."

Jake replied, "I couldn't have done it without you, Julie. There is nothing better than having someone you can count on. I hope whoever the Bureau assigns you to appreciates you as much as I have."

With a warm smile, Jake went into his office, hoping to use his remaining time before the reception began to finish up the last of his work.

Sean King woke up early as well. While Jake was getting ready for the day, Sean was making his own preparations. He had not slept well, carefully considering all the aspects of the fateful decision he had made the afternoon before. It seemed whenever he did manage to doze off, the dream about the crow came back, jolting him awake. Knowing what the rest of the day would hold, Sean saw no reason to clean his room, make his bed, or even pack. Instead, he too dressed in the clothes he knew all the Agents-in-training would wear, with one big difference.

One of the important rites of passage for all the students at the Academy was the day they passed their firearms qualification test. Tony Chen had been a knowledgeable but demanding instructor. He expected every student to understand the gravity of the use of deadly force, and to exercise that force as responsibly, carefully, and effectively as they could. While the instruction included the use of long guns, shotguns, and assault rifles, the use of the Bureau-issued sidearm was the most important. As Chen repeatedly told his charges, effective use of the sidearm was the tool most likely to save your life because it was often used in unplanned, and therefore fluid situations.

Sean had a bit of a head start on his classmates thanks to the years of training he had received from Matt Horn in Freedom at their makeshift range. But Chen had used that experience to demand a higher level of competence from Sean. While Sean's scores for accuracy on the range were consistently higher than his peers, for Tony Chen, it still wasn't good enough.

But it was in the dynamic "Shoot or don't Shoot" scenarios, where agents were expected to make snap, life-or-death decisions, that Chen was the most demanding. And in those exercises, Sean had consistently proven his ability to shoot, and to shoot well, under high levels of stress. As a result, Sean was the first in his class to pass the firearms qualifications test. As a reward, Tony Chen had held a small ceremony, where he gave Sean his first Bureau-issued weapon, and the authority to use it. It was a 9mm Glock, the weapon carried by law enforcement officers everywhere because of its reliability, stopping power, and relatively small size and weight. It was a beautiful weapon.

Today, Sean double-checked the magazine, drew back the slide to ensure a round was in the chamber, and slipped the Glock into the pocket of his blazer. Checking his appearance in the mirror, Sean was satisfied the weapon wasn't noticeable. Now he just needed the courage to use it.

Nadia had enjoyed a peaceful morning before heading to the Academy. For her, over twenty years of planning was coming to an end today. She would pull the trigger that would end Charlie's life, and make Mott begin to feel the loss Nadia had been suffering for all these years. Even though she knew she would spend the rest of her life in prison, it would be worth it. After all, she thought, she has been in a sort of prison ever since her beloved Bill had been killed. Now that Sean was all grown up and out of the nest, she would be alone with her thoughts for the rest of her life anyway. That may as well be in prison as anywhere else.

She was sad that Sean would have to live his life on the run, but she had done it for twenty years, and had found some joy in it. She'd made friends in Freedom and believed Sean could do the same wherever he settled down. The money she had left for him in the trunk of the rental car would help him find that place. She hoped he'd be happy. While Sean's parting words to her yesterday about trying to get away if things didn't go as planned worried her, on balance, Nadia was at peace with the decisions she had made. And best of all, Jake Mott would suffer.

She did one final check of her appearance in the hotel mirror. She had pulled her now blonde hair back into a ponytail. She hadn't been adept enough at using the hair dye to change her dark eyebrows, but there was nothing to be done about that now. She then pulled on the COVID mask and secured it below her chin and behind her ears. Taking a long look, Nadia was satisfied nobody would be able to recognize her, even if they had her picture. Checking to be sure her small handgun was carefully hidden in the bottom of her purse, Nadia turned out the lights and headed out to her rental car.

As Nadia waited in line at the security entrance to the Academy, she was glad she had decided to rent a car. The Marines guarding the entrance were carefully checking license plates. If she had used her own vehicle and the plates she had stolen had been reported, she would never have gotten inside. She had a moment of worry when the guard asked her to remove her mask to check her picture ID, but he simply nodded and waved her through. She made the short drive to the parking area in front of the admin building, and saw that many of the students and their guests were already on the plaza. After she parked, she tried to spot Sean, but because nearly every student was dressed in the same outfit, she quickly gave up. Calm and confident, Nadia locked the car, squared her shoulders, and walked up the slight rise to the plaza and to her destiny.

As Kathy drove through the security entrance a mere four cars behind Nadia, she felt the excitement of the day start to build. Looking to the passenger seat, she could tell Charlie was happy to be back on campus again. Even though they had all been relieved when Charlie had been exonerated by Arroyo's fingerprint check, the entire experience had been stressful and disappointing. She knew Charlie wondered whether the near-arrest, and the public nature of the accusations, would follow him around for his whole career. Only time would tell. Jake had arranged for Charlie to sit next to him with the VIPs in the front row, but they had agreed Jake should be the one to tell him, so Kathy had remained silent. Maybe that outward sign of support would help Charlie's reputation.

Jake had reserved a parking spot for Kathy and Charlie in the staff section. Kathy pulled into her spot, and she and Charlie walked to the plaza together.

"Your father and I are both proud of you, you know. I hope you can enjoy this day as much as we will."

Charlie smiled that easy-going smile of his. "I know I will. It's a great day! Thanks to you and Dad for helping me get here. I love you guys."

Between the 200-plus students, forty or so instructors, and "no more than two guests each" according to the memo Jake had issued, there were nearly 500 people milling around on the lower level of the plaza. As the head of the Academy, Jake knew he had an obligation to mingle and greet as many of the guest as possible before the ceremony began. But he would start with his own family. He spotted Kathy and Charlie as they entered the plaza, and he made a beeline for them. After giving Kathy a hug and a peck on the cheek, he turned to his son. Smiling, and shaking his hand, Jake said, "Congratulations, Charlie. You've earned this. I just want to say how fortunate I am that on the day I officially leave the Bureau, you officially join it. It has a certain symmetry, don't you think?"

Charlie responded, "I'm honored. Thanks, Dad. Oops, sorry. Can I call you Dad now, Mr. Mott?"

Jake just laughed. "Of course, you can. And after 5:00 today, you can call me anything you want. And by the way, when it comes time for the ceremony, don't sit with your classmates. You'll be sitting right next to me in the front row."

Charlie began to protest, but Jake said, "I wanted this, but the Director himself insisted. He felt you had been put through the wringer with this fingerprinting issue, so a little positive attention might be nice."

Charlie smiled. "Okay. Don't argue with the boss, right, Dad? Also, I've been looking around for Mr. Chen. Is he here?"

Jake hesitated, then replied, "No. He has a special assignment and couldn't make it. He sends his regrets." Jake then made his apologies to his family and turned to greet as many other people as he could in the forty-five minutes remaining before graduation.

It seemed every student at the Academy wanted his or her parents, spouse or significant other to meet Jake Mott. Some, Jake thought, because they liked him, but others because Jake had become somewhat infamous due to the deaths on the Academy grounds and the surrounding publicity. Whether their motives were pure or perverse, Jake greeted everyone he met warmly and genuinely, and then moved on.

A few minutes before 11:00, Jake spotted the Director with Steve Marks glued to his side. "More like his backside," Jake thought. Knowing this was part of the job as well, Jake made his way over to them.

"Director Anders, welcome. I'm glad you could make it. I really appreciate it, as do the students, I'm sure."

The Director shook Jake's proffered hand, and spoke, "I know this has been a rough few months for you. Steve here has kept me updated all along."

"I'll bet he has" Jake thought, but didn't say.

Anders continued, "Jake, I wanted to let you know that I put together a Side Letter with the Agent's Association this morning. They have agreed in principle, and their Executive Board will meet at noon today to formally approve it. In short, anyone who has not already volunteered will be fingerprinted as a condition of starting their next assignment with the Bureau after graduation. If any students leave employment with the Bureau before then, the Agreement allows us to withhold their final paycheck until they comply. I know the timeline is not what you would have liked, but we are going to get this guy, you have my word on that."

Jake had already resigned himself to the fact that the killer, whoever he or she was, would be walking off the campus today. The Director's news was appreciated, though.

"Thank you, Director. And I'd like to add that I understand the Union leadership's position. I've worked with most of them in the past. They are good agents, and good people. Their interests and mine didn't mesh well this time, but I have no hard feelings. And you're right. We will get this guy."

Turning away from the Director, Jake spotted Sean King talking to an older blonde woman, presumably his mother, Jake made his way over.

Sean looked nervous, but politely said, "Mr. Mott, this is my mother, Maria King. Mom, this is Mr. Mott."

Jake smiled and stretched out his hand towards the attractive woman. Maria had blonde hair, but her dark eyebrows proved it came from a bottle. She was wearing a full COVID mask, which covered her nose, mouth and chin, but it did not cover her eyes. And those eyes! They bored into him with an intensity he had never experienced. They studied him like a butterfly collector might examine her newest specimen. There was an anger in those eyes, for reasons Jake could not begin to fathom. As she took his hand, and shook it, her eyes never left his.

"Nice to meet you, Mr. Mott." The tone of her voice echoed her eyes, and Jake was glad to have his hand back in one piece.

Jake couldn't speak right away. Throughout the exchange, Jake saw that Sean's eyes darted back and forth between the two of them, nervously shifting his feet. Finally, glancing at his watch, Jake said, "Nice to meet you as well, Maria. It looks like we need to get started. Sean, could you start making your way to the upper level?"

Before Jake could move, he felt a hand on his arm.

"Mr. Mott, I made it back in time!"

Jake glanced away from Maria, and saw Katie Arnold. Despite having driven all night, Katie looked professional, as always.

"Sean, aren't you going to introduce me?"

Again, Sean did the introductions. Katie grabbed her cell phone from her jacket pocket, stepped back, and said, "I think we need a picture."

She quickly took several photos of Jake, Sean, and his mother.

"Thanks, everyone. Mr. Mott, did I hear you say we are about to start?"

Jake nodded and turned. As he walked away, he stole one more backward glance at Sean's mother. Her stare back at him never wavered.

# Chapter 20

## The Ceremony

Jake stepped up to the microphone. The assembled students at his back had promptly taken his cue and settled into their seats on the risers. Except for Charlie, they were seated in alphabetical order, the same order their names would be called. The audience would watch as each graduate would file down the right side of the risers, turn, walk past Charlie, then Jake. They would receive their certificate center stage from Kyle Gulya, the student-selected speaker, with their left hand, while shaking the Director's hand with their right. They then would proceed back up the left-hand side and back to their seats. Jake figured that with military efficiency, they should get through all 200 or so graduates in under forty-five minutes.

The guests had taken a little longer to settle down, but only five minutes behind schedule, Jake cleared his throat and began his remarks.

"I'd like to welcome our distinguished guests, students, faculty, and mostly you, the family and friends of our graduates today, to the Graduation Ceremony of the Summer, 2020 Class of the FBI National Academy."

There was the expected cheers and applause.

"I want to begin by thanking our incredible instructors, staff, and students, who put up with being separated from their families during the pandemic, but were able to deliver the highest quality education available to law enforcement anywhere in the world. The decision to quarantine for the last three months was difficult, but we all got through it. I would especially like to extend those thanks to my lovely wife, Kathy.

"Next, I would be remiss if we did not take a moment to remember three men who are not with us here today. Frank Steele, Bullet Davis, and Fritz Hemmer. I'm pleased that my son Charlie here has been cleared of any involvement in their deaths, and that we are committed to finding those responsible. But that does not take away the loss we all feel.

"And finally, I want to thank all of you, the families of our graduates. Many years ago, Branch Rickey, the famous manager of the Brooklyn Dodgers, was asked what he looked for in a young ball player. He replied that he looked for speed. He could teach anyone how to play the sport, but as he said, he could not teach 'fast'. When I look at our graduates today, I know we taught them how to do their jobs. They received the best training available in evidence, forensics, interviewing skills, tactics, weapons, driving, investigations, and criminal law, among others. But what we can't teach them is integrity. A commitment to do the honorable thing. To make the good choice. That can only come from you, their parents, grandparents, spouses, or anyone else who passed along the values they hold dear. You did that. So, thank you. Today is just as much for you as it is for them."

Jake stepped away from the podium to thunderous applause. He suspected the reason was more because he had been brief than for the content of his remarks, but he felt he had done his job.

Stepping back to the microphone, he said, "And now I'd like to introduce the instructor selected by the graduates to deliver his remarks. Kyle Gulya teaches legal issues and ethics here at the Academy. He has been an Agent and instructor for nearly eighteen years, and has always been respected by his peers. It is nice to see that respect is shared by his students. Kyle, the podium is yours." Jake sat down to more applause, his work for the day complete.

Sean watched as Jake took his seat, feeling surprisingly at peace with his decision. Certainly, without intending to, Jake's remarks about doing the right thing only reinforced what Sean was about to do. As he looked out into the audience and spotted his mother, he was sure of it.

When he met with his mother the day before, he had hoped to be able to talk her out of following through on her plan of revenge. But once those hopes were dashed yesterday at the mall, Sean had to re-examine the entire situation. To his mind, one thing was certain: Charlie was going to die today. His mother would make sure of that, and as a result, she would spend the rest of her life in prison. Yet, he knew that his own hands were already bloody. In support of his mother's thirst for revenge, he had killed three innocent men. Somewhere inside, he knew he should be the one to suffer the consequences of that decision.

Moreover, he knew his mother remained innocent. Yes, she had planned and executed the botched bank robbery with his father many years ago, but she and his father had been wronged by the bank and his mother had not personally harmed anyone. Her plan to kill Charlie would change all that. After everything she had already suffered in her life, Sean did not want to see his mother caged forever.

So, Sean had come up with the only solution that would satisfy his mother's obsession, keep her out of jail, and ensure that the truly guilty would pay. He would be the one to kill Charlie before his mother ever had the chance. By sacrificing himself for his mother's freedom, perhaps he could begin to atone for all the pain he had caused.

As Mr. Gulya was finishing his remarks, Sean went over the careful steps he would take in the next few minutes. He would make the slow walk down the risers to the front of the stage. His name would be called. As he passed in front of Mott, he would reach into his jacket pocket, pull out the Glock, turn, and shoot Charlie. He would then drop the gun, surrender, and admit everything. His mother would have her revenge, but she would also go free. To Sean's mind, it was the best solution to an impossible problem, and he was ready to make the sacrifice to save his beloved mother.

Jake was pleased that Kyle had taken his lead and kept his remarks brief. The distribution of the certificates could now begin. Steve Marks stepped to the podium to read off the names of the graduates. Director Anders stood next to him, ready to shake over 200 hands. Gulya stood facing the graduates immediately in front of Jake, next to a table holding the stacks of certificates he would put into the graduates' left hands. The well-oiled machine was ready. As Marks read the first name, the row of graduates behind Jake rose as one, and began filing to the aisle. Susan Aaron stepped forward, took her certificate, shook the Director's hand, and stoically moved on. And so, it began.

The eighth graduate in line was Katie Arnold, but she was anything but stoic. Rather, as she stepped in front of Jake, she whispered, "Look at my text right away. Please."

Then her name was called, and she moved forward. Intrigued, Jake opened his phone, and seeing her text from ten minutes ago, clicked on it.

"Mr. Mott, I think you need to look closely at the three photos attached. There is a connection here. I can feel it. Please don't think I'm crazy."

The attachment had three photos, side by side. The first was the enhanced photo his Seminar Team had enhanced of the blurry image captured by the video in Milwaukee. The second was the photo from Indianapolis. And the third was a cropped version of the photo Katie had just taken of Jake, Sean, and his mother, isolating Maria's head. Peering carefully, Jake noticed the striking similarity in the eyes of all three photos. The shape of the eyebrows, the cheekbones, even the ears, were eerily similar. But what really struck Jake was the head position in both the photo from Indianapolis and the one from today. In both, the woman was turning her head in exactly the same way, trying to avoid the camera. The angle of the head, the turn of the neck, and the slight raising of the shoulder were all identical.

Oblivious to the parade of graduates, Jake continued to scan back and forth from one photo to the next. Jake started to think, "Maybe Katie isn't so crazy." The comparison certainly wouldn't hold up as evidence in a courtroom, but it made Jake's mind start to chew on the possibilities. "Let's see," he thought. "The bank robber's accomplice burns down the house in Madison. To cover her own identity maybe? The gold coin sales then switch to the Pacific Northwest right about the time Sean is born. And didn't the bank robber say something about his unborn child? The math worked out. Sean's mother lived in southwest Idaho during the entire time, but days before Sean's graduation, the sales moved across the country, first to Salt Lake City, then to Indianapolis. Could Sean have some sort of connection to the gold sales? To the bank robbery?

Jake scanned the audience as he continued to turn the possibilities over in his mind. His eyes finally found the person he was looking for: Maria King. Second row, near the aisle. Their eyes locked as they had at the reception an hour earlier. Again, Jake was taken aback by the intensity of those eyes. He saw anger, and hatred, and resolve. Katie was right. Something was going on here.

Jake was interrupted in his thoughts by Charlie, who leaned over and said, "It's almost my turn." It's odd how the slightest variation from a routine can stand out. The constant repetition of a name being called, a student stepping forward, a left hand taking the certificate, a right hand stretching for a handshake, and a continued walk across the stage, had become mindless background for Jake as he was alone with his thoughts. Nothing in that routine changed as the name "Sean King" was called. Sean stepped forward. His left hand took the certificate. But then his right hand didn't stretch forward but went into his jacket pocket. That deviation from routine registered somewhere in Jake's mind, and he became instantly alert.

The first thing Jake saw was the gun in Sean's hand swinging around towards him. Jake would recall later how everything seemed to move in slow motion from that moment. The Glock continued its arc, but passed by Jake, stopping to point directly at Charlie. Jake's stomach clenched, but his legs were already moving by that point. He surged forward towards Sean, placing himself between the muzzle of the gun and his son. Jake then distinctly heard not one, but two shots ring out, and at the same time felt a blow like a sledgehammer hit him in the left side of his chest. His entire left side went numb.

Jake's momentum carried his body forward, hitting Sean and knocking them both to the ground. He was aware of the sounds of screams all around him, and people running for cover. Jake looked over his shoulder, and saw Charlie, still standing and apparently unharmed. Good. But where did the second shot go? As he tried to focus, he ran his right hand over his chest, and felt the wetness of copious amounts of blood, his own blood, and he knew he had been badly shot.

Jake was lying on top of Sean King. As he pushed himself up with his good arm and looked down, he could see Sean's chest covered in blood. At first, Jake thought it was his own blood, but then saw the gaping wound in Sean's own chest. Sean's wound was foaming with air bubbles, confirming to Jake the shot had punctured the lung. Jake had also attended enough autopsies to know from the jagged edges that the hole in Sean's chest was an exit wound. Jake tried but couldn't make sense of what he was seeing.

Sean reached for Jake, grabbing him by his jacket and pulling him close. Sean's face was twisted in pain, and he was crying. "Mr. Mott, I'm sorry. For everything. I'm so sorry."

Jake knew Sean was dying. He placed his good hand against Sean's cheek, looked into his eyes, and said, "I know, Sean, I know. Rest now. I forgive you."

Sean looked up at Jake with gratitude as his eyes fluttered closed, then opened again. "Mr. Mott. The crow. It's gone. I know it's gone."

Jake then watched as Sean's face relaxed, and his eyes closed, finally at peace. He felt his own body go cold, knowing he was not far behind Sean. He felt hands roughly pulling him off Sean's body and laying him flat.

He heard someone yell "get some compression on that wound, now!" Then he saw Charlie kneeling over him, pushing down on his chest. The pain was excruciating, and Jake's body couldn't take any more of it. He thought to himself, "So this is what it feels like to die. Hmmm. Not so bad." Then everything went black.

# Chapter 21

## Overwatch and Recovery

Tony Chen was nothing if not a consummate professional. Not only was he an excellent marksman, but he had good instincts about people. For twenty years, Tony had trusted Jake's leadership and his judgement. So, when his friend called him two days before graduation, he knew it was for a good reason. Jake had explained that he was concerned about something happening during the graduation ceremony. He knew somebody was willing to kill innocents to embarrass either the Bureau or Jake personally. What better place and time to do that again than in the most public of settings, the graduation ceremony itself?

When Tony asked what they could do about it, Jake told him what he wanted. "I know it's a big ask, but I've decided to move the Ceremony to the outdoor plaza. I want you on the roof of the admin building with your best sniper rifle and scope ready. Scan the crowd, as well as the students. Watch for anything out of the ordinary. If you see something, let me know by text right away."

Tony asked, "What if there's no time? How are you going to get me authorization to fire in a fluid situation?"

Jake looked Tony in the eye. "Let's hope it doesn't come to that, but if it does, there is nobody I'd rather have making that decision than you. I am officially ordering you to use deadly force if you believe it is necessary to protect innocent human life. I'll put my order in writing for the file. That should protect you with the Bureau if something goes wrong. But you know that the lives of my family, our students, and all our guests are going to be in your hands. I sure hope I'm wrong, but I think a little insurance is not a bad idea."

So that was how Tony Chen found himself on the roof of the admin building when Sean King's name was called. Tony had just finished scanning the visitors and had returned his attention to the stage. It was pure luck that had his high-powered scope trained on the area around the podium at the exact time Sean began to draw his weapon and take aim in Jake's direction. From his vantage point well above the crowd, Tony had already considered his firing angles to various potential targets. For this reason, he had selected a lower velocity ammunition that would not pass through the body of the target as readily as his preferred ordinance. This particular line of fire was the trickiest, as there were several people immediately behind the target. He would need to hit his target center mass, and hope the lower-velocity ammunition did not exit Sean's body.

Almost simultaneously with hearing Sean's gun fire, Tony squeezed his own trigger. He saw Sean pitch forward from the hit from the rifle directly into Jake, where they both collapsed to the ground. He could see both of them moving slightly, but knew Sean was no longer a threat. Following his training, and knowing there was nothing immediate he could do for Jake, Tony reloaded his rifle, and continued to scan the crowd for other threats. Initially, he saw what he expected. The students took cover behind the risers or the front doors of the admin building, then immediately began scanning for potential threats. The Academy had done its job well, Tony thought with pride. The audience was another matter. Most of them were civilians, and they scattered in every direction imaginable, creating complete chaos on the lower level of the plaza.

Then Tony spotted one person in the crown who hadn't panicked. Standing frozen in the second row, a blonde woman simply stared at the stage as people all around her fled. Drawn to her, Tony watched through his scope as she reached into her purse and pulled out a handgun. She shouted something he couldn't hear, and then pointed the gun towards the stage. Taking aim and preparing to fire again, Tony saw a flash of color as someone tackled the blonde woman. Two more guests ran to help, and within moments, the blonde was pinned to the ground, and the handgun secured. Tony let out a breath and sat back. The day was over. But, Tony wondered, at what cost? Had he been too slow to save the life of his friend?

Jake felt like he was floating in a sea of white. He wondered if it was clouds. Then he saw a hazy but beautiful face. An angel? There was a bright light off to his left, and he turned his head away from it as his vision began to clear. The face of the angel came into sharper focus, and he realized it was Kathy, concern etched deep into the lines on her face. But she never looked better, Jake thought.

She looked away, and said, "Get the nurse. He's waking up," then turned back to him and gave him a reassuring smile.

He saw he was in a hospital room, white sheets and white walls, with the sun streaming through the window to his left. That explained the vision he had upon waking. "I'm not dead yet," he thought, and tried to sit up. The pain that shot through his shoulder and chest made him wish he was.

He focused on his wife, and asked, "What happened?"

By then, a nurse in blue floral hospital scrubs had entered the room, a uniformed gentleman with a Captain's insignia carrying an I-pad right behind her. The nurse immediately checked the tubes attached to Jake's arms, and the various monitors next to his bed, somehow making sense of the flashing lights, scrolling numbers, and beeping noises they gave off.

She turned to the captain, saying, "Everything is looking stable, Doctor. No changes in his vitals."

"Thank you, Cheryl, and good morning, Jake. I'm Dr. Bob Martinez. You probably have a lot of questions. Let me try to bring you up to date. First of all, you are going to recover. But it's not going to be easy or fast. You were hit by a 9mm bullet in the left side of your chest, about two inches to the left of your sternum. It slammed into your fifth rib, and angled upward, seemingly going out of its way to miss hitting anything truly vital. It nicked the top of your left lung, narrowly missing the artery that feeds your left arm. It then tore into the tendons and bone that make up your shoulder, before coming to a stop against your left clavicle. When you were brought in here, we put together our surgical team, and operated immediately. You had already lost a lot of blood, largely due to the injury to the lung. Frankly, if your son hadn't kept pressure on the wound from the time of the incident until you arrived here, you might have bled out.

"Once we stopped the bleeding, we were able to remove the bullet and get you stable and out of surgery. X-rays and an MRI allowed us to survey the damage further and develop a surgical plan for repair of the shoulder. The next day, after fully briefing your wife, she gave us permission to operate, and we did what we could. As you know, the shoulder is a very complicated joint. We attached a plate, several screws, and re-attached several of the tendons as best we could, given the damage we saw. That's about all we could do. The rest is going to be up to you and the rehab specialists.

"I can tell you this. You are lucky to be alive. But you will be facing some very painful rehab, lasting several months, and even with that, you may never regain the full use of your shoulder."

Jake tried to take it all in but had so many questions. "Doc, where am I? And are you saying it's Saturday? The last thing I remember, it was Friday."

The doctor answered, "You are at the medical center on the Marine base at Quantico. You may not have survived transport to any medical facility farther away. We have one of the best trauma facilities in the Washington, D. C. area, so you were lucky to be brought here. And today is Monday, not Saturday. Between the anesthetic from both your emergency surgery and the shoulder repair, plus the healing your body needs to do after the trauma you suffered, you've been in and out of consciousness for over three days. For what it's worth, Kathy has never left your side. We tried to get her to leave for a few hours to get some rest, but she insisted on staying. She's been napping on the cot we brought in for her, and only leaving long enough to get some food from the cafeteria."

Jake turned to Kathy, who looked at him with a mix of love and gratitude.

"Jake Mott, if I get any gray hairs from this, you will not hear the end of it. And we have a cruise to take, so don't you even think about slacking off on your rehab, understand?"

Jake couldn't help but smile, as did the doctor and the nurse.

"Yes, dear," was all he said, a smart move, he thought to himself.

The doctor continued, "You're going to be here for at least a couple more days, but after that, we'll be able to send you home. You can do the rehab on an out-patient basis. But again, I warn you, it is going to take four to six months, and it will be painful." His phone buzzed. Looking down, he said, "That's my wife, Christina, so I need to go. There have been quite a few people who want to talk to you, but I want you to take it easy, okay?"

Before Jake could respond, Kathy jumped in, "He will, doc. I'll see to it!"

Dr. Martinez laughed and left the room. After the nurse finished tending to her duties, she left Jake alone with Kathy. Jake looked at his lovely but very tired wife.

"I'm so sorry about all this, my love. I'm still unclear on everything that happened, but I never wanted to put you through anything like this. How are you doing?"

Kathy said, "I'm doing ok, now that I know you are going to recover. When the shooting first happened, I couldn't get to you right away. The Director, Mr. Gulya, and several of your students formed a perimeter around you and wouldn't let anyone inside of it. I saw Charlie working on you, covered in blood, and I feared the worst. When the ambulance arrived, I ran to our car and followed you here. It was terrifying waiting for news from the surgeon. When he finally told me you were going to make it, I started to cry with relief and happiness. Jake, the scene at the graduation was awful. I'm just glad nobody else was killed."

"So, Sean is dead, I guess."

Kathy nodded. She went on. "Look, that's enough for now. You need to rest, and there is so much to tell you. And I need to get out of these clothes and get a hot shower and some healthy food. Charlie has been checking in regularly over the weekend, and is on his way over here. Now that you are awake, I'm going to drive home, get cleaned up, and sleep in my own bed tonight. Charlie will be here in a few hours, and I'll be back bright and early tomorrow. I'm leaving strict instructions for the staff not to let anyone in here except Charlie until tomorrow. So, get some rest."

Kathy came over to Jake's bedside and took his hand. Leaning over him, she tenderly kissed him, and looked into his eyes. "I wasn't ready for you to leave me, yet. Thank God you didn't."

After a pause, she nodded and left Jake alone. It didn't take more than a few minutes before he was sound asleep again. It was dark before Jake stirred awake. Even though his shoulder had been immobilized, he could feel it throbbing. Looking to his right, he saw Charlie slumped down in a chair, scrolling through his phone. He savored being able to look at his son for a few moments, thankful that he was safe and unharmed. When Charlie glanced up from his phone and saw that Jake was awake, he typed in a quick message, hit send, and tucked the phone away. Then he smiled and said, "Hey, Pops, how are you feeling?"

"Well, I'm hungry. Can I get some decent food around here?" Jake asked with a smile. Charlie called the nurse, who popped into the room a moment later. Jake asked for some dinner, and after reviewing the rather limited and unappetizing menu choices she gave him, told the nurse what he wanted.

After she left, Jake asked, "And how about you? How are you doing? What have you been doing since Friday? Catch me up on everything."

Charlie jumped right in. "On the home front, I've been trying to help Mom get through this, but I never fully appreciated what a strong woman she is. She wouldn't leave your side and handled all the medical decisions more calmly than I could have. So, I ran interference on all the outside distractions, especially the media."

Jake cast a questioning eye at his son. "The media? What do you mean?"

Charlie broke into a wide smile. "Dad, you are the hottest item around. Cellphone footage of the shooting went viral. Now everyone is talking about the FBI agent that took a bullet in the chest to save his son's life. It's a great story. Despite the junk the media usually puts out, people love a positive story line like this. All the big media outlets have been trying to get an interview with anybody involved. Mom has refused, but many of the students and their families are talking. You're a hero."

Uncomfortable in the spotlight, Jake demurred. "I'm no hero. Everything happened in a split second. How does anybody know what really happened, anyway?"

Charlie gave his father a hard stare. "Well, I know what I saw, and I know what you did. But if that isn't enough, Nadia Trulenko is making it crystal clear what happened. There is no doubt you saved my life, and maybe many more lives."

Jake was puzzled. "Who? Who is Nadia Tru... whatever-her name is? How does she know anything about this?"

At that point, the door to the room opened, and Sgt. Arroyo peered in, "Is now a good time?"

Charlie motioned him in, and said to Jake, "I know Mom said no visitors, but I knew you would have lots of questions. I texted him when you woke up, and he came right over from his office across the street. To answer your question, Nadia Trulenko is Maria King's real name, and she won't stop talking. I'll let Sgt. Arroyo take it from here."

Arroyo smiled at Jake. "How are you feeling? We were all pretty worried there for a while. I'm glad you pulled through."

Jake said, "I'll be okay, but somebody better start talking. What do we know for sure?"

The big Marine sat down and opened his file.

"Like you, I had similar concerns about security at the graduation ceremony. So, I had two MPs from my unit in plainclothes circulating among the guests. And by the way, I'm a little pissed off that you posted a sniper on the roof without sharing your concerns with me. If you weren't in a hospital bed right now, I'd be chewing you a new one.

"Anyway, when the shooting started, my guys charged up the steps to the upper level, one preventing anybody from approaching the scene, and the other providing emergency medical assistance. They report that Charlie here followed directions perfectly. He was the one who kept pressure on the wound from the scene all the way to the hospital. You probably owe him your life.

"During the chaos, a woman in the second row pulled a weapon and pointed it at the stage. Before my guys could react, a retired NYPD officer, father of one of the graduates, tackled her to the ground and pinned the weapon under her body. Two women, the mother and sister of another graduate jumped in, and helped wrestle the gun away. By then, the MP arrived, handcuffed the woman, and took her into custody. Ya gotta love law enforcement families. They have no fear when it comes to protecting their own."

Jake interrupted, "What about Sean? What happened to him?"

Arroyo replied, "We'll get back to that in a minute." Returning to his file, he told Jake, "From the minute she was handcuffed, she was practically bragging about what she and her son had done. I wanted to be sure there were no screw-ups with use of her statements, so as soon as we had her printed, photographed, and in a cell, I personally began recording the interview and read her Miranda. She said she wanted to tell us everything so, and I quote, 'we would all know what that bastard Mott did to me and Sean,' end of quote."

Jake's eyes widened. "What I did to her? I'd never even met her before Friday."

Arroyo continued, "True, but she has a hell of a story, equal parts tragic, clever, and vengeful. She grew up the child of migrant workers. She says her father killed her mother before Nadia was forced to kill him to stop him from raping her. We're still checking some old police reports on that, but her story rings true so far. She bounced around for a while before settling in Madison, Wisconsin. It turns out her boyfriend, and Sean's father, was William Landry, the bank robber from Milwaukee you had to take down."

Jake did the math. "Sean isn't old enough. He would have never known his father."

Arroyo nodded. "Right. But that didn't prevent Nadia from doing everything in her power to infect him with her own personal brand of vengeance. Jake, you should hear her... I don't know... 'bragging' I guess is the right word, bragging about how she taught her son, from birth, to seek your personal ruin. She has been talking about how she manipulated him, controlled his education, his friends, every part of his life, so he would do anything she asked. She is one scary woman!"

Jake pondered that. "Why would she be acting so triumphant if I survived and her son is dead? That doesn't make sense."

Arroyo shrugged his shoulders. "When she first started talking about what she had done, she seemed to think that you had been shot, and had fallen on top of Sean. She didn't know about Tony Chen's shot." Seeing Jake's quizzical expression, Arroyo brightened, "Oh, you didn't know. Your well-placed sniper shot Sean a split second after he shot you. Tony Chen is one helluva shot.

"Anyway, I just didn't bother to correct Nadia's assumption that you were dead, and Sean was still alive, at least at first. So, on and on she went, filling in all the details we would never have discovered on our own. One item you would be particularly interested to know is that she had planned on killing Charlie, not you. Apparently, Sean, acting on his own, decided to do it for her. It cost him his life."

Charlie spoke up. "See, Dad, you did take a bullet meant for me."

Jake replied, "And you provided the first aid that saved me, so I guess we're even. Except you still owe me for your college tuition, so don't get cocky."

Father and son smiled at each other over the long-running family joke then Jake turned back to Arroyo. "So, what happened when you told Nadia I was alive, and Sean was dead?"

Arroyo's face fell. "She simply snapped. It was one of the saddest things I've ever seen. Stunned silence, then tears, turning into wailing and sobbing you wouldn't believe. She started pulling at her wrist restraints hard enough to draw blood. I had one of our shrinks observing, just in case. He had her sedated, and she's currently on suicide watch. How does any mother recover from that?"

Charlie asked, "What will happen to her, do you think?"

Arroyo told him, "That's not clear yet. I'm working with the federal prosecutor. Final charges will probably include conspiracy to commit murder, attempted murder, and a whole range of lesser state and federal charges. But I suspect none of that will matter. Her mental capacity to stand trial is so compromised right now, she will probably be hospitalized for years. If she ever gets better, she might get a plea deal, but either way, she never breathes free air again. She is the real reason Steele, Hemmer, and Bullet are dead, and your dad is in here. She gets no sympathy from me."

Turning back to Jake, Arroyo checked his notes, "I guess that's all I have in terms of an update on this case. But now I need something from you, Jake. Witnesses say you and Sean exchanged words immediately after the shooting. I need to know what was said so I can finalize my reports."

Jake went silent for a moment, then said, "He really didn't say anything relevant to the case. Let's just leave it at that."

Arroyo looked annoyed. "Come on, Jake. Relevant or not, at least in your humble opinion, I need to know what was said."

Jake shook his head. "Okay, how about this: He didn't say anything that I could understand. Satisfied?"

The look on Arroyo's face showed that he clearly wasn't, but he made some notes in his file, and closed his folder. "That's all I need for now. Take good care of yourself. I'll keep you posted." Arroyo then extended his hand. "Jake, thank you. It was an honor to work with you." They shook hands warmly. Arroyo then nodded to Charlie and left.

After the door closed, Charlie sat down at his father's side, scowling. "Dad, I heard what you and Sean said to each other after the shooting. How could you tell Sean you forgave him? He killed Frank, and Fritz, and Bullet, and he tried to kill me! What were you thinking? I don't get it."

Jake looked at his son with love. "Charlie, think about it. The reason this happened, the three murders, the shooting, Sean's death, all of it, was that Nadia wouldn't forgive. You heard her life's story. What she felt when Sean's father was killed was something I can't understand. But if she had been able to forgive, she might have lived a good life. If I don't choose to forgive Sean, am I any better than her? Are you?"

Charlie's expression softened.

Jake continued, "Two weeks ago, you gave me a plaque for my desk saying that I didn't tell you how to live, only that I lived and let you watch me do it. Well, this is how I choose to live. You will need to make your own decisions about how you will live."

The two men sat in silence for a long time, until Jake drifted off to sleep.

# Chapter 22

## Retirement

By Tuesday morning, Jake was starting to get antsy. His shoulder still hurt like hell, but he had demanded the medical staff reduce his painkillers. He had eaten some hospital food, which gave him some energy but also motivated him to want to get out of the hospital as soon as possible, if only to avoid eating any more of it. Kathy had returned, looking fresher and more rested than she had the day before, as was expected, while Charlie, who had stayed the night on Kathy's cot in Jake's room, was looking tired. Dr. Martinez had stopped by to look at Jake's wounds, declaring them to be healing normally, but continuing to prescribe rest.

When the nurse came to clear Jake's breakfast tray, she announced, "There is a very persistent man who has been waiting outside for over an hour. He is demanding to see you. His name is Steve Marks. Says he's your boss. Should I let him in?"

Jake rolled his eyes and looked to his wife. She said to nobody in particular, "I'd rather not, but I suppose there is no avoiding it. Sure, let him in."

Marks entered the room, but to Jake's pleasant surprise, he had brought Katie Arnold with him. Also unexpected was the sling holding Marks' left arm.

Charlie spoke up quickly, "I'm pretty tired. I'm going to head out and get some rest."

As he moved to leave, Marks asked him, "Have you told him yet?"

Charlie paused. "Um, Dad, the Director talked to me yesterday. He said as a 'thank you' for what I went through, he'd let me choose my first assignment after graduation. Last night, after our talk, I made my decision. I'm going to the Milwaukee office. You started your career there, so I guess I can, too. I mean, I was born there, but never have been back. It could be interesting."

Jake was touched. "Thanks, son. Just hope that nobody remembers me. I could be more of a hindrance than a help. Get some sleep. We will talk more about it when I get out of here."

Jake turned to Marks. "Please thank the Director for me. That was a nice gesture. But you didn't need to come all the way down here for that. What's up?"

Marks gestured towards Katie. "I know Arroyo briefed you on the criminal case against Nadia Trulenko, but I thought you might like an update on Katie's work wrapping up the Nazi Gold case. It's been quite interesting. Katie?" Katie's eyes shone with the pride every agent gets for their first big case.

"Mr. Mott, we managed to recover nearly all the gold that had been sold over the past twenty years. We suspect there may be a piece or two still held by a private collector, but we currently have seventy-eight of the eighty original coins that Ms. Trulenko said she started with.

"What has been interesting is figuring out what to do with them. With the help of the Bureau's legal counsel and the State Department, I contacted the governments of Bulgaria and Romania, where Ms. Trulenko's grandparents lived, and the German Government, which minted the original coins. Everyone wanted them initially, both because of their historical value, as well as the fact that gold is currently trading at about $2000 an ounce. But it turns out that none of those governments wanted the bad press that would go along with fighting over them.

"So, I thought about what you told us about seeking justice, and made a suggestion, which everyone accepted. All potential government claims are being waived, and the coins are being donated to Israel, to be put on permanent display in the Holocaust Museum in Jerusalem. Everybody wins."

Jake smiled at the young and eager agent. "Nice work, Katie. Creative solution. I like it. Where did you learn that?"

Remembering Jake's handling of the bank loans at the end of the Milwaukee case, Katie just smiled.

Marks stepped in. "Jake, the Israeli government has asked for a representative of the Bureau to be on hand for the opening of the exhibit. The Director would like you to do it."

Jake didn't hesitate, "No but give my thanks to the Director. This has been Katie's case. If not for her persistence, who knows what might have happened. Please, send her."

Katie's eyes went wide, "Do you mean it, Mr. Mott? I'd be honored."

Getting a nod from Steve Marks, she gave out a yell, and moved to give Jake a hug. But Jake held up his good hand and said, "I'll take that hug in about six months when this shoulder heals, okay?" They settled on a quick handshake, and Katie left the room.

As Steve Marks opened his briefcase and started to speak, Kathy stopped him,

"Mr. Marks, I don't want to overstep, but you need to hear it from me. Jake is done. He is no longer an employee of the FBI, and don't even think of trying to get him to stay. Not for any reason. Understand?"

Surprised at first, Marks gathered himself, and began speaking directly to Kathy.

"Mrs. Mott, you may think Jake is no longer an employee of the Bureau, but he is. You see, your husband is a very smart man. Smart people know what they don't know. When Jake submitted his paperwork to retire, I told him that if he didn't withdraw his request in writing, any work he did for the Bureau at the Academy would be as an independent contractor." Jake's heart sank. He knew he had never signed or returned the paperwork Marks had given him rescinding his early retirement.

"Kathy, Jake knew he had no idea how to buy liability insurance, or disability insurance, or do all the other bureaucratic nonsense associated with being an independent contractor. He knew that if he was injured at the Academy as an independent contractor, he would have to pay for his rehab and all medical treatment on his own. But if he remained a Bureau employee, not only would the FBI cover all his medical costs and rehab, but if he were later determined to be disabled as a result of his injuries, he would get a full pension, not the reduced pension based on his early retirement date. You see, that is why I'm here. I found a copy of the paperwork from several months ago withdrawing his retirement and signed by Jake, just sitting on my desk. I need to have Jake verify his signature."

Marks opened up the forms and showed them to Jake. Jake was stunned.

After a moment, Jake turned to Kathy. "Hon, could you go down the hall and get yourself a cup of coffee? I'd like a few minutes alone with Steve, okay?"

Kathy looked at Marks with a measure of distrust, nodded, and left without another word. Jake turned to Marks. "You and I both know that is not my signature. What is going on, Steve?"

Marks took a deep breath and let it out before speaking. "Jake, I know you think of me as a bureaucratic weenie, and I guess I am. I see you, and others like you, on the front lines of law enforcement every day. You are the tip of the spear. You get your hands dirty, risk your lives, and stop the bad guys. Me, I'm not cut out for that kind of work. Never have been. But that doesn't mean I don't respect, even envy, the work you are able to do every day. And here you are, in a hospital bed, because of something I asked you to do. So, I'm asking you to let me do something to thank you for what you did, and have been doing, for your whole career. Can you do that?"

Jake looked at the paperwork again, then thought for a long time. With a new sense of respect for Marks, Jake said, "Hmmm. I guess that is my signature. You should probably get that filed right away before someone loses it."

The two old adversaries smiled at each other. Marks took the paperwork, folded it, and put it into his briefcase. As Marks turned towards the door, Jake said, "You're still a bureaucratic weenie, you know."

Marks smiled. "Yes, I suppose I am. But I'm a good bureaucratic weenie. And I can live with that."

Kathy came into the room just as Marks was leaving. Jake stopped him.

"Hey Steve, you never told me. What happened to your arm?"

Marks smirked, "You weren't the only one who was shot at graduation. The bullet that killed Sean King passed through him and hit me in the wrist. Broke two bones but didn't have enough force left to hurt anything else. I'll be fine."

Jake smiled back. "Good for you. Chicks dig scars. Right Kathy?"

Kathy could only stare, wondering where the jovial banter had come from. Marks waved with his good arm and was gone.

Kathy asked Jake if he wanted to rest.

"No, I'm fine. The old energy is coming back."

Kathy told him that she ran into Tony Chen in the coffee room, and he'd asked to visit. "Okay with you?"

Jake nodded, and Kathy went to the door and waved Tony in. Tony shook his friend's hand warmly, but then the banter began.

"When are you going to get out of bed, old man? They need the room for people with real medical problems."

Jake retorted, "Hey, show some respect. You're in the presence of a hero. Haven't you heard?"

"Hero my ass," Tony countered. "I've been telling everyone you are so clumsy; you probably tripped and fell into the bullet."

Both men chuckled.

"Seriously," Jake said, "You saved my life, and maybe Charlie's as well. Thank you."

Kathy said, "Amen," and gave Tony a bear hug. "This hug is from Jake, too, even though you men would never show it."

Tony was moved. "Jake, did you hear about my next assignment? I saw Marks leaving a few minutes ago and thought he might have told you."

"No."

Tony grinned.

"They offered me your old job. I'm running the Academy for the next class. Big shoes to fill, but I've got big feet, so I'll be just fine. I'd like to be able to pick your brain from time to time, though. If it's okay with Kathy, of course." They both smiled and nodded.

Tony looked at his friend.

"You look a bit tired, and I don't blame you. I'll head out. We can catch up when you start your rehab. Take care!"

Before he could leave, Jake asked him, "Tony, one quick question. Did you really shoot Steve Marks?"

Tony looked surprised by the question, then a little ashamed, and said quietly, "Yes, I guess I shot Steve Marks."

Jake said, "You shot Steve Marks?"

Tony looked at Jake, and said a little louder, "Yes, I shot Steve Marks." Then, getting the joke, Tony puffed out his chest, and proudly shouted, "I shot Steve Marks!"

When Jake started to chuckle, so did Tony. Soon, they were both roaring with laughter, causing the nurse to charge in to see what all the noise was about. She and Kathy could only shake their heads in disbelief, as the nurse said, "What a couple of loons! He's going to be fine."

# Epilogue

## Barcelona, Spain

**Six Months Later**

Jake was jolted awake as the plane touched down in Barcelona. Glancing at Kathy sitting next to him, he saw she had already freshened up and was ready to go. The Mediterranean Cruise Kathy had dreamed about began here in Barcelona and ended in Greece. Checking his watch, Jake saw they had plenty of time before they needed to be at the ship. He had made a promise to himself during the long, painful rehab sessions, and today he would fulfill that promise.

Jake gingerly moved his left shoulder and was happy to know the long flight hadn't had any ill effects. He had healed well, but the doctors had concluded he had a partial disability, which allowed Jake to receive a disability pension from the Bureau, nearly thirty-five percent higher than the early retirement pension they had expected. Jake would never do a pull-up again, but otherwise he would be fine.

After clearing customs, Jake and Kathy headed for the taxi stand, knowing their luggage would be transferred to the ship directly by the cruise line. Jake stopped briefly at a currency exchange booth, walking away with five, two-Euro coins.

Jumping into the first taxi, they enjoyed the twenty-five minute drive to their destination.

The Sagrada Familia Cathedral has been under construction since 1882. The brainchild of Antoni Gaudi, the soaring Catholic Church had always captivated Jake's interest. He wanted it to be the place he finally closed the book on the past year of his life. Exiting the taxi, Jake and Kathy entered the church, and were overwhelmed by its beauty. Squeezing Kathy's hand, Jake left her in a pew in the main section of the church and went in search of the Chapel dedicated to Saint Joseph, the patron saint of fathers.

Approaching the altar, Jake dropped in his five coins, and lit five candles. Kneeling, he said five prayers: For himself, to be a better father and husband. For Kathy, that she would have joy and contentment with him. For his two children, that they would return to their Catholic faith. For Nadia Trulenko, that she would find peace. And lastly, for the poor, tortured soul of Sean King, that he would receive forgiveness.

Satisfied, Jake rose, and returned to his lovely wife. Pausing to look around once again, they held hands at the door.

"Ready?"

Jake nodded, and they stepped out into the Mediterranean sunshine together.

**THE END**

Made in the USA
Columbia, SC
28 February 2023